thunder
city

By Loren D. Estleman from Tom Doherty Associates

Loren D. Estleman

thunder
city

a novel of Detroit

A TOM DOHERTY ASSOCIATES BOOK new york

MYSTERY

THUNDER CITY

Copyright © 1999 by Loren D. Estleman

All rights reserved, including the right to reproduce this book, or portions thereof, in any form.

This book is printed on acid-free paper.

A Forge Book
Published by Tom Doherty Associates, LLC
175 Fifth Avenue
New York, NY 10010

Forge® is a registered trademark of Tom Doherty Associates, LLC.

ISBN 0-312-86369-1

First Edition: November 1999

Printed in the United States of America

0 9 8 7 6 5 4 3 2 1

For Dale L. Walker,

a very smart man

The American Beauty rose can be produced in all its splendor only by sacrificing the early buds that grow up around it.

—John D. Rockefeller, Jr. (1905)

part one

The Seed

The Irish Pope

At half past six every morning except Sunday, James Aloysius Dolan awoke to the polite knocking of his houseboy, Noche, who then opened the bedroom door and wheeled in his breakfast.

While the great man arranged himself into a sitting position in his massive mahogany box of a bed, the servant placed a footed wicker tray astraddle Dolan's imperial paunch and laid out the courses, removing the covers from the green majolica dishes, unrolling the heavy silver from the linen napkins, and filling the stemware from pitchers of water and fresh-squeezed orange juice. He used tongs to drop two lumps of sugar into a white china cup, poured thick cream over them, and topped off the cup with strong black coffee from the silver decanter, stirring the contents just twice with a short-handled spoon; his employer enjoyed anticipating the caramelized confection at the bottom. All this was accomplished with a minimum of noise and no conversation, as silence was strictly enforced until after Dolan had dined. Just before withdrawing, the servant transferred four morning newspapers from the bottom shelf of the cart to the top.

The breakfast menu varied little from day to day. It included a sixteen-ounce T-bone steak, served rare under a dozen scrambled eggs; a large platter of corned-beef hash; four thick slices of ham, well marbled and fried in lard; a quarter of a pound of bacon; six pancakes smothered with honey and maple syrup; a loaf of fresh bread, sliced into inch-thick slabs, toasted lightly on both sides, and slathered with butter and blackberry jam; a three-minute egg in a silver cup; four medium apples, sliced thin, deep-fried, and dusted with cinnamon; and a piece of chocolate. He ate everything without hurry, washing it down with four cups of coffee and wasting nothing. As he ate, he read each newspaper from the banner beneath the masthead through the shipping reports at the back, skipping the fiction supplements and making mental note of items he intended to discuss with his associates. One of the papers was in Hebrew, a language he did not read, but by studying the cartoons and rotogravures he was able to glean something of what his minority of Jewish constituents had on their minds. Armed with this and a fair command of Yiddish, he had managed to deliver a substantial percentage of the vote from the downtown corridor to his candidates in the last election—no small feat with a ballot top-heavy with Phelans, Murphys, Sullivans, O'Donnells, and Boyds.

When he was through eating, he mopped his lemon-colored muttonchop whiskers with the napkin he used as a bib and rang the silver bell on the tray. Noche came in to remove the breakfast things while he drew on an old dressing gown over his nightshirt and retired to the bathroom to move his bowels.

He was a man of many names. Friends who had known him since school called him Jimmy. Those who dealt with him through third parties referred to him as Big Jim—which, at six foot four and 350 pounds, with hand-lasted brogans on his size fifteens, he was, quite apart from his influence. The opposition press tagged him Boss Dolan, while his supporters in the Fourth Estate preferred the Honorable James A. Dolan or, whenever his sporting interests were the subject, Diamond Jim. He disliked the monicker hung upon him by the newspapers outstate: the Irish Pope. It assumed a self-deification of which he considered himself innocent. He did confess to a certain satisfaction with the good-humored nobility of the title conferred upon him by his cronies in the Shamrock Club and the beer gardens downtown; he enjoyed answering to "Himself." He was the only Himself in the Detroit area, except when the great John L. Sullivan paid a call to the city. On those occasions he graciously surrendered the office and honors to the man with the more resonant fame.

He pulled the chain on the tank and set out his shaving things. Shaving was an operation which for thirty-three years he had performed with an artist's meticulous care and some pleasure. He lathered his big red face with a badger-hair brush from a cake of lime-scented soap in a mug bearing his initials in gold, selected an ivory-handled razor from among seven in a leather case, each labeled with a different day of the week, and scraped his cheeks and round knob of chin and the underside of his jaw with the same long graceful strokes he used to whet the blade on the strop that hung beside the basin.

It amused him in a mildly cynical way that most people who responded to his name could not identify his formal title. The specific duties of Detroit street railway commissioner he delegated to clerks, while the office itself allowed him access to halls of government that would have been closed to him as chairman of the state Democratic Party, yet did not distract him from this important work with the more time consuming responsibilities of a higher station. In this way he managed to elect mayors, governors, and congressmen. Although he was powerless against Theodore Roosevelt's popularity as the Republican president, he could and did hobble the damn Rough Rider through the representatives he had sent to Washington.

Serene in these ruminations, he returned to the bedroom, where Noche had laid out his black morning coat, striped trousers, pressed shirt, union suit, socks, and garters on the freshly made bed.

James Dolan dressed as carefully as he shaved, picking lint off his broadcloth sleeves, buttoning on a crisp collar from the box on the huge carved mahogany bureau that had come over with his father and mother from Limerick, and tying his green satin necktie, which he secured with a ruby horseshoe. He left only his black patent-leather shoes and dove gray spats to the manservant, who appeared at the very moment he was required to tie the laces and fasten the buttons and buckles; the magnificent Dolan belly made bending an exertion of energy best reserved for matters of broader import.

"Mrs. Dolan is up, I suppose?" Dolan asked then.

"Yes, sir. She is in the salon."

"The children, too, I suppose?"

"Yes, sir."

The exchange was ever the same. Mrs. Dolan was always up ahead of her husband, performing her ablutions in the bathroom they shared between their separate sleeping quarters (an arrangement of peace; Charlotte Dolan snored, James did not) and descending the stairs to awaken the children and dress them for school. She would have no maid or governess, and only tolerated Noche's presence in the house because her husband's needs and habits took time that she would rather devote to her issue.

Noche arranged the cuffs of Dolan's trousers over his insteps with two sharp tugs, rose, and asked if there would be anything else. Dolan said there would not. There never was, but one of the servant's many virtues was that he never failed to ask. The houseboy—he was over fifty, wrinkled and brown like tobacco leaves, with a streak of white in his short black hair—ducked his head a quarter of an inch and left, walking softly on the balls of his feet. This practice gave him an air of stealth he did not in fact possess. Noche was a former Cuban insurrectionist who had been freed from a cell in Morro Castle by the Americans at the end of the war with Spain, after the Spaniards had spent four months burning the soles of his feet with hot irons. He could stand to wear nothing on them more

substantial than paper slippers. Dolan had discovered him literally on his doorstep seven years ago, barefoot and carrying a
cardboard suitcase and a letter of introduction from a captain
in the Thirty-first Michigan Infantry, the son of an old friend,
for whom Dolan had arranged a commission one week after
the U.S.S. *Maine* blew up in Havana Harbor.

The great man went downstairs to find his wife in the dining salon as reported. She was a small woman, inclined toward
stoutness since turning forty, in a high-necked white blouse and
a dark skirt from beneath which poked the shiny toes of her
shoes, as tiny as her husband's were huge. She wore her brown
hair swept up in the elaborate coif that had been common in
the past decade, now eroding from a landscape filled with
bright-eyed lady typewriters whose hairstyles were simpler and
easier to maintain. Dolan had forbidden her to modernize her
appearance, and she had decided to allow him to. She believed
women in the workplace were a disruptive influence, and could
not understand why they would abandon the advantages of their
gender in order to spend twelve dreary hours in an office.

After exchanging cordial greetings with his helpmate, Dolan took his place at the head of the long maple table that was
too large for the rather small room. Its chairs crowded the East-
lake sideboard and china cabinet, behind whose beveled glass
was displayed the seventy-two piece china set Charlotte had
inherited from her late sister, and which only came out at
Christmas and on St. Patrick's Day. Oval frames canting out
from the flock-papered walls contained photographic portraits
of James's and Charlotte's parents and smaller cabinet photographs of their own children in communion clothes. Sentimen-
tal St. Valentine's Day cards and ornate wedding invitations
stood open atop the cabinet and sideboard. The dining salon
was emphatically a woman's room, just as the book-lined and
tobacco-smelling study at the other end of the house was a
man's.

James accepted his fifth cup of coffee of the morning, poured by his wife, and left it on its saucer to cool while his children trooped in to greet their father before leaving for school. Nine-year-old Sean, small for his age and slight, resembled his father not at all except in coloring. Light-haired, with luminous eyes and a bright pink complexion, he was an excitable youth who studied hard and received failing grades in every subject. He would once again this year attend classes throughout the summer in order to avoid being left back. Seven-year-old Margaret, tall and horse-faced, with white ribbons in her dark hair to match her Catholic collar, was altogether a brighter student and seldom allowed what she was thinking to show in her expression. One of the crosses James bore was that his male and female progeny were born backwards. Sean was ill-suited for a career in either business or politics, while Margaret's talents, eminently practical to both, would go to waste when he married her off to the relative of a prospective ally. If he could manage to do even that; it grieved him to admit that his daughter was not comely. He loved and respected his wife, and she was devoted to him, but between them there was a dark place because she could bear no more children.

When the couple were alone, Charlotte sipping her coffee at the opposite end of the long table, Dolan asked if he had not heard the telephone bell earlier. He spoke of the instrument with distaste. He rarely used it and regretted that he had allowed it to be installed in the front hallway. Very quickly he had learned that a king's castle had no meaning when anyone with the power of speech could breach its walls.

"That polite Crownover boy called," replied his wife. "He asked if you would be home to him at three o'clock this afternoon. I said you would."

"Which Crownover, Abner the Third or Edward?"

"Neither. It was Harlan."

"*Harlan?*" He set down his cup with a click. "Whatever can he want to see me about? He's feeble-brained."

"He is not. He is shy. You would be as well if your father were Abner Junior. The man is a tyrant."

"The tax base could use a dozen more tyrants like him. He saved his father's business from bankruptcy after the old boy threw in with John Brown. Any self-respecting horse in the country would be proud to step into the traces of a Crownover coach. Our phaeton is a Crownover. You've never been ashamed to be seen riding in it up Piety Hill."

"The coach is not the man. Anyway, I hope you won't be after keeping Harlan waiting. He had to plead for the hour off and if I know Abner Junior, he'll dock the poor boy another hour if he's one minute late getting back."

Dolan consulted his pocket winder and made rumbling comments about having to cut short his afternoon to meet with the idiot son of a man who forbade politicking on company property, but they both knew the argument was over the moment Charlotte had introduced her view. He resigned himself to spending a bleak hour with a young man whose own father trusted him with duties no more pressing than those of foreman of the loading dock.

He finished his coffee, kissed his wife, and trundled out into the front hallway, where Noche waited with his hat, a soft dove gray one to match his spats with the brim turned up jauntily on the right side, and his stick, black walnut with a gold knob. It was a fine spring day, unseasonably warm for Michigan, and Dolan left his overcoat in the closet as he began his stroll. There were those who said he should move out of the narrow brick saltbox and into one of the more spacious homes on Jefferson Avenue facing the river. He was not among them. His father had laid each brick of the house in Corktown, he had grown up there, and it was over that high threshold he had carried his bride when he was a twenty-two-year-old switchman with the Michigan Central Railroad. In the small lumber room that became his study he had pored over borrowed books in preparation for the bar. In the parlor on the ground floor he had rehearsed the opening arguments of his first case, with Charlotte as his audience, practicing the gestures and finding the breath control that would win him his first elected office. Both his children had been born there, and he had fed William Jennings Bryan, George M. Cohan, and the great John L. in the dining salon and shared his golden Irish whiskey and General Thompson cigars with them afterward in the study. He intended that his wake should be held in the parlor; when he vacated the house for good he would do so on his back in a coffin made of sturdy white pine from the Upper Peninsula.

His daily rounds took him first to the Erin Bar in the next block, where he climbed a rubber-runnered staircase between horsehair plaster walls to the Shamrock Club on the second floor. He never drank alcohol before noon, and breakfast was too recent for him to partake of corned beef and cabbage, the chef's specialty, but he accepted yet another cup of coffee—in summer it would be a glass of lemonade—in the private curtained room where he conducted business, selected his first cigar of the day from a humidor proffered by Fritz, the club's German headwaiter, clipped off the end with the miniature guillotine attached to his watch chain, and lit it carefully with a long wooden match. The club's mahogany panels were hung with pictures in plaster frames of prizefighters and the ornate back bar was stocked with more mature whiskey than its somewhat larger counterpart downstairs.

For the next three hours he greeted his appointed visitors with courtesy, offering them cigars and the hospitality of his bill, and sat down with them at his table to hear their requests and complaints. A contractor wanted to arrange a permit to build a hotel on Woodward Avenue. A streetcar conductor named Hanrahan had fallen from the platform at the end of his shift, breaking his wrist, and wanted the city to pay his doctor's bills. A maker of moving pictures had a contract with the owner of the Temple Theater on Monroe Avenue, but had been denied permission to show his feature because it included a scene of two women undressing to their chemises and bloomers. Dolan vetoed the contractor's petition on the grounds that his hotel might cause hardship for Jim Hayes, a friend and party supporter who owned the Wayne Hotel in that block. He shook a stern finger at Hanrahan, whose accident was well known to have been the result of having made his last stop at Dolph's Saloon; but Dolan produced a roll of greenbacks from a pocket of his morning coat and peeled off enough of them to satisfy the man's doctor. (Hanrahan worked as an unpaid volunteer during elections, conveying Democratic voters to the polls without charge and tearing down Republican posters on his Sundays off.) There was nothing to be done for the moving-picture man, as the Temple was a private enterprise and not beholden to the city. Dolan softened this blow by giving the fellow the name of the manager of a burlesque house in Toledo that might have room on the bill for his ecdysiastic display. Judge Collier stopped by to pay his respects and accept the offer of a glass of beer, which he sipped through a straw to avoid staining his immaculate white beard. Brennan, the assistant party chairman, spent ten minutes discussing the November ballot, during which he drank three whiskeys, then shook half a dozen pieces of Sen-Sen into his mouth straight from the box and left, as steady on his feet as he had been arriving. His bantam body, tightly vested and topped with a shiny brown bowler, burned off everything he put into it within minutes. The man's nervous animation exhausted Big Jim, who valued the man's energy but preferred something more stationary in a companion.

At twenty minutes to twelve, Jimmy Dolan retrieved his hat and stick and boarded a streetcar to downtown, ostentatiously slotting a nickel into the fare box, which as street railway commissioner he was not required to do. He disembarked on Woodward Avenue with time to exchange small talk with familiars he encountered on the street. He inquired after the health of Johnny Dwyer's saintly mother, remarked upon the comeliness of Jerome and Cathleen Whelan's infant daughter Josie, elicited a promise from Casey Riordan to send him an invitation to his sister Mary's wedding. It was a matter of some speculation in Corktown whether the Honorable James A. Dolan left off campaigning when he slept.

At his customary table in Diedrich Frank's saloon, in a booth upholstered in tufted leather beneath a poster showing Eva Tanguay, the Queen of Perpetual Motion, in tights and an hourglass corset, he shoveled in a platter of sauerkraut, three kinds of sausage, and a wheel of Pinconning cheese, chasing each course with a glass of lager. When the boy arrived with the first of the afternoon papers, he tipped him a nickel, lit a cigar, and read with keen interest the details of yesterday's National League baseball match between the Tigers and the Orioles at Bennett Park. He scowled upon learning that a routine ground ball hit by Uncle Robbie Robinson to Pop Dillon at first base had turned into a game-winning RBI for Baltimore when the horsehide bounded off an exposed cobblestone and past Dillon's ear. For years Dolan had been after Georgie Stallings to dig up all the stones and prevent such "cobbies" in future, but the general manager, bound by club owner Sam Angus's Scotch purse strings, could offer nothing more permanent than an occasional application of fresh loam. Big Jim was fond of repeating that he'd lost fifty cents in a friendly wager on the old Detroits in 1895 and had spent five thousand dollars trying to win it back. Betting on baseball was the most scrupulously managed of his vices. Jakob Wiess, proprietor of the Star of Israel chain of cleaning stores in Cleveland, boasted that he owned the most modern steam pressers in the Middle West and magnanimously declared that he owed this distinction to the Indians and James Aloysius Dolan of Detroit. Dolan acknowledged this with an outward show of bluff good humor and an inward loathing for Wiess, whom he considered an unscrupulous businessman and a Christ-killer into the bargain.

Next he reported to Falco's Barbershop (haircut, fifteen cents; shave, ten cents), where amidst the sparkling white tile and endless mirror images he sank back into a leather armchair and pretended to amuse himself with *Harper's* and the *Police Gazette* while eavesdropping upon the conversation between the barbers and the customers seated in the five Union Metallic chairs. He found these exchanges more enlightening than the newspapers, and considered his decision to eschew the status of an in-home tonsorial visit a signal advantage over his equals. Moreover, the man on the street pointed to his presence in such establishments as evidence of Big Jim's accessibility and democratic nature.

When Sebastian, his favorite barber, was free, Dolan sat for a trim, then, pink-necked and freshened with witch hazel, gave him a quarter. He snapped open the face of his watch, sighed, and took a streetcar back to Corktown, where Abner Crownover II's backward son awaited him in his study.

Jimmy Dolan loved this room. Small compared to those of many men less important than he, it was packed with mustard-colored law books in a walnut case that filled the wall to the right of the desk, a massive slab of carved and inlaid hickory supporting a stained blotter, a heavy brass inkwell and pen stand, and a bust of Socrates done in green marble with a chip out of one eyebrow that made the old pedant look as if he were winking slyly. A full-length oil portrait of Himself with his thumbs in his vest pockets hung behind the desk, still smelling faintly of turpentine; it had been finished just last week. Over everything, Turkish rug and leather humidor, Regulator clock and elephant-leg wastebasket, hung a pungent and masculine odor of bootblack and tobacco and decaying paper and dust;

21

no feminine invasion with feathers and lemon oil was tolerated. The English sparrow that had built its nest on the sill outside the leaded window seemed unaware that it had settled so near the center of the great machine that drove the city of Detroit, and by extension the state of Michigan and a large part of the Midwestern bloc in Congress. The bird alone accepted such crumbs as were sprinkled before it with no thought of returning the boon.

Not so Harlan Crownover, who sprang up from the leather armchair in front of the desk when Dolan entered. He was a rather stocky twenty, darker than his father, but he possessed the long Gallic upper lip that to some degree bore out the family's claims to descendancy from the French who had settled the region two hundred years before. This distinction was in no small part responsible for the gulf that separated the Crownovers from the Dolans in the New World; in a hundred years of continuous residency, Big Jim's great-grandchildren would still smell like peat to the Abners and Harlans of the next century. The Irish Pope noted with distaste his visitor's costume of faded flannel shirt, stained dungarees, and thick-soled work boots; he hadn't even bothered to go home and change on his way there from work. Well, Charlotte had said he only had an hour. Still, he might have put on a necktie. If Noche had answered the door, he would have told the son of one of the city's richest men to go around back.

No trace of Dolan's displeasure showed as he wrapped his big soft hand around Harlan's small calloused one. "Merciful Mary, can this be Abner Junior's middle boy? I'm after remembering a skinny lad in knickers with a swollen nose. You slid down the Washington Street hill into the wheel of a milk wagon."

"That was Edward," Harlan said. "I think it was a coal wagon."

Dolan grunted and indicated the armchair. He was vain

about his memory for personal details and didn't care to be caught in error. Seating himself between the wings of his great horsehair swivel, he asked after the health of Harlan's parents.

"Mother's very busy with the Orphans' Asylum. I'm afraid Father's working himself to death, but he won't be dissuaded."

This literal answer displeased Dolan, who preferred to reserve such straight talk for matters of greater gravity. It was no secret that Abner III, Abner Junior's eldest son, had been promoted to an executive position of no real authority when his incompetence in the office of president had driven the company to the brink of bankruptcy, and that Abner Junior had been forced out of semiretirement to assist young Edward with his new presidential duties. Edward was his father's rubber stamp, an adequate functionary but incapable of arriving at a decision that differed with Abner Junior's nineteenth-century fundamentalism. Harlan, the dimmest star in the family constellation, had been passed over entirely. A long tradition of genius had ended with old Abner.

"Will you have a brandy?" Dolan asked.

"Thank you, sir, no. I reserve my drinking for the Pontchartrain bar."

So far nothing the young man had said had elevated his station. Less than six months old, the Pontchartrain Hotel had replaced the fine old Russell House, which for half a century had sheltered such world luminaries as the former Prince of Wales. No one of a certain vintage had been encouraged when it was demolished to make room for a pretentious palace for transients whose bar catered to a particularly disagreeable clientele: motormen who tracked grease and oil across the Oriental rug in the lobby and hoisted their pistons and things onto the mahogany bar for the admiration of their cronies.

"Are you a frequent customer?" Dolan asked.

In his eagerness to curry favor, Harlan misunderstood the motive behind the question. "I'm a two-drink man, sir. Never more nor less. I don't mind saying most of those fellows enjoy tipping the tankard and distrust those who limit themselves to one glass. Henry Ford is the exception. He's a total abstainer, but he is a genius."

"A genius, is it?" Dolan was amused. "You're a fortunate young man. In forty years I've never met one."

"You would if you visited the Pontchartrain."

He shifted in the swivel; the sauerkraut had begun to work. For a young man without much time the fellow was taking the long way around the barn.

Harlan sensed his discomfort. He leaned forward, clasping his hands between his knees as if in prayer. "I intend to invest in Mr. Ford's automobile company. If you'll agree to lend me the money. I intend to repay it with interest within a year."

Dolan was suddenly serene. Pleas for money were solid ground. He'd been afraid he was going to be asked for a job. Charlotte, who for some mysterious female reason had taken a liking to the young man, would make life difficult if he turned him down, yet he didn't want to alienate Abner Junior by employing a son who had decided to desert the family enterprise. Money was another thing entirely. To challenge a man's decision in regard to his funds was as indelicate as questioning his religion.

"I heard this fellow Ford was out of the automobile business."

"He closed his plant for lack of capital. Now he has the support of Alexander Malcolmson."

"The coal dealer?"

"He has faith in Mr. Ford, as have I. Five other men are interested: John Gray, a banker, and John Anderson and Horace Rackham, who are successful lawyers. Another John and Horace, the Dodge brothers, have agreed to manufacture engines and other parts in return for shares. Mr. Ford feels that he can arrange a hundred thousand in capital if he can raise a quarter of that amount in cash. Five thousand would entitle me to twenty percent of the common stock. I own a thousand dollars in shares in Crownover Coaches. I wish to borrow the rest."

"Have you approached your father?" Dolan asked with a smile.

"My father is a traditionalist." Harlan clamped his mouth tight at the end of the statement.

"Surely nothing so bad as that." This young man had begun not to amuse him. "Why did you come to me? There are banks."

"I've been to the banks. The bankers are all very patient until they learn my father isn't interested. They're business-men."

"Automobile manufacture is not a business?"

"It's more than that. It's the future. It occurred to me that a politician such as yourself might be expected to see beyond the next fiscal year. When I was small, I saw a picture of you in the newspaper, wearing overalls and leaning on a hoe in one of those vegetable gardens Hazen Pingree started throughout the city when he was mayor. I never forgot it. When everyone else was complaining about the bad economy, you and Pingree were doing something about it, to feed the hungry. Men who take action is what the automobile industry is all about."

So now it was an industry. Dolan remembered the picture very well. It had elected him to city council, his first public office. Charlotte had had to let out his old switchman's overalls, and he had borrowed the hoe from an unemployed bricklayer who was tending the garden. Ping's Potato Patches, as they were called, hadn't done a jot to improve conditions among the poor, but they had gotten the old man a statue in Grand Circus Park, if they ever got around to finishing the thing.

"The last time I invested money, I lost every penny," Dolan said. "Although *lost* is not accurate. It's on the bottom of Lake

25

Michigan with the Great Lakes Stove Company's first and only shipment."

"I'm not asking for an investment, but a loan. I intend to repay it with interest come fire or flood. The risk is mine."

"The money is not."

"Are you turning me down?"

"I am. We live in an age of interesting inventions, of which the automobile is just one. I'm afraid I haven't the vision for which you credit me; I can't tell which will survive and which will be supplanted by the next interesting invention. If you lose your investment, you will remain indebted to me, and you will come to resent me for it. I value my association with your family too much to jeopardize it."

"The decision is final?"

"I'm afraid it is." Dolan smiled. "Please give my regards to your father and mother. I haven't seen them since the last bicycle race I attended on Belle Isle. The elections," he added by way of explanation.

"You're making a mistake, Mr. Dolan."

He frowned. The boy was no gentleman. Dolan was not either, by way of birth and occupation; he had long ago resigned himself to that truth, but it upset him that someone could take the privilege so far for granted as to reject it out of hand. It was like a man born to wealth telling a poor man that money was not important.

"Good luck to you, Mr. Crownover."

After Harlan had shaken his hand and left, Big Jim Dolan sat back down and set fire to a cigar. Had he not made it his business not to muck around in another man's business, he might have considered warning Abner Crownover that he was risking too much to trust his loading dock to his middle son.

chapter two

The Coach King

In contrast with the princely portrait of James Aloysius Dolan that hung behind Big Jim's desk in Corktown, the likeness of the founder of Crownover Coaches might have been lost in his son's office at the corner of Shelby and Jefferson were it not for the oversize frame in which it was matted and mounted. It was a three-by-five-inch tintype, orange and wrinkled, of a bulldog face in a stiff collar and pale side-whiskers, a fleshy badge of mid-Victorian prosperity with an incongruously hollow stare, as if the eyes had been punched out of a mask. The picture was made in 1859, the year John Brown hanged for treason. Abner would stand trial that same year for conspiracy in the raid on the federal armory in Harpers Ferry, Virginia; although the jury would vote for acquittal, the ardent abolitionism that had driven him to meet with Brown and Frederick Douglass at the Detroit end of the Underground Railroad and agree to help finance their bold plan to arm the slaves would destroy his reputation as a stable businessman. He sold his wagon-making business and died, a broken man, shortly before the Second Battle of Bull Run.

Abner Crownover's descendants weren't quite sure what to do with him. They felt little concern about the wife and three children he deserted in England to build wagons for pioneers departing the Northwest Territory for Oregon; such footnotes were infinitesimal in the book of the Great Expansion. They pointed with pride at the site in Miami Square where the wheels and sideboards were fitted, reminded people that A.

Crownover & Company had been the largest private employer in antebellum Detroit, and insisted that its founder's name be included in the roll of those who were present under the oaks in Jackson when the Republican Party was created in 1854. That he should have thrown all this over in favor of an idealistic dream was a subject upon which they chose to remain silent. Treason was one thing, and a bad enough job at that; it was the poor business implicit in the decision that they abhorred.

Abner Crownover II seldom mentioned his father, and since the age of eleven, when he had gone to work as a grease boy in the firm that had once belonged to his family, had corrected people when they addressed him as "Junior." He considered himself as much the founder of the company as was his father. Hard, uncomplaining work and perceptive suggestions made deferentially and through channels had earned him an executive position at an age at which the sons of most successful men were starting college. In that capacity he persuaded his superiors to acquire a bankrupt manufacturer of short-haul freight vehicles and passenger coaches. The day of the great wagon trains was coming to an end; within five years Crownover & Company had abandoned wagon making altogether for the business of providing brass-fitted carriages for the well-to-do. A mechanic at heart, Abner worked out an ingenious suspension system that smoothed cobblestones and potholes and delivered the 400 to their destinations with diamonds and silk tiles intact. The Crownover opera coach, bearing the firm's elegant coronet in gold leaf on the door, became a staple among the gentlefolk of the Gilded Age.

Then came the Panic of '73. Overextended members of the board of directors had reason to thank young Abner for buying out their shares at a more favorable rate than the stunned market offered, and at an age when most young men of good family were attending college, "Junior" acquired controlling interest in Crownover Coaches. His story was written up in *Harper's* and inspired a laudatory book written by a journalist from Toledo, handsomely bound in green cloth with gold, circus-style lettering, entitled *The Coach King*. It sold well throughout the end of the nineteenth century to readers whose shelves sagged beneath the weight of volumes by Horatio Alger and G. A. Henty. In the meantime the plant moved from Miami Square to its present larger quarters, with two floors of offices separated by soundproofing from the hammer clatter and wailing steam saws at ground level. Crownover vehicles had been made to order for Governors Pingree of Michigan and Cleveland of New York, William Randolph Hearst, and Sarah Bernhardt. A grateful nation had presented Admiral Dewey with a Crownover cabriolet in mahogany with ivory side panels in honor of the victory at Manila. William McKinley rode to his second inauguration in a one-of-a-kind Crownover phaeton with gold-plated headlamps and the presidential seal inlaid in the door.

The nation's youngest tycoon was now in his fifties. Long hours and total responsibility for the operation of his company had added twenty years to his appearance, disappointing those visitors who expected, on the evidence of *The Coach King*, to meet a man in whom some semblance of youth still resided. His pale hair, fine as spun sugar and cropped close to his pink scalp, was so little removed from total baldness that it might as well have fallen out years ago. The long upper lip, which in the tender years had contributed to his boyishness, gave him in age the face of a mummified monkey. His glittering black browless eyes did nothing to detract from this impression. In recent years he had formed the habit of sitting motionless and unspeaking behind his plain desk, staring with his bright simian eyes at speakers, then dismissing them with nothing more than a reference to the time. These speakers repaired directly to the bars of the Pontchartrain and Metropole, as much in search of human contact as refreshment. Abner II was not a warm man. It was said his first wife had committed suicide because of loneliness.

In fact she had simply died, albeit of neglect and a related condition; Scarlet fever, however, was announced as the cause. He had married again in 1876, scandalizing Edith Hampton's eastern aristocratic family with the notion of a grease boy entering its halls. Edith gave birth to six children, four of whom survived infancy. The daughter, Katherine, eloped at fourteen with an adventurer bound for the Oklahoma territory and vanished from the family history. Abner III, the oldest of the three boys, became president of the Detroit office of Crownover Coaches in 1898, and was reassigned to an executive position with fewer responsibilities and a more impressive-sounding title when it became clear that pressure did not bring out the best in him; he was, in truth, incapable of making a decision and holding to it. For his replacement, Abner II passed over Harlan, his second son, and promoted young Edward from the upholstery shop. He would assume control of the company upon his father's retirement.

Harlan was the family disappointment. His reluctance from an early age to take part in discussions related to the business was interpreted as evidence of a slow brain, an affliction common among the Hamptons, who spent their days lawn bowling and adding new wings to the ancestral mansion in Rhode Island. The foremanship of the loading dock in Detroit went to Harlan.

On this day early in the new century, Abner II directed Winthrop, his secretary, to place a telephone call to the Cincinnati office. Cincinnati bought most of the materials consumed in the manufacture of Crownover vehicles. Abner had suspected for some time that the director culled the quality items from each shipment for use in Cincinnati, sending inferior grades to Boston and Detroit. Despite all his best efforts to persuade his branch managers to subordinate the interests of their fiefdoms to the good of the company as a whole, some stubborn pockets of feudalism remained from the dark days of his father's tenure. If this morning's conversation did not go well, he was determined to dismiss the man. He hoped it would go well. Roosevelt's trustbusters were making it difficult to find executive replacements who had not been disgraced in the Republican press.

While he was waiting for the call to go through, he instructed Winthrop to admit his son Edward, who had been lingering in the outer office for twenty minutes.

"Good morning, Father."

"It is. I saw a robin." Abner seldom failed to treat conventional greetings literally. "Sit down. How is your wife?" He never remembered his daughter-in-law's name. He could; he did not. In so far as he subscribed to scientific theories, he believed that the human memory was finite, and that if one were not selective, the time would come when for every new fact one admitted, an old one would have to be evicted. Beyond that, he approved of his son's choice. The woman was practically invisible.

"She's well, sir. I'll tell her you asked." Edward hesitated. He resembled his father, except for his eyes, which were large, soft, and bovine. His wire-rimmed spectacles were largely unnecessary and served merely to create severity. His old-fashioned muttonchops, long and thick and combed straight out from the corners of his jaw, fulfilled a similar purpose. Unlike Abner he was inclined to be fleshy, and such adornments gave his portliness an air of nineteenth-century gravity, more stable than self-indulgent. In ten years he would be morbidly obese. "I wish you would have a talk with Harlan. He's neglecting his duties at the dock."

"In what way?"

"Well, to begin with, he asked for an hour off yesterday. He was fifteen minutes late returning."

"You timed him yourself?"

"Of course not. I was informed of the fact by Mr. Daily."

"Did Harlan give Ted Daily a reason for his tardiness?"

"No. He did apologize," he added, in a sudden show of sibling support.

"Did he say why he wanted the time off?"

"Mr. Daily says no." He seemed about to go on. He did not.

"I assume Daily subtracted the fifteen minutes from his card."

"Of course."

"That being the case, I cannot see why you felt compelled to bring this to me. Particularly when it involved waiting twenty minutes to report fifteen minutes of delinquency. Given that, which of you is more guilty of neglecting his duties?"

Goaded into defending himself, Edward abandoned his show of discretion. "During that hour he was seen going into Jim Dolan's house."

"By whom?"

"I can't reveal the source."

"I see. I hope you are paying the security men you assign to follow your brothers around out of your salary. They are employed to protect the plant."

"If Harlan is cooking something up with the Irish Pope, the entire company is in jeopardy."

"Dolan is a politico. I pay this company's taxes and be damned with him."

"The Democratic Party lends money to those who serve its interests. Dolan controls the party. I think Harlan went to his house to borrow money to invest in his damn go-devils."

"Surely he's outgrown that whim."

Edward spread his soft meaty hands. "Why else would he meet with Diamond Jim?"

"I made it clear how I felt about automobiles when he

approached me with the idea of joining hands with that man Ford. The machines are too expensive and complicated ever to catch on with the general public. Rich men grow bored with their kickshaws. They move on to other things."

"Logic is wasted on Harlan. He's weak in the head."

The telephone jangled.

"I'll have a talk with him." Abner unpegged the listening cup. When Edward remained seated, he placed his hand over the mouthpiece. "Cincinnati."

"Ah." His son shoved himself to his feet and trundled out.

Abner hung up on his branch manager's obsequious farewell, donned his trilby and light topcoat, and told Winthrop he would return in thirty minutes. He rode the caged elevator to the ground floor. Hector, the operator, had been a cabinetmaker in the firm's employ until his right hand was mangled by a drill press. That was the hand, clothed in a mitten, with which he operated the lever. The work was less demanding than his old job, and so his salary had been cut from five dollars per week to three. He was a dark-skinned Greek with pewter-colored hair who in nine years had not exchanged more than a greeting with his employer.

The clangor of coach making was a shock to Abner's system after the quilted silence of the office, but he welcomed it, along with the smells of turpentine and sawn wood and fresh lacquer, the scorched-metal stench from the boilers that powered the steam machinery, the clatter of tools dropped to the broad oaken planks of the floor. The sight of coaches, buggies, depot hacks, and carriages in various stages of construction, seen through a golden haze of sawdust, never failed to carry him back to his youth. His rheumatic hands felt the metal bail of the heavy grease bucket cutting into the folds of the fingers, he tasted his own sweat trickling into his mouth from his streaming forehead, heard the wheelwrights cursing him when he was slow to slather the hubs with handfuls of the thick viscuous brown stuff in the bucket. He knew every bevel and join in every vehicle that rolled out of every plant in the Crownover empire; at one time or another he had planed and fitted them all. None of his competitors had managed to improve upon the suspension system he had patented. To achieve parity they were forced to pay him for its use in their own product. If he never made another vehicle, his invention would continue to pay him millions.

He paused to watch a young carpenter tapping a peg into place where a side panel met the back of a Victoria coach. The young man's shoulders tensed, aware that he was being scrutinized by the owner of the company. After the first tentative raps, Abner begged the fellow's pardon, relieved him of his mallet and, gripping it near the end of the handle, drove the peg home with one sharp blow.

"Leverage." He handed back the mallet. "I dined with a university professor who told me he spent an entire semester teaching the principle to an auditorium full of student engineers. I learned it from an illiterate Negro my first day on the job."

"Thank you, sir." The carpenter fumbled in his wooden toolbox for another peg.

Abner went out through the great open bay doors to the loading dock, a platform erected three feet above the ground so that material and equipment could be transferred smoothly from the boxes of delivery wagons into the building. The concept was another of his own improvements, borrowed from a flour mill he had seen on a visit to a Michigan farming village; although he did not get the credit for it that he received from his suspension, he calculated that the addition saved the firm two hours each day, enough time to complete the chassis of an extra coach or carriage. That meant two more per week, and eight more at the end of each month. Genius, he was fond of repeating, is the art of making things simple.

It was a warm day for early spring and he could smell the sun reflecting off the surface of the river. The brick factory buildings of Windsor carved square chunks out of the sky on the opposing bank. A native Detroiter, he felt pride at the thought that a worker on the Canadian side might even now be gazing across the water at the mighty height of the ten-story Hammond Building and, nearby, the fourteen floors of the Majestic. Businesses like Crownover Coaches and the Michigan Stove Company made such things possible. He was a major investor in the stove manufacturer, whose president had entered into an exclusive contract with Crownover to provide the wagons that delivered the heavy cast-iron conveniences to stores and private customers who ordered them direct from the factory. He had only to turn his head a few degrees to see that factory and its great display piece, the Biggest Stove in the World, standing in front of it. The construction, as big as a house, had been moved there from the Chicago Columbian Exposition of 1893, where in demonstration of the greatness of the project the wooden replica had sheltered an entire family on salary to the stove maker.

There were those who told Abner he should erect a monstrous coach for the same purpose. He demurred, explaining that Crownover had not gotten where it was by imitating the actions of others. In private he considered the big stove a vulgar blot on the Detroit skyline. He had the self-made man's horror of public exhibitions of gaucherie. For this reason he had filled his closet with suits made to his order by the Prince of Wales's tailor during his visits to London and had hired, in strict secrecy, a valet formerly employed in the Benjamin Harrison White House to teach him which fork to use and where to place his napkin during a formal dinner. He was aware that some of his earthier competitors muttered among themselves that Abner Crownover took too seriously the honorary title of Coach King, but he wasn't troubled by it. He had had an audience with Pope Leo XIII, and he could not think of another thirty-third-degree Freemason who could claim that.

As it happened, the episode of the Church of Rome had threatened to expel him from the Detroit order. From this controversy he also remained aloof, trusting that the High Priest would not forget who provided the funds that forestalled an investigation by the membership into cost overruns incurred in the construction of the Masonic Temple. He did not forget, and in time the muttering ceased. The example of his father had taught Abner II that honorable causes and charitable deeds were best embraced when they bore favorably upon one's livelihood. He had joined the Freemasons because many of the men with whom he did business were members. He had met with the Pope because most of the politicians who voted for and against taxes on private enterprises and established commercial zoning ordinances were Irish and Catholic. (He had spent the time with His Holiness attempting to interest him in a new papal vehicle.) In 1896 he had publicly contributed to the presidential war chest of William Jennings Bryan because Detroit was a Democratic enclave, while quietly pledging three times the amount to the McKinley campaign, Republicans having demonstrated support for American business. After the assassination and Roosevelt's rise, Abner had sent the new chief executive a beautiful silver-chased Winchester rifle with a carved stock, custom-made at the factory in New Haven. He had no fear that the Rough Rider's vow to smash the eastern trusts would include Crownover, but at a modest seven hundred dollars the gift seemed a sound security investment.

Harlan was busy supervising the unloading of packing cases from the back of a dray. The stenciling on the cases identified them as the erstwhile property of a plant in Erie, Pennsylvania, that made brass coach lamps. The lamps, which arrived packed

in straw, were made from copper mined in the Upper Peninsula; an arrangement resulting in a triangulated course across
two Great Lakes and eight hundred unnecessary miles, but one
that had to be made in order to obtain the cooperation of a
Pennsylvania senator in a matter involving a federal harbor tax.
The senator's jurisdiction acquired a new industry, and Crownover gained an exemption. As a bonus, Abner had realized a
profit when he sold the equipment from his own lantern plant
to the Pennsylvania firm, which was owned by the senator's
brother-in-law. So far the new century was starting out where
the old one had left off.

His satisfaction at this reminder of an old windfall was
marred by his son's appearance. Harlan insisted on dressing as
the men beneath him dressed, in dungarees worn soft and cor-
duroy shirts with the ribs rubbed shiny where his elbows
brushed his sides. It was clear that he helped with the physical
labor. Like most men who had worked their way up from the
ground, Abner made it a point of honor to spare his sons similar
indignity; not because he wished them less hardship, but because the sight of young Crownovers heaving and sweating
along with the men in their employ would please his enemies.
He regretted deeply that he could not trust his second-born to
make even a show of competence at a desk, as Abner III had
managed to do once he'd been removed from the directorship
of the Detroit operation. The duties of a glorified file clerk had
suited his eldest son as the pressures of decision making had
not. Young Harlan's silences during family discussions had convinced his father that the boy was incapable of understanding
simple business. The fact that he was his mother's favorite confirmed his weakness. Edith was the kind of woman who rescued
fallen birds and selected the runt of the litter, attempting to
foil the Darwinian principles that Abner had applied to business, with brilliant success. If she liked a person, a creature, or
a thing, it followed that the object of her affection was damaged

in some fundamental way. He treated his wife at all times with cordial reverence and held her in contempt.

As always, he made a mental note to upbraid Harlan for his misplaced democracy when they were alone, and busied himself inspecting boards from a stack of lumber laid at the edge of the dock. They were mahogany, shipped at great expense from Central America and reserved exclusively for use in custom vehicles. Company policy was to protect the wood with a tarpaulin at all times when it was outside and to move it inside as quickly as possible. He had slid a fourth board out from under the cover and was sighting down its length as if it were a billiard cue when his son approached him, mopping his hands with a stained rag.

"This is a surprise, Father. You never come down to the dock."

"Obviously a mistake. These boards are warped."

"The entire shipment is defective. It's been left out in the weather. They're dumping it on us."

"Have you made arrangements to return it?"

"I'd planned to talk with Edward about it this afternoon."

"There's nothing to talk about. Return it."

"If we return it, it will be two months before it's replaced, if Nicaragua agrees to replace it. We've had trouble with them before. They'll insist upon inspecting it before authorizing a second shipment. If we simply put in another order, we'll have it in four weeks."

"And eat the cost of Nicaragua's incompetence?"

"This isn't the first time we've been dissatisfied with that firm. We'll of course place our order with a competitor. Meanwhile we can make up part of the cost by selling this shipment to Wilson."

"Who the devil is Wilson?"

"C. R. Wilson Body Company," said Harlan, using a tone in which he might have said "King Edward of *England*." "They make bodies for Olds, the automobile manufacturer. I know Fred Fisher there. Automobile customers are less picky about such details. What they can't use in the bodies they can burn for charcoal."

"Meanwhile we're still operating at a loss."

"We'll make up for it by remaining liquid. We paid for the mahogany in advance. A refund would take as long as replacement, by which time it may be worth less than what we get from Wilson now. The economy is on the upswing. Prices are rising."

"Where did you read that, in the Hearst press?" Withstanding a lecture in economics from his backward son soured Abner's stomach. Of late he had been forced to give up coffee in favor of warm milk.

"Hearst is saying the opposite, actually. He's running again."

Abner dropped the board he'd been inspecting on top of the stack. The sharp clank turned heads among the workers unloading the brass lamps. He kept his voice level. "Crownover isn't in business to help your friends in the automobile world. Return the shipment."

The expression on Harlan's round face was unreadable. His father thought it blank. "They won't go away because you ignore them," Harlan said.

"Is that the reason you went to see Jim Dolan behind my back?"

"It wasn't behind your back." The young man didn't seem surprised that he knew of the visit.

"You took time off from your work here to go see him."

"It was personal time."

"Someone had to do your work while you were gone. Someone had to do *his* work, and so on. It left us a man short."

"The company was still solvent when I returned. Meanwhile seventy-five minutes were deducted from my card."

"Then you admit you went to Dolan for money after I refused you?"

"I went to see him. I have nothing to admit."

"He's a politician!"

"Some men are. You needn't make the word sound like an oath."

Pain began to gnaw at Abner's stomach. It never did when he spoke to Edward. Abner III was always too busy considering what to order for lunch to unsettle his father's digestion. He adjusted his tack. "And did your populist friend oblige you with a loan?"

"He declined the offer I made him."

"Of course he did. The man is not a fool, despite his transparent attempts to appear as simple as his constituents. Now will you abandon your scheme?"

"Did you abandon your spring suspension when your superiors told you it wouldn't work?"

"It isn't the same thing."

"That's the idea, Father."

Needles jabbed at his abdomen. "From now on you will not leave your job except in case of emergency. A doctor's signature will be required before you are allowed back on these premises."

It is no small thing for a man to see his own eyes glaring back at him. For a moment he thought his son would quit, and for a rarity he was not sure whether he dreaded the gesture or hoped for it. He did recognize the instant when Harlan acquiesced. It was less an indication of surrender than it was an indirect kind of defiance. In his youth, Abner had worn the same expression often enough to know it when it was shown him. "All right," said his son.

As victories went, it was as sour as his stomach. He pressed for more. "I didn't ask if you approved. Say you understand."

"I understand."

"Arrange to have those boards sent back to Nicaragua to-day."

"Yes, sir."

Abner left. On his way to the elevator he smelled not the smells nor heard the sounds nor saw the sights of the factory he had built. He thought only of warm milk in a glass and fifteen minutes alone in the cloistered silence of his office. It was as much of a retirement as he would ever feel secure enough to take.

chapter three

The Sicilian Prince

Drawn along ethnic lines, a map of Detroit in the small years of the twentieth century would have resembled a butcher's chart; one of those largely unnecessary wall decorations presuming to divide an overstuffed cow into chops, steaks, ribs, and sweetbreads, each section tinted its own color and promising a set of pleasures and disadvantages unique to itself.

In the center, bisected by Joseph Campau Avenue, lay Hamtramck, populated almost exclusively by second-and third-generation Poles. Of all the local neighborhoods designated by the national origin of their residents, Hamtramck alone was a fully incorporated city with its own mayor and police force, a distinction conferred upon it because of the seniority of its citizens and their invited status. In 1838, commissions agents met these hardworking, ox-shouldered refugees from Czarist Russia at the gangplanks in New York, Boston, and Baltimore, and carted them inland to grade and lay track for the Detroit and Pontiac Railway. Later they smelted iron for the stove industry and tilled the fields for the D. M. Ferry seed farms. They saved their wages, bought and built houses, and closed ranks against all the groups that followed, none of whom came by invitation. Tint Hamtramck rusty red for a living earned as hard as iron.

Corktown occupied the near west side, named for those immigrants from County Cork who led the exodus from Ireland in the time of the blight. Unlike the Poles and Germans, they knew English, and so assimilated quickly, albeit in numbers that horrified an earlier generation of Americans and drew inordinate attention to their preferred vices. They laid brick, ran streetcars, fought for prizes, wore police uniforms, and elected themselves into positions of power, establishing feudal fiefdoms copied from the examples of their former absentee English landlords. Color Corktown green, because that's what they would prefer.

East of central belonged to the Germans, now giving grudging ground, block by block, before the Italians. In residence as long as the Irish, they shared political influence with them, but did not patronize their pubs as the Irish did their beer gardens. The Germans were by and large educated and cultural, drinking their lager and eating their sauerbraten while reading Goethe and listening to Wagner on the phonograph. At the same moment Bismarck destroyed Napoleon III's army at Sedan, the French families who had traded Detroit away from the Indians were withdrawing from St. Antoine, Beaubien, and Lafayette to make room for the vendors of music boxes and German silver. The victory was complete; the Gallic tongue was no longer heard except when someone mangled the names of the original streets. Paint the near east side the dusty old gold of the Prussian double-headed eagle.

Bounded by Macomb, Monroe, Randolph, and Beaubien streets, Greektown sang and danced to the frenetic strings of the eastern Mediterranean. Brown-necked men in cloth caps and thick moustaches played checkers in the coffeehouses and washed down moussaka and sticky baklava with ouzo and retsina in restaurants larded with the smell of hot grease from lambs roasting. Cheeses and slaughtered ducks hung in the windows of shops where dried apricots and bottles of olive oil were sold. It was said that while the Poles worked and the Germans learned and the Irish stole, the Greeks ate. Shade in Greektown the deep blue of the Aegean Sea.

Negroes teemed in the area east of Randolph and south of

Congress. Their fathers and grandfathers had settled there at the northern end of the Underground Railroad, freed from the southern plantations first by radical abolitionists, then by government decree. They swept the streets, cleaned the houses of the well-to-do Irish and Germans, sweated in the stove foundries, and portered the Michigan Central and the Grand Trunk railroads. At night the men cast dice in the back rooms of the saloons and occasionally squared off with knives over disputed points. Elsewhere in the city, they took off their hats and spoke low and politely, with their gazes on the ground at their feet. East of Randolph and south of Congress, they walked down the center of the sidewalk, smoked cigars and drank dago red and ate pigs' knuckles and danced to piano-roll rag and bet their tips on Jack Johnson. The area was as separate and as self-contained as Hamtramck, without the paperwork. Make it black.

Between Gratiot and the river sprawled Italy in all its variety, segregated into blocks representing each of the regions of that boot-shaped peninsula and the boccie ball of Sicily, poised at the toe to career off the coasts of Africa and Spain. Here was Abruzzi, with Naples next to it, with Firenze two blocks down; Calabria and Venice and the rest, dug up separately and transported a third of the way across the globe and replanted side by side, with all their local traditions and enmities intact. Their sons and daughters married within the block, they spoke the dialects of their villages at home, their toothless grandfathers and barrel-shaped aunts never ventured outside the neighborhood except to attend church or be buried. They were janitors and building superintendents, they laid cobblestones, smeared tar on the roofs of buildings downtown, and straddled the girders of infant skyscrapers prickling the flat cityscape with long black lunch pails in their laps. On Columbus Day they marched in the big parade and bet on horses named Nina and Santa Maria in the chalkboard back rooms of barbershops and drank Chianti from basketed jugs in restaurants hung with pictures of Garibaldi and Italian prizefighters with Irish names. In the sopping heat of summer they slept on fire escapes on bare mattresses while Caruso sang on phonographs heard through window screens, drowned out from time to time by loud arguments and shattering china. Sometimes by a gunshot. Then a coffin would be borne down the street before moaning horns and a death-beat bass drum played by men sweating in black wool suits and celluloid collars, trailed by widows in black scarves. Drape Little Italy in the red, white, and green of the Italian flag.

In the heart of the Sicilian neighborhood, seated at his favorite table in a tiny restaurant splattered with tomato sauce, with fishing boats in the Gulf of Castellamare painted on the plaster walls, Salvatore Bornea ate a small plate of linguini in a light cream sauce, chasing each forkful with a sip of mineral water. Bornea was a student of the radical health theories of John Kellogg and C. W. Post of Battle Creek, Michigan, and eschewed his fellow countrymen's taste for starchy fats and red wine in deference to his trim waist. This consternated those Sicilians who expected their *padrones* to exhibit the swollen vests and puffed-out cheeks of the prosperous dons who ran things back home. The older residents did not come to his table, preferring the well-upholstered company of "Uncle Joe" Sorrato, who mediated disagreements among families and between landlords and borders. But Uncle Joe was dying at seventy-eight of a stroke brought on by too many clams fried in butter and too many gallons of forty-nine-cent wine. They would come around.

Salvatore Bornea, who was better known as Sal Borneo among the younger residents who did jobs for him and came to him for his patronage, had first seen the light of day in Siracusa, Sicily. To that he was willing to admit; but whether the year was 1870, 1871, or 1872, he declined to confirm. He had come to America in March 1884, bearing a birth certificate proving that he had attained the age of fourteen in February of that year, empowering him to enter the country without a legal guardian. When, however, he was arrested by the Detroit police in 1890 for assault with intent to commit great bodily harm less than murder, he produced a birth certificate dated September 11, 1872. He was prosecuted as a minor, and upon pleading guilty to a reduced charge of simple assault, spent ninety days mopping floors and emptying chamber pots in the Detroit House of Corrections. In truth, he was uncertain about the month and year of his birth. He had seen a notation of December 1871 in a family Bible when he was small, but was led by a conversation he had once overheard between relatives in an adjoining room that the date was a perjury intended to cover up a pregnancy too short for even the common explanation of a premature appearance. The 1870 certificate belonged to a cousin, also named Salvatore, who had died at the age of three months. The 1872 document was a forgery. Six years in the New World had been sufficient to acquaint him with the skilled people necessary to allow him to ply his trade.

The assault episode was an embarrassment. A barber named Gilberto Orosco, who owned three chairs and employed two additional barbers and a manicurist, had received a letter; not delivered by Borneo nor written by him, but the text of which he could guess: "You have more money than we have. You can afford to give $1,000 to the young man who comes to ask you for it." When Borneo went to the man's shop, Orosco threatened him with a razor. He agreed to leave, making a joke of it, saying that if he had come there to have his blood spilled he would ask for a shave. For three days he did not return to the shop, although he did go to the shoe store across the street each day before closing, to try on shoes facing the window and observe that Orosco was always the last to leave his establishment, drawing the shades himself and locking up, then turning left to stroll home to his house around the corner. On the fourth day, Borneo stepped out of the doorway of the apartment house on the corner and cracked open the barber's skull with a two-foot length of billiard cue. He had the misfortune of having been seen, and of all things by a magistrate with the Wayne County Court, a position which put him outside the category of citizens who could be intimidated into withdrawing their police report. He witnessed the assault upon leaving his tailor's, supplied an accurate description to the officers in the local precinct, and within a quarter of an hour, Borneo was taken from his room and put in handcuffs. Orosco lived, and was sufficiently sobered by the event to say nothing of the extortion demand, and so intent to commit murder was not included in the charge. Borneo had certainly intended to commit murder, and he had not intended to be seen. He regretted both mistakes. The frightened barber paid the thousand dollars, and Uncle Joe Sorrato, who had sent the demand, was pleased with the young man's refusal to identify his employer during nine hours of interrogation that left him with three broken ribs and a punctured eardrum; upon his release he received five dollars in silver for his silence.

Borneo became Uncle Joe's enemy then. He was planning to visit the old don with something better than a billiard cue when Sorrato suffered the first of the series of strokes that would chain him to his bed. This was better satisfaction than Borneo could have hoped for. He declared a truce—with Uncle Joe.

The old man listed himself in the Detroit directory as a greengrocer. He had not operated a fruit-and-vegetable cart in fifteen years, but no Italian merchant in the city could sell produce without his permission. Those who had tried, and had ignored the warnings, had their carts upended by toughs and their pears and cantaloupes squashed and kicked apart, had paraffin bombs hurled through their shop windows and buckets of excrement dumped over their inventory. Some of the reluctant merchants were stomped and kicked along with their wares, or were in their shops when the bombs exploded and flung flaming liquid in every direction. One who had made himself particularly clear about where he stood on the subject of blackmail had been forced to watch with a knife at his throat while his daughter was raped on the floor between his display cases. All of these incidents were investigated by the police, who inspected the scenes, asked questions of the victims and their neighbors, and reported that the crimes were the result of centuries-old vendettas going back to the Old Country, and hence outside the jurisdiction of the local constabulary. The officers were by and large Polish and Irish. Some of the residents shrugged and said the police were paid off, just like back home. Others argued that it was worse than that; they just didn't care. They said that the people who had told them the streets of America were paved with gold hadn't lied, their information was just outdated. The gold had all been torn up and banked long ago by the people who came before them, and they, the newcomers, were expected to replace it with cobblestones and asphalt for a dollar a week.

Sal Borneo was unmoved by these complaints. It was the crudity of Giuseppe Sorrato's methods that offended him. Left unchecked, such arrogant savagery must eventually fill too many columns in the English-language newspapers, ignite the gentry, and through its indignation overcome the authorities' inertia, sparking wholesale raids and ruining the protection business for everyone. Only a generation earlier, mobs armed with truncheons and torches had ripped through San Francisco's Barbary Coast, smashing saloons, setting fire to brothels, dumping craps tables and roulette wheels into the harbor—closing the frontier as surely as screwing shut a tap, and all because one too many sailors got his brains bashed in and his body dropped through a trap with all his pockets turned inside out.

Nothing, Borneo had learned, was permanent, though everything was cyclical. Goodness and vice must each take its turn, but neither could hold it forever. He had followed with interest the formation of various antisaloon leagues across the country, most notably the one headed in Ohio by the Reverend Howard Hyde Russell, a dried-up old raisin with white hair and spectacles, Carrie Nation in a vest and without her bonnet. The idea seemed to be catching on, and with a teetotaler in the White House, there was no telling how long that fire would burn or how much it might consume. Better to sit it out, or fan it in a direction more beneficial. There was money to be made from fighting fires, once people had had enough of them, and if one took care not to step in the path of the flames.

Uncle Joe was safe on his deathbed. Not so his son Carlo, who at age thirty was even fatter than his father, and who had announced the old man's retirement by having himself listed as a greengrocer in the city directory. His first official act was to target a butcher on Heidelberg, in what was until recently Germantown.

Vito Grapellini was no ordinary purveyor of steaks and chops. When he closed his shop at night, he changed out of his apron and straw boater into blue-and-white flannels, white spats, and a Panama hat, and struck off toward the streetcar swinging a bamboo cane like Eddie Foy. He supplied the finest cuts to wealthy homeowners on Jefferson and through Big Jim Dolan had contracted to fill the larders for twenty-five-dollar-a-plate fund-raising dinners thrown by the Democratic Party. For this boon the Irish Pope received a 20-percent return on every slice of corned beef sold. Grapellini had been known to drop what would have been a month's wages for a bricklayer on a single race at the fairgrounds, and to be seen in Dolph's Saloon an hour later, drinking beer and eating bratwurst and laughing. When Carlo Sorrato gave Borneo a letter to give to the butcher and said he should be good for five thousand if he didn't want to see his shop burn down, Borneo thought Carlo was inspired less by Grapellini's prosperity than by national pride; had the man sought comfort in cannoli and Chianti instead of that German rot, one or two thousand might have been satisfactory.

Borneo accepted the commission and delivered the letter. He had decided that if the butcher took fright and agreed to the demand, then his plans must be postponed and the matter treated as an ordinary transaction. When Grapellini opened the envelope and moved his lips over the words, his features lost all color; Borneo turned to leave. Then the blood returned to the butcher's face all at once, a deep, liverish red, the hue of rage. Borneo waited while both paper and envelope were torn in two, then the pieces shuffled together and torn again. The scraps fluttered to the sawdust covering the floor. Borneo was distracted by them for an instant. When he looked up, the butcher had jerked his cleaver from the block between them and was holding it like an axe.

"Get out of my shop, you damn Sicilian nigger!"

Grapellini, he realized at that moment, was a Calabrise. There was a special hatred between the two regions, separated only by the hair's breadth of the Strait of Messina, that amounted almost to love.

Borneo held up a palm. "Put down your weapon, Vito Grapellini. I have a proposition."

He spoke in English, lest his island dialect goad the butcher into violence. His face was already the same shade of scarlet as the stains on his apron.

"I read your proposition already." The cleaver remained where it was.

"You have been here ten years, long enough to know that not much is different here. If you refuse to pay the money, a fire in your place of business is the least you have to fear. You may lose your life."

"We will see what Jimmy Dolan has to say about that."

"Dolan is a mick. He will not interfere with what goes on in Little Italy. If he roars, Carlo Sorrato will give him a street-sweep he has paid to plead guilty to manslaughter. Dolan will be satisfied, and you will still be dead. He will find another butcher."

"I will not be dead alone."

"No one is dead alone. The cemetery is crowded. Why should you tax its capacity further? I am offering you a way by which you will keep your life and most of your money."

"Why not all of it?"

Borneo smiled. The moustache he had started turned down at the corners, and the expression was melancholy. "Like you, I must live."

The cleaver came down slowly. "How much?"

"Five hundred dollars."

Grapellini's smile was not melancholy. Borneo saw in it that the butcher now considered him a tenth as important as Uncle Joe's fat son.

"Five hundred dollars a month for as long as Sorrato and everyone else leaves you alone to do business."

The smile went away. The cleaver ground curls of white maple out of the block.

"I will let you think about it," Borneo said. To aid him in his decision, he gave the butcher the names of three men to whom he might turn for references. One of them was Gilberto Orosco, the barber.

When Borneo returned the next day, Grapellini did not pick up his cleaver. He finished wrapping a package of veal for a woman with thick ankles and a faint moustache, fumbling a little with the string, and thanked her for her order. When the bell tinkled behind her, he addressed Borneo as Signor Bornea and said that he was very much interested in the proposition he had made.

Borneo was grave. "It was no less interesting yesterday. It is true that at the end of ten months you will have paid me as much as Carlo Sorrato is asking, and then the payments will continue. However, Carlo Sorrato does not offer a guarantee that he will not return in six months to demand another five thousand. Nor does he promise that you will not be bothered by others who will say that if Vito Grapellini can afford to pay Uncle Joe's fat son five thousand dollars to leave him in peace, he can give us two hundred in return for the same service. It goes on, you see. There is no unity among these fellows. I will see that you are not bothered by them."

"I have no doubt that you can, now," Grapellini replied. "The Sorratos are a different matter. The old man is dying, but Carlo has three brothers."

"A cockroach has six legs. They are harmless once you cut off its head."

"I will not pay for murder."

"I do not murder for pay. We are discussing an arrangement to insure your business and your person against loss and injury. Grapellini, I did not come here to say all over again what I said yesterday. Do you accept my proposition or not?"

The butcher turned around. His cleaver and a number of knives with blue-edged blades were laid out on the back counter. When he faced Borneo again he was holding a thick envelope, smeared with bloody juice.

Borneo did not take it. "You will pay me when we meet next. Do you open your cash register before you have cut and weighed your meat in full view of the customer? Satisfaction comes first."

The next day, Carlo Sorrato was found lying facedown on Riopelle Street, north of the Eastern Market, with his pockets turned inside out and his throat slit from ear to ear. The coroner's physician who performed the autopsy, a young man named Edouard, reported that he hadn't enough blood left in him to float a five-cent cigar. It was decided at the inquest that he had died at the hands of robbers. Salvatore Bornea was among those brought in for questioning. A salesgirl at Partridge & Blackwell's department store named Graziella Carbone told police that at the time of the atrocity she and Borneo were watching the vaudeville show at the Temple Theater, after which they went roller-skating at the Pavilion. She produced ticket stubs in support of her claim. Borneo was released. Three weeks later, the couple married in St. Mary's Roman Catholic Church. Vito Grapellini provided the meat for the reception at the Wayne Hotel.

The murder of Carlo Sorrato was never solved. His brothers, Vincenzo, Gaetano, and Giuseppe Jr., offered a reward of a thousand dollars for the name of the perpetrator, but it was withdrawn after Vincenzo fell into the path of the Woodward Avenue streetcar and his right leg was amputated. His claim that he was pushed was investigated by the police, who reported that the incident was a regrettable accident caused by the eagerness of the homebound crowd to board the car. The same night, Gaetano found a note under his door advising him to forget about Carlo. A program for a dance recital featuring Gaetano's five-year-old daughter was included in the envelope. Upon Vincenzo's release from St. Mary's Hospital, all three Sorratos and their families moved to Toledo, where they opened a market.

Shortly after Vincenzo's accident, other merchants began paying Sal Borneo to insure themselves and their businesses against injury and loss. He recorded the amounts in a ledger as dues paid to the Unione Siciliana, a benevolent organization of which he was founder and president. Two years went by, a period remembered as a time of peace within Detroit's Italian community. Then Borneo entered Vito Grapellini's shop on a day when his dues in the Unione were not expected. He said, "I have a proposition."

"Another one?" The butcher wiped his bloody hands on a rag.

"This one will not cost you." Borneo reached inside the coat of the suit he had ordered cut to his measure at C. R. Mabley's in Cadillac Square and placed an envelope on the maple block. It contained $12,000 in crisp new hundred-dollar bills. "That is the money you have paid me for protecting yourself and your business since we made our agreement. I offer it back in return for controlling interest in your shop."

Grapellini smiled, but his eyes were troubled. He had grown to admire Borneo as a man of his word, but he feared him more than ever. "You want to be a butcher?"

"Certainly not. I don't know chuck from sirloin. I seldom even eat meat. I want you to go on running Grapellini's Meats just as you have from the beginning. I will be your silent partner. We will share in the profits and I will not presume to tell you how a butcher's shop should be run."

"Twelve thousand would buy the whole thing."

"As I said, I am not a butcher. I wish merely to share in the profits and to declare on government forms that I am a businessman in the city of Detroit."

"You could do that anyway. Who would dispute you?"

"No one here, whom I can persuade by reason, or kill if he does not see things as clearly as I. The government is an ant heap. You can neither reason with it nor kill it."

The proposition was accepted, as both men knew it would be. Salvatore Bornea had himself listed in the city directory as a butcher, and entered the business community. Less visibly, he entered into Grapellini's unspoken agreement with James Aloysius Dolan to furnish the Democratic Party with meat in return for 20 percent of the proceeds.

Thus began the relationship that would carry the hidden

city machinery into the twentieth century. The thing was not written about in the newspapers nor discussed except in back rooms in Corktown and in the public rooms of saloons among those who had nothing to gain or lose from it, but it was understood by people who could make neither head nor tail of the city charter, and accepted as far away as the state capital in Lansing as an essential ingredient in the grease that kept the democratic gears turning. At election time, young hooligans were paid by Borneo to tear down posters advertising the campaigns of candidates who opposed Dolan's ticket; telephone lines into their headquarters were cut, vociferous supporters were beaten and robbed in the very streets their champions had pledged to make safe. Pugs employed by the Unione Siciliana plucked ballots from the hands of voters at the polls, made their marks next to the correct names, and dropped them into boxes, glaring silent challenges at would-be objectors. Dolan in his turn kept police away from Borneo's brothels and horse parlors and, when the Sicilian received a note threatening the life of his newborn daughter if he did not put out ten thousand dollars with his empty milk bottles, stationed officers in front of his house twenty-four hours per day until the danger had passed. The officers were able to give witness to the fact that Borneo was secure at home the night an extortion suspect, a hooligan of Neapolitan descent, had his heart cut out on Mt. Elliott Street. (Two others involved in the attempt apologized, saying that they were forced into the scheme by the Neapolitan, of whom they were afraid. Borneo hired them to perform various errands, and was impressed with their efficiency and loyalty. He sincerely regretted it when they were taken by carriage to a point on the river near Flat Rock, forced to kneel on the bank, and shot in the back of the head. It was said in Sicily that your enemy is not your friend, no matter if he marries your daughter and fathers your grandchildren.)

The Dolan-Borneo tie increased the wealth and influence

of both parties, even as it caused grumbling among some of their acquaintances. Older Sicilians, not reconciled to Borneo's ascendancy over the still-stricken Uncle Joe, referred disparagingly to him and his confederates as "the Irish," and Assistant Party Chairman Brennan complained that you could trust a greaseball guinea to stick you in the kidneys when your back was turned and not a bit further; but even detractors could not dispute the advantages of the arrangement, and gave both men credit for not flaunting their association. Indeed, they had never met.

Sal Borneo was built slightly and stood below the average height for his race, having survived a bout with smallpox at an age when most young men experienced their final growth spurt. The bones of his face were prominent, particularly the bridge of his nose, which hooked like a Sioux Indian's. He had in fact grown out his moustache because it was less disadvantageous to be thought a foreigner than a New World savage. The pox had spoiled his complexion, made it mealy, but he had fine dark eyes with long lashes and excellent teeth, which he attended as closely as his diet. Some women thought him handsome. He was a good family man, however, and kept only one mistress, a waitress who lived in an apartment he maintained on Vernor Street and who led her friends to believe her benefactor was a stove-company executive living in one of the fine homes on Jefferson.

What meals he ate outside his house he preferred to take in the little restaurant on Charlevoix Street. The food was only adequate, but the service was good without being effusive and he liked the wall murals, which reminded him of his boyhood in Siracusa. His father had been a fisherman there until he was mistaken by a vendettist for an enemy and murdered. Borneo was cheated of his vengeance when the man for whom his father was mistaken murdered the murderer. He shipped for America soon after to escape his grief and disappointment. New

York City was too noisy for a boy from a small fishing village, and he had lacked the train fare as far as Chicago, where he had cousins; while stopping off in Detroit to seek employment to raise the difference, he had discovered something of home in the smell of the river, the elegant brick houses facing Canada, and the pushcarts and pomp of the saints-day parades in Little Italy. The stove makers and carriage builders were hiring immigrants and paying well. Chicago, he had felt, could get by without him. It had taken him just twenty years to rise from a common day laborer and street tough to a power in the city. In private, a great deal of argument would have been required to convince Sal Borneo that there was no gold beneath the asphalt.

He had finished his meal and was reading the book he had brought, volume III of Gibbon, when he became aware that Bernardo, his waiter, was standing in front of his table. The old fellow was reluctant to interrupt his reading by addressing him or clearing his throat.

"Yes?" He marked his place in the book with his finger.

"Your pardon, Don Salvatore. A young gentleman wishes to approach your table."

Borneo looked past the fat waiter but did not recognize the stocky young man standing inside the entrance. He wore work clothes stained with grease and sweat.

"Did he say what his business is?"

"No, sir." Bernardo appeared mortified that he had not this information to report.

"What is his name?"

The waiter closed his eyes, the better to concentrate upon the pronunciation. "Harlan Crownover."

"Crownover?"

"Si, Don Salvatore. That is what he said."

Borneo closed his book. "Tell the young gentleman I would

be delighted if he would join me. And please bring us a bottle of your best Chianti."

"Chianti?" The fat fellow beamed.

"Yes, Bernardo. On certain occasions, health must walk behind."

chapter four

The Prodigal

At the dawn of the century, news items relating to the manufacture and operation of automobiles were researched and written by sports reporters. Articles on "motoring" appeared beside photographs of gangle-jointed baseball pitchers and lists of first-, second-, and third-place finishers in the bicycle races on Belle Isle. Motormen were identified as fellows in goggles, ankle-length dusters, and leather gauntlets, a uniform as distinctive as the leather helmets and padding worn by college football players, and their arcane jargon peppered their interviews with the frequency of *knucklers* and *breadbaskets* in boxing pieces.

Like most sporting men, these figures, manufacturers and race-car drivers alike, congregated in places that catered to them in herds. When Ransom Olds's auto plant on Jefferson burned to the ground and the owner was sought for comment, when the rumor took flight that Henry Ford had decided to make a third run at the automobile business and reporters wanted to ask him why this attempt should be any more successful than the others, when one or the other of the Dodge brothers was out on bail on a complaint of discharging a firearm in a crowded restaurant and his side of the story was required, the men on the sports desks at the *News, Times,* and *Free Press* had only to send their reporters to one of five bars set yards apart along Detroit's Campus Martius downtown. This was the toplofty designation set aside for the stretch of Woodward Avenue where the Seventh and Twentieth Michigan marched on their way to put down the Southern Rebellion, and where older residents remembered gathering in 1865 to bow their heads in memory of the martyred Abraham Lincoln.

The Normandie, around the corner on Congress, offered a Louis Quatorze atmosphere of gilded paneling, a Brussels carpet, and bottles of imported liqeuer, sparkling in rainbow colors along the back bar. On Woodward, Louie Schneider's served dark ale and bitter German beers beneath Wagnerian prints, with the smell of sauerkraut sunk stud-deep into the walls. The Metropole was redolent of good cigars and aged brandy, its woodwork polished to an improbable finish, as if mirrors had been melted and poured over every horizontal surface. Up the block, across from the white porcelain and gleaming stainless steel of Sanders' ice cream store, stood Churchill's, paneled in mahogany, trimmed with brass, and decorated with cut crystal and Julius Rolshoven's *Brunette Venus* reclining in nothing but a beaded frame behind the bar. The illuminati of the motor crowd went to the other places to celebrate the invention of a new fuel pump or to commiserate with one another upon a bank foreclosure; the vintage wines and single-malt Scotches of Churchill's were reserved for impressing prospective partners or closing a deal involving thousands. Most of the auto men were separated by only a few years from a time when the batwing doors at the end of the entryway were as close as they dared come in their greasy overalls and muddy work boots.

But ever and again they returned to the Pontchartrain. In the bar of that upstart hotel, in the company of prizefighters in photographs and Theodore Roosevelt's abstemious portrait scowling above the beer pulls, they drank, ate the free lunch, compared war stories, and to the chagrin of hotel manager Bill Chittenden, who feared for the Persian rugs in the lobby, occasionally brought in pieces of their engines for the admiration and advice of their colleagues. There were dents all over the bar's glossy oaken top where pistons had slipped through oily fingers and where manifolds and short blocks had been heaved up and slammed down with too much force. Most bars smelled of beer and cigars and moustache wax; the Pontchartrain smelled also of gasoline.

Harlan Crownover found the bar nearly deserted at half past three Saturday afternoon. He'd expected nothing else, but he'd hoped for better. His news was too good not to share, but too big to wait until evening, when the ball game let out at Bennett Park and the room filled with friends and strangers stinking of bleacher sweat and mustard, rushing the season by wearing straw boaters before Memorial Day; the Jefferson Avenue elite, most of whom would not set foot in the Pontchartrain, sniffed and said the next thing you knew some motorman would show up at the opera house in a woolen bathing suit.

At that hour, Harlan shared the dim interior with the bartender, a new man whose name he hadn't yet learned, a pair of strangers in derbies smoking cigars over brandy snifters in a booth at the back, and Horace Dodge, seated at the bar with a shot glass in his hand. Harlan sighed and went over to sit next to him. In general he found the Dodges, John and his brother Horace, loud, obstreperous ruffians, whose natural inclination to seek trouble wherever it resided, and to create it where it did not, was refined by drink into methods of torment not normally encountered outside the child's battlefield of the playground. No one who told the story was sure whether it was John or Horace who had fired his revolver at the feet of a bartender at Schneider's in order to persuade him to demonstrate an Irish jig, but it sounded more like John, who of the two was the more honest bully. Horace was the kind who crept up behind a victim on hands and knees for his partner to push the fellow over his back.

This Harlan had learned from observation rather than experience, for he was exempt from their hectoring by reason of his birth. These two sons of the owner of a machine shop in rural Niles, Michigan, were always polite in their rough-hewn way to Harlan, a second-generation heir to an American business dynasty, whose father had saved the company from ruin and in the process created a national institution. To them he was old nobility, and their behavior toward him was the traditional bowing and scraping of the typical bully before a power greater than his. If they called him by his first name and pounded him on the back in greeting, it was merely an American face-saving substitute for tugging their forelocks. They were equal parts proud of having attracted his company and contemptuous of him for having lowered himself to associate with the likes of them. He in his turn found them as comfortable to be around as a pair of iron stoves stoked up to white heat.

Horace's round fleshy face, when he turned to answer Harlan's greeting, was flushed as deep as the flame-colored roots of his hair, a lock of which had sprung free from the sweatband of his derby and dangled Napoleon-like over his bulbous forehead. The flush, together with the pink tint in the whites of his eyes, indicated that the shot glass in his hand had been filled more than once. The brothers, beefy and running to fat, still in their thirties but with broken blood vessels in their cheeks as if they'd been drinking heavily for forty years, had big appetites and thirsts to match. The hand with which Horace took Harlan's in a bone-pulverizing grip was broken-knuckled, with years of grease under the nails, and nicked all over with old white-healed scars and fresh bleeding ones; owners of one of the most successful machine shops in the Midwest, the Dodges couldn't resist picking up a wrench and barking their knuckles alongside those of their employees. Harlan considered this democratic streak their one saving grace.

He didn't bother to ask Horace what he was drinking. He and John invariably started their day with boilermakers, then around noon jettisoned the beer in favor of straight rye. Harlan, who disliked strong drink, ordered a bock.

"I got the money," he said, when the beer had been brought and the bartender had retired to the opposite end of the bar.

"No shit, how much?" Horace raised his glass and knocked the top off a fresh refill.

"Five thousand."

"I'll be damned. From the old man?"

"No."

"Not the bank. They all run when they hear Henry's name."

"No." He swallowed some beer and tried not to make a face. Ford's temperance was a raw spot with both Dodges and he didn't want his potential partners to think he was opposed to alcohol. "Do you know if Mr. Ford is coming in today?"

"What for? He don't drink, he don't eat, he don't smoke. The only reason he makes cars is so he don't have to stay home and fuck." He jerked down the rest of his drink in one movement and signaled the bartender with a finger.

"Why do you do business with him if you disapprove of him?"

"I don't disapprove of no one. John and me are the kind that other folks disapprove of. Ford's all right, I guess. If he works out that problem with the rear axle he might even sell somebody a car. I just don't like no one preaching at me any day but Sunday."

"He's a bit of a stick."

"That's why he ran away from his old man's farm. If he stayed put longer than a minute, somebody would of strung a fence to him."

"Where's John?" It occurred to Harlan as he asked the question that he'd never before seen the brothers separated. Most of the time they even dressed identically, as if they were twins.

"Learning to be a typewriter."

"A what?"

"He went and bought him a typewriting machine and locked himself up with it for two days, but he said he couldn't bang it any faster than a turtle fucking a snail. He went and enrolled himself in a course at the YMCA."

"Can't he afford a secretary?"

"He says dictating letters and then having them typed and then reading them takes too long. I think he just likes having another contraption to play with. I bet he took it apart and put it back together three times in them two days. Also it keeps him from thinking about Ivy." John Dodge's wife had died the previous October. His and Horace's mother, seventy and confined to a wheelchair, had promptly moved into John's house to care for his three children.

"He's going to work himself to death."

"If he does, he'll die rich. Me too. Every penny we make goes back into the plant. We're putting up a new building at Monroe and Hastings."

"I wondered what was going in there. What was wrong with the Boydell Building?"

"It shrunk. We just took over all the machinery at Canadian Cycle and Motor."

"You bought them?"

He drank and shook his head. "They swapped us their equipment for the royalties they owed me for that bicycle ball bearing I invented. We needed a place to put it, so we're building one."

"It seems like the only industry that's doing any building in this town is automobiles. I wish I could get my father to open his eyes."

"Well, you can forget that."

Other customers were trailing in. Harlan didn't recognize any of the faces, although Horace nodded to several and twisted around on his stool once, to pump the hand and slap the shoulder of a thick-necked young man in a gray flannel suit with a humorous expression on his face. When the fellow left to claim a booth, Harlan asked who he was.

"Barney Everitt. He runs the upholstery shop at Olds."

"Olds burned down."

"Sooner or later everything does. That don't mean you leave the business. And just because your old man don't throw in with you don't mean you got to go it alone. John and I took over the shop because the old man couldn't juggle the books with both hands and his feet."

Harlan laughed and spun his glass between his palms. "I could never do that."

"Why the hell not? If we didn't, the shop would of closed down. Family's family, but a man's business is his living."

"Crownover Coaches isn't a machine shop in Niles."

"Suit yourself. You can't stop a man from hanging himself if he's bound and determined, John says." Horace drank.

Henry Ford walked in ten minutes later. Lean and bony-looking in a charcoal three-piece suit too heavy for the weather and a round collar, he appeared taller than he was, and older than his years, his hawk nose, deep-set eyes, and straight slash of a mouth giving him the resemblance of a Maine farmer dressed for church. Horace spotted him first and hailed him. Harlan saw a brief expression of pain cross Ford's face when he recognized the younger Dodge. Recovering quickly, he strode over and shook the man's hand. Horace's bone-mauling grasp appeared not to distress him. When it came Harlan's turn to stand and greet the newcomer, he found out why; years of tinkering in his backyard with wrenches and pliers and countless laps with his hands gripping the wheel of a racing car had strung Ford's fingers with steel wire. Harlan's own loading-dock grip barely answered.

"I want to talk to you about that rear axle," Horace said.

"I'm working on it," Ford said.

"I got a couple of ideas."

"So have I." His eyes moved nervously in their sockets. They had a steely sheen, not unlike Horace's patented ball bearings. "Mr. Crownover and I have a spot of business to discuss."

Harlan, who had not had an appointment with Ford, responded to the implied plea. He spotted the two derby-hatted strangers sliding out of their booth and, excusing himself to Horace, steered Ford in that direction, cutting off John Kelsey, the wheel maker, and a companion. Kelsey muttered an oath, but without conviction; Harlan had heard the man was too tender-hearted even to expect anyone but himself to wash his underwear. An unconventional business attracted unconventional men.

"Are you a friend of the Dodges'?" Ford asked when they were seated.

"We've barely met."

"Well, that's the way to keep it, if you can't avoid knowing them at all."

"I hear they're rough customers."

"That's no disadvantage. It's a rough industry. What color would you say their hair is, auburn?"

"Red, definitely."

"Not reddish brown?"

"Red. I'd think they were Irish if I hadn't heard otherwise. Is it important?"

"Not if I can find a white horse." Ford looked around the room as if he might spot one there.

"Are you superstitious?"

Ford shook a finger at him as long as a darning needle. "Don't underestimate the element of luck. If you weren't born the son of a millionaire, you'd be mopping out stables. If my grandparents hadn't been evicted from a tenant farm in Ireland in 1847, my boy Edsel would be planting potatoes in County Cork. If I hadn't seen a steam thresher puffing down a dirt road when I was fourteen and impressionable, I'd be plowing my father's farm in Dearborn. I built my first steam engine that day, using a five-gallon oilcan as a boiler. So when I see a white horse I have to find a red-headed man, and the reverse. Either one is bad luck without the other."

"If you feel that way, I'm surprised you went into business with John and Horace."

"They have the best machine shop in the Middle West."

To which statement Harlan might have added: *that will have anything to do with a twice-failed manufacturer of automobiles.* But he did not. The very fact that the Dodges had agreed to provide engines for Ford cars had decided Harlan to throw in with this odd angular man whose eyes burned like pinpoints in the steel jacket of a foundry. Ransom E. Olds, the anointed royalty of the tiny realm of the motorcar, had found the brothers adequate to build transmissions for the curved-dash Oldsmobile, whose sales had been sprightly before the fire. In fact, Harlan had been considering approaching Olds with the proposition of a partnership when the plant burned. Of the smattering of prospects that remained, Henry Leland, Ford's own former senior partner, was too well established in the machine-tool business with some dabbling in automobiles on the side to need or want a new associate, and the rest were either parvenus who frittered away their capital buying drinks for one another in the Pontchartrain and talking about machines they would never build, or crooks and con artists. Ford, on the other hand, had ideas; and he certainly knew and loved automobiles. He had built his first fully operational machine from scratch in his shop in 1896, had raced cars with Barney Oldfield, the former bicycling champion, and had quit the Edison company when his supervisor offered him a general superintendency if he agreed to abandon his experiments with gasoline-powered vehicles. Harlan, no stranger to heated family business discussions (although he himself had never taken part until the invention of the automobile), could imagine the conversation that had ensued between Ford and his wife, Clara, when he brought home this news. For all that he was a queer fellow who held that the fumes from internal combustion engines cured tuberculosis and heart disease, and refused to eat sugar because he believed the sharp crystals would shred his stomach. It amused Harlan, when the bartender approached them, to hear his companion order only a glass of mineral water with a slice of lemon; Sal Borneo, whose background was as far removed from Ford's farm-country upbringing as possible, had drunk the very same thing, without the lemon slice, after helping himself to a single ceremonial sip of Chianti from the bottle he had ordered.

Harlan asked for another glass of bock and ignored Ford's disapproving frown. He was not the supplicant here, as he had been with Borneo and Jim Dolan before him; the weight of five thousand dollars in hundred-dollar bills in an envelope in the inside breast pocket of his season-rushing seersucker jacket felt like a secure plate of armor against his ribs.

"I've got the money," he said, after the drinks had been brought.

"What money?"

The question unsettled him. "Well, the five thousand. That's the amount we agreed upon in return for a twenty-percent share."

"I'm up to my neck in partners now. Malcolmson's saddling me with that Daisy man."

Alexander Malcolmson, a self-made millionaire who had begun as a simple coal merchant and within a few short years had bought out all his competitors to dominate the Detroit market, was the most upright and legitimate of Ford's backers. "I don't know what a daisy man is," Harlan said.

"Bennett. The air-gun fellow in Plymouth. He'll invest if I agree to build my automobiles in the Daisy plant. He even wants to call it the Daisy. I told him no."

"Was that wise?"

"I don't much care if it ain't. I never asked Malcolmson to ask him in. If I listen to every damn fool with money in his pocket, I'll wind up making cars for the emperor of Russia in St. Petersburg, complete with sled runners up front so he and his wife and that nut Rasputin can go motoring through Siberia."

"You need partners to operate."

"If I had two nickels to rub together I'd tell every last one of them to go back to their coal and their banks. If they refused to leave, I'd drag a dead skunk across their trail and stink them out. Absolute control is the only way anything ever got done in this country worth shouting about."

Harlan smiled over his beer. "I'm beginning to understand why some people call you Crazy Henry. Only a crazy man would try to talk someone out of giving him money."

"Crazy like a fox." Ford tapped his bony forehead. His tight grin betrayed Yankee pride at having coined a phrase. "Take back your money. I can use it, but I need bodies more."

"Bodies?"

"Good stout wooden ones on elmwood frames. I want Crownover Coaches to make the bodies for the new Ford car, and I'll pay fifty-two dollars apiece. Cash up front. That's the same deal I offered the Dodges."

"You had to. They wouldn't have done business with you otherwise."

The tight grin tightened another notch. "Sure they would have. Those boys love to gamble."

Harlan shook his head. "I want to be part of something that doesn't involve my father."

"Now who's crazy? Everything a man does involves his father. I might go sixty, if you'll give me permission to use the Crownover suspension system."

"I can't. That patent belongs to my father."

"I'll steal it, then. But I still need bodies."

"I wish you'd just take my money. There are plenty of carriage shops in town."

"There are, and most of them are every bit as good as yours. Don't look at me like that, you know it's true. Abner the Second hasn't done a new thing since he invented his spring. But those other shops haven't his name. Motorcars are like skyscrapers; new enough to excite people, but how many of them actually climbed into an elevator and rode it to the top until J. Pierpont Morgan set foot in one for the first time? Godevils won't seem so new and scary once it gets out Crownover's making them. Crownover carried the pioneers to California. If it was good enough for Grandma and Grandpa, I guess it's all right for Junior."

"Are you going to include a history lesson in your advertising?"

"History is bunk. We're living in history, but you can trust the writers to get it all wrong. Think about it. A Dodge engine in a Crownover body paid for by Malcolmson coal. Nothing so new and frightening about that."

Harlan, hemmed in by Ford's relentless logic, had no exit but confession. "My father will never agree to it. He thinks automobiles are a thing of the moment and will have nothing to do with them."

"He didn't feel that way when he junked his father's covered wagons and started making opera coaches."

"He was young then. No one had written a book about him." It came out more bitter than he'd intended. "I wish you'd just take my money."

After a moment Ford picked up the envelope, lifted the flap, and thumbed through the corrugated stack inside. It did not appear to have occurred to him that to count the bills in the presence of the man who had given them to him—an American gentleman by birth—might give offense; but Harlan wasn't offended. Like the Gold Rush, the boom in automaking had attracted goldbricks and four-flushers from all over the forty-five states. It was not in the habit of those who followed the profession to expect honesty. When he was through counting, Ford slid the envelope into his inside breast pocket and emptied his others in search of his receipt book, ejecting in the process an odd assortment of machine screws, washers, spark plugs in white porcelain jackets, and various bizarre-shaped bits of metal, hard rubber, and cardboard that defied identification onto the table. At length he produced a swollen pad stuffed with folded sheets of notepaper scribbled all over with figures and abbreviations and borrowed a fountain pen from Harlan to record the transaction. Harlan accepted the carbon and his pen and watched Ford gather up his baubles. He noted that they all went back to the precise pockets from which they had been taken; crazy Ford might be, and certainly eccentric in his habits, but he was a walking file cabinet.

"When do you go into production?" Harlan asked.

"I'm dickering over a place on Mack. If I get it, I'll have the first car on the road by next spring, if those Jews at Hartford Rubber don't hold me up too high on the tires." He took a bite out of his lemon slice, making Harlan's own tongue shrink inside his mouth. "What's your favorite color?"

"Blue, I suppose. Why?"

"I've been looking at paint chips for a week. Seems it don't matter what kind of engine or transmission a motorcar's got as long as the customer likes the color it's painted, or so C. H. Wills says."

"Who's Wills?"

"My design engineer. He helped me draw up the nine ninety-nine. Maybe he's got a point."

The 999 was the racing machine Barney Oldfield had driven to a first-place finish in the five-mile Challenge Cup race in 1900. Oldfield had spent the week before the race learning to drive, and had steered the 999 and himself into modern history a few weeks later when he set a world's record for the mile in 1:01. Harlan said, "Red lacquer is our most popular color. It's the same shade Napoleon ordered for his coronation coach."

"What did that squirt know? Fulton offered him the steamship and he showed him the door. I'm leaning toward black."

"What are you planning to make, a car or a hearse?"

"Japan black dries fastest."

"There's one car for every one and a half million people in the country. I don't think the demand's so great they won't wait for the paint to dry."

"Perhaps not. Now." Ford applied his linen napkin fastidiously to both corners of his mouth as if he'd had a seven-course meal instead of a single slice of lemon. The steely eyes were more brilliant than ever. "Where'd you get the money?"

The crudity of the question surprised Harlan into giving an honest answer. "I borrowed it from Sal Borneo."

"The mafia man?"

"So they say. We didn't seal the arrangement with a black hand, so I can't be sure."

The darning needle wagged. "I won't have a wop telling me how to manufacture automobiles."

"It was a straight loan, not an investment on his part. When I told him what I wanted it for he wasn't even interested. All he cares about is that he gets his money back."

"He was interested. When that butcher comes back for his cut, it comes from you, no one else. I've got enough partners as it is. If Bennett comes in I'll have too many. No greasy dago is going to get his spaghetti hooks on an American automobile company."

"I promise you he won't."

"I promise *you*." Ford's voice cracked. The forty-or-so-year-old mechanical genius sounded like a querulous old man. He scooped up his glass and emptied it. It was as if he'd poured water into the radiator of one of his automobiles; the patches of red that had appeared on his sallow cheeks faded, his eyes seemed less bright. Their gleam now was speculative. "You know your father's a hidebound fool."

Harlan, unsettled already by the previous scene, felt the need to put up some kind of filial defense. "He has a blind spot when it comes to automobiles. Everyone has one about something."

"Think he's senile?"

"He's only in his fifties."

"That doesn't mean anything. That jackass Bryan's only in his forties, and he tried to ride a silver sled into the White House. The Abner Crownover who saved his father's company wouldn't have closed his ears to a new idea, even if he thought it was crackpot. He'd have heard it out."

"The family decision is I'm an idiot. He wouldn't listen to me if I brought fire from heaven."

"He's right about that one thing. You are an idiot."

Harlan was nettled but amused. "If this is how you treat someone after he's given you five thousand dollars, I wonder how you've managed to attract any backers at all."

"You're an idiot if you let him throw away the business he built up from a hole in the ground, your birthright. An idiot or a coward."

He was no longer amused. He had begun to realize that as far as bullies went, the Dodges were far less sophisticated, and therefore far less effective, than this son of an Irish-American farmer with gasoline in his veins and a fuel pump for a heart. "I'm gambling money I may have to pay back with my life on your third swing at the plate and your last strike. That may make me an idiot. It makes me anything but a coward."

"Cowards often do brave things to avoid doing something they're more afraid of."

"Tell me what it is and I'll tell you if I'm afraid."

"Taking Crownover Coaches away from Abner the Second."

Harlan had lifted his glass. He put it down without drinking and looked at Ford. "You're the second person today who suggested that," he said.

part two

The Plant

chapter five

Memorial Day

Memorial Day was always an important date in the life of James Aloysius Dolan.

He was too young to have served in the War between the States, too old to have fought against Spain in Cuba and the Philippines, and though he spoke often of his regret that his country had never found need to put him in uniform, he had an Irishman's instinctive distrust of the military and shed few tears in private for those who had Given Their Lives. His patriotism ran more toward brass bands and bunting, and his chest swelled nearly as large as his belly when all four Dolans, in all their late-spring finery of red satin, starched white cotton, and blue gabardine, paraded with stepladder and trifold flag through the dewy grass shortly after dawn to affix the Stars and Stripes to the brass pole canting out over the front door of the house in Corktown. It was a matter of considerable pride on national holidays that theirs be the first staff in the neighborhood to display Old Glory; when on July 4, 1899, the McCorkingdales' flag was discovered already aloft next door when the Dolans rose, Big Jim consulted *The Old Farmers' Almanac* in order to determine the exact hour and moment of sunrise, then telephoned the party conduit to the *Free Press* and arranged to publish a column accusing Seamus McCorkingdale of violating the Flag Code by hoisting the sacred banner before the sun was decently above wicked Windsor. McCorkingdale, a conductor with the Michigan Central Railroad, a notoriously nonpartisan voter, and a Protestant into the bargain, responded with a withering letter to the editor in which he proclaimed his innocence, identified his neighbor as the instigator of the column, and suggested that Dolan had failed to raise his flag first because he was dissipated by drink and debauchery during a premature celebration the evening before of the birth of the Republic. Dolan wrote an open letter in answer, insinuating that McCorkingdale's father had given McCorkingdale's sister's dowry to an official with U.S. Immigration to overlook a vile disease on the old man's health chart that otherwise would have kept him out of the country.

The war raged on into August and might have continued indefinitely had not the Michigan Central Railroad dismissed Seamus McCorkingdale for drinking on duty and the Detroit Savings Bank called in his mortgage, forcing him to move himself and his family into his brother's home in Cleveland. There was a hearing to review the justification of his dismissal, at which it was established during testimony that a nearly full bottle of Old Eagle imported bourbon had been found in McCorkingdale's locker in the depot on Third Street during a surprise inspection by Pinkerton detectives. This was clearly against regulations and prima facie evidence of dereliction of duty, and the insistence of the accused that he had never seen the bottle before the inspection, and that moreover he was a lifelong teetotaler and a charter member of the Anti-Saloon League, did not alter the decision. Six weeks after his neighbor of eighteen years moved out, Dolan's second cousin, a recording secretary with the local Democratic Party and a high-ranking official in the Knights of Columbus, moved in with his wife and eight children. In three years, Big Jim's cousin had never once hoisted his flag first.

But the business of the flag, and the speech Dolan would make later at a rally on the Campus Martius, had little to do with the importance of today's date for him. Memorial Day was

the day he laid out the first of the outfits in his extensive summer wardrobe.

Noche, reliable valet that he was, had no part in the ritual
beyond picking up the clothes at the cleaner's, where they were
sent without fail on the first business day in May. Dolan's dour
and indestructible winter woolens were one thing, and in excellent hands with the manservant; but the master would no
more brook interference with the first rite of summer than he
would invite a companion into his confessional. Noche was
given the holiday off to visit his sister, whose family he had
moved from Santiago de Cuba to Detroit with the money he
had managed to save from his salary.

The first item to be laid out on the mattress of Dolan's
formidable bed was the blue gabardine with which he ushered
in warm weather. Most of his colleagues preferred seersucker,
but he did not care for the billowy nature of the fabric, and
despite the gentle hint implicit in Charlotte Dolan's suggestion
that the stripes were "slimming," he held to the belief that they
made him look like the big top in the circus. The steep cotton
twill was woven so tightly that the unlined gabardine felt slick
and cool to the touch, like silk; a material he restricted to neck-
ties and the socks he wore with evening clothes, lest he create
an unfavorable impression of wealthy decadence. With the
comfortable informality of a white oxford shirt, crisp linen collar
and cuffs, sporty yellow spats on his black, high-laced brogans,
and a daring explosion of yellow necktie, he felt that he had
shucked off the chrysalis of winter at last; emotions such as this
were too fine to share. He didn't wish to be taken for a fop or,
what was worse, a poet.

The last item to come out of the deep walnut wardrobe in
the corner of his bedroom was his straw boater, veteran of a
hundred rallies and a thousand ball games, from which he lov-
ingly removed the blue tissue and from whose red satin band
he plucked the last bit of lint between thumb and forefinger,

unwilling to risk snagging the threads with a brush. It was the only boater he had ever found that fit his big head; all the others rode up to his crown in minutes, where they were prey to the first breeze stiff enough to carry them south. As such it was not to be launched skyward with thousands of others when Jimmy Barrett tapped one past the shortstop with the bases loaded in the ninth. Dolan had found it at Mabley's five Aprils ago, just when he had resigned himself to life in a Panama hat of foreign manufacture; C. R. Mabley himself had rescued it from a box in which an employee had repacked it for return to the factory as an oversize item, and had presented it to Big Jim with his compliments. Dolan treasured the gift as he would a blessing from the Pope in Rome. It was as stiff and as light as a new playing card, woven from pure white wheat straw, and when he tilted it over his right eyebrow at a thirty-degree angle and exchanged his heavy stick for a bamboo cane, he felt ten years younger and as light on his feet as a two-hundred-pounder, every inch the *boulevardier*—in so far as he ever cared to follow the example of a sinful Parisian. And so, after a light breakfast with his family downstairs consisting of six waffles with honey, twenty Blue Point oysters, a platter of fried potatoes, half a loaf of French toast, and a half-gallon of coffee, he piled wife and children into the hired carriage waiting in front of the house and started downtown. It was said in Corktown that the awnings were not unrolled nor the parlor rugs removed to have the winter dirt beaten from them until Diamond Jim was observed cruising down Michigan Avenue, tipping his summer hat to the ladies and signaling the driver with his summer stick. So vocal was he on the conventions of seasonal dress that if he were to appear in his gabardine and straw a week early, his neighbors would doubt the evidence of their calendars.

As the Dolan carriage rolled down Woodward toward the Campus Martius public assembly center, the boatered and bonnetted throngs lining that broad thoroughfare cheered it as the lead vehicle in the Memorial Day parade, notwithstanding the fact that Mayor Maybury, the city fire brigade, and the members of the brass band sweating in their heavy woolen uniforms would not make their appearance for another twenty minutes. The parade could not take place until Detroit's most prominent citizen and his family had taken theirs. When the driver drew rein, mounted patrolmen made a path through the crowd for the Dolans to walk to the steps of the speakers' platform, where an officer on foot touched his helmet and uncoupled the velvet rope that they might mount to the folding chairs arranged inside the red-white-and-blue bunting. Male spectators in straw hats and derbies who had braved police chastisement by reaching out to shake the hand of the Irish Pope pumped circulation back into their fingers with cries of wonder at the strength of the man's grip, while the women in their ribbons and lace admired or criticized Charlotte Dolan's remarkable bonnet with its spray of real peonies and brim as large as a carriage wheel. It was a sunny day, and not a few of the younger men present— notably those in belted coats and striped vests—wore tinted cheaters in blissful disregard of the danger that they might thereby acquire reputations as "sports." Seated in the reinforced armchair especially selected to accommodate his tonnage and girth, Big Jim lamented aloud to his wife the general relaxation of standards in masculine dress and deportment since the war with Spain. She in turn patted his hand and reminded him that it was a new century. "The president himself allows his daughter to be photographed wearing a shirtwaist."

"Roosevelt is a buffoon." He had put on his horn-rimmed half-spectacles—studiedly unlike the despised chief executive's gold-framed pince-nez—to look over the notes for his speech. Although he had written them in large letters on squares of white cardboard that had come back with his shirts from the cleaner's so that he wouldn't have to wear the glasses when he mounted the podium, he found that he still couldn't read them without squinting. This put him in a dark humor. He did not fear aging, and indeed welcomed each new strand of silver in his temples that brought him that much closer to the enviable rank of Distinguished Elder Statesman. However, he had a railroad switchman's distaste for the loss of youthful powers. Next to go would be his hearing. A demoralizing picture came to him of Old Jim Dolan, sitting bent over in the front row at a Knights of Columbus meeting with a white beard to his ankles and a tin horn screwed into one ear.

"Why is the president a balloon?" asked young Sean.

His mother began to correct him, but was interrupted by Dolan, whose eyes twinkled above the top edge of his spectacles. "What else would you call a large bag filled with hot air?" he replied.

Little Margaret, horse-faced as ever in her fluffy white pinafore and red-and-white-striped hair bow, punched her brother's shoulder. "He didn't say balloon, stupid. He said baboon."

"Stop, now! I'll have the driver take you home, and you will miss the parade."

"Let them be, Charlotte. They're both right."

His wife sighed, said that he was spoiling his children and that they would grow up to be vaudevillians or worse. He paid her no attention. With offspring such as these, he reflected, he would never grow old. For that brief moment it didn't matter to him that his son was a nincompoop and his daughter as plain as a washtub.

The parade started on time, and Dolan, who was secretly bored by loud bands and the spectacle of the city's many fraternal orders marching in all their gold braid and swinging sword tassels, consulted his pocket winder and resigned himself to the wait. He rose to his feet for "Columbia, the Gem of the Ocean" and its fellow contender for the title of national anthem, "The Star-Spangled Banner"; nodded a greeting at the fire marshal, his wife's cousin; applauded with the rest of the spectators when the mounted police appeared in their orderly ranks with gold-chased helmets sparkling and the coats of their well-curried mounts glistening like stretched satin; and sighed in relief when the musicians gathered on the bandstand and played their final four selections, finishing with a mournful "Tenting Tonight on the Old Campground," to which many sang along in honor of the fallen in four formal wars and the Indian conflicts. He stood throughout the benediction, presented by Bishop Michael O'Shea of Most Holy Trinity and his own confessor, with his chins on his chest and his boater in his hands and made copious use of his great lawn handkerchief, during Mayor Maybury's windy forty-minute speech on the subject of Sacrifice to keep from wilting his collar. Nothing had dehydrated him so much since his last twelve hours at the switch in the Michigan Central yard.

At last it was his turn to speak. He jettisoned most of his prepared comments ("When the gentleman ahead of you holds forth for an hour," he was fond of advising young elocutionists, "finish in five minutes"), retaining only the reminder that a short ninety years before, the British under General Sir Isaac Brock had staged their own parade up Jefferson Avenue on the occasion of the surrender of Fort Detroit to the enemy, and that, "as that great American and founder of the Democratic Party, Thomas Jefferson, once said, 'The price of liberty is eternal vigilance.'" Using his great moustaches as counterweight to his mighty diaphragm, and rounding his vowels further with huge oracular motions of both hands, he transfixed his listeners with the same speech he had been using, with minor adjustments, on every public occasion since his first bid for office. He had learned early that large open-air groups were like children demanding their favorite story at bedtime, who resented even the slightest deviation from the way it had been told a hundred times before. This time he was proved right as always, as with bows and hands raised for merciful peace he resumed his seat to cheers and the requisite flurry of heaven-bound headgear. Charlotte touched his hand and leaned close to tell him how proud she was, as without transition she cuffed Sean on the back of the head and instructed him to remove his finger from his nostril at once.

The assembly broke up. Dolan wrung the bishop's hand and then the mayor's, acknowledged with ducked head the congratulations of admirers, and saw his family to their carriage, where he kissed his wife on the cheek and assured her he would meet them at Belle Isle later for their picnic. He then walked to City Hall in company with the mayor, ironing out a disagreement over the relative virtues of cobblestones and macadam in resurfacing streets on the way. Cobblestones it would be, for the time being; Dolan's brother owned the quarry with which the city had a contract. Inside they parted, and Big Jim entered the office he seldom visited, a small corner room in the clock tower but with fine views of the Civil War Memorial and the framework of the new Wayne County Building through the windows. The latter construction, with its dozen varieties of marble domestic and foreign, its miles of interior oak and curly maple, and heroic bronze charioteers flanking the portico, enabled the state Democratic Party to funnel a significant amount of public money into its war chest from the overrun, as well as the personal savings account of the party chairman.

The room was painted dark green above the oak wainscoting, contained a bowl fixture suspended by chains from the ceiling and connected by an exposed cable to a button switch next to the door, two plain desks with captain's swivels, four more or less dependable Windsor chairs for visitors, and a calendar with a color-tinted photograph of the Peoples State Bank Building at Fort and Shelby, in whose design Stanford White was said to have taken a hand. The office smelled of cigars and varnish and the disagreeable disinfectant that was partially the reason Dolan spent less time there than at any of the other stops on his official route.

This was not true of the deputy street railway commissioner, who when Dolan came in was seated behind his desk, making entries in a calf-bound ledger the size of a dining-room table. Randolph Strick was a small, pudding-faced German with startling blue eyes and straw-colored hair that he parted above his left eyebrow and combed in perpendicular directions with simultaneous jerks of a set of silver-backed brushes that he said had belonged to his father, an adjutant to Otto von Bismarck. He wore, on this hot late May day with the windows shut tight, heavy brown tweeds that made his superior itch just looking at them, yet he had never been seen to sweat, nor had Dolan seen him anywhere but in that office, seated at that desk. The top was heaped with papers, books, and rolled street charts, and as he balanced the ledger between his lap and the edge of the desk a fresh fall of sheets joined the litter around his feet. Six feet away stood the desk reserved for the commissioner, its leather top naked but for a pristine blotter pad and an inkwell whose contents, if indeed it had any, must have set as hard as concrete since the last time a pen had been dipped into them. Dolan himself could not remember ever having done any paperwork there, but he was as certain as he was of anything that Strick would never consider extending his territory even temporarily to include his superior's work space. He was a born soldier, obeying orders without question. He ran the street railway system with no interference from anyone, including the man who had been elected to run it.

There was not, in point of fact, much to run. Local streetcar service was provided by Detroit United Railways, which held the city franchise. The private company laid and maintained its tracks, replaced its rolling stock, and hired conductors, then submitted its invoices to City Hall. Randolph Strick drew up bank drafts to cover the expenses, meticulously recording the transactions in his ledgers. Every penny was accounted for, and two separate and well-organized petitions for reform had failed to uncover anything improper in the deputy commissioner's neatly ruled columns. This was because the improprieties existed only in the offices of the DUR itself, whose officials paid James Aloysius Dolan a comfortable monthly stipend in return for his continued successful opposition to public ownership of city transportation. He was in the plum position of being able to monitor just how much money was paid to the DUR by the city, and thus to ensure that nothing was held back from his end. Strick was one of the very few absolutely honest men he had ever met, contented with his eighteen-dollar-per-week salary and the sandwiches he brought from home to eat at his desk while he worked. Dolan had become convinced of this when he had a nephew employed with the accounting office of the DUR try to induce the deputy to keep a second set of books in return for 50 percent of the resulting profits. Strick had politely declined.

The polite part was important. The commissioner delighted in his deputy's total lack of sanctimony. An honest man who did not expect honesty of others, or resent its absence in strident tones, was as rare as a beautiful woman who did not condescend to those of her sisters who did not possess beauty. Dolan was certain that Strick, who would pay a messenger service two dollars to return a penny pencil that he had absent-mindedly put in his pocket, would not even make a face if Dolan were to trip an old woman with his stick right there in the office and steal her purse as he was helping her to her feet.

On this holiday, Dolan had stopped in to learn if Strick's sources in Monroe County had confided to him the various routes being discussed for the construction of a new interurban line between Detroit and Toledo.

"There is not a thing new from here to Monroe." The man's heavy Ruhr Valley accent, despite his emigration to America at the age of six, indicated that he still did most of his thinking in German. He continued to draw lines through his sevens and refer to the last letter in the alphabet as *zed*. "There is some discussion of moving it inland from the lake south of Monroe to avoid flooding the tracks in high weather."

"How far inland? I need to know the exact property being discussed."

"My friend was not specific." On the rare occasions Strick ate lunch outside the office, he always ate it in Diedrich Frank's saloon with Gunter Klaus, a Monroe County farmer who also sat on the planning commission. Neither man was married, although both were approaching middle age. Whatever dark doubts Dolan entertained about his deputy, he neither spoke of them nor confronted them in private. Bees' nests were not to be disturbed when honey was free.

"You had a call." Strick indicated the brass upright telephone standing aslant atop a heap of foolscap on his desk. "That man Borneo."

Dolan frowned. "What did he want?"

"He heard your speech. He said to tell you it made him proud to be in America."

"Anything else?"

"He said it amazed him how you find time to rehearse your oratory and still manage your busy schedule."

The message lay heavily atop Dolan's breakfast. The Sicilian never called unless he wanted to remind Dolan he existed. That meant he was feeling neglected. Maybury's police must have hit one of Borneo's brothels. Dolan and Borneo had never met, but there were times when the damn arrogant wop seemed to consider himself the senior partner in their arrangement. He wondered if it might be time to kick in a couple of the man's horse parlors; show him how the cow ate the cabbage.

Probably not, however. He preferred to save public demonstrations of good government for October, so that the details were still fresh in the minds of voters come the first Tuesday in November.

He changed the subject. "See if you can get your friend in Monroe to be specific. I don't want to have to buy up every acre of farmland in the county and wind up planting potatoes on most of it."

"Haven't you sources of your own?"

"They're all Lutherans down there."

"I am Lutheran," Strick said.

"You are, but you're the only one I've ever met who I didn't think would nail his damn manifesto to my front door." He adjusted his boater, popped the crown, thumped his cane on the rug, and caught it on the bounce. He was feeling uncommonly good after his successful speech, in spite of the disturbing telephone call; the prospect of a little punitive raid in woptown in four months put the shine back on things. "I'm off to fried chicken and Kraut potato salad. You ought to get out and into the sun, Randy my lad. It's a national holiday, or haven't you heard?"

"I have sensitive skin. And these ledgers are not going to keep themselves."

"I'm going to see you get a two-dollar raise. Not that you'll have any fun with it."

Strick smiled faintly. "I have a sister in Düsseldorf. She can use the money."

"We all have sisters in Düsseldorf," Dolan said, and left for his picnic.

On the dock at the foot of Woodward he stood still for more congratulations upon his speech, some of which patently came from acquaintances who had not been present when he gave it, and when the ferry bumped to a rest against the hemp fenders and a crew member swept off his cap and motioned for Big Jim to board first, he had the opportunity to shake his head and stand aside for a lady in a seersucker dress with matching hat and parasol. She bowed her head graciously and caught his eye with a knowing glint that he interpreted as acknowledgment of a previous acquaintance. He did not remember her, and it bothered him all the way to the island. He stood near the bow, smoking a cigar and contemplating the betrayal of his phenomenal memory, the greatest weapon in his arsenal.

Jimmy Dolan was a loudly vocal supporter of monogamy, and it was his secret pride that he practiced it in private in so far as a man of his prominent stature could expect to maintain his sacred vows. In a public life of twenty years he had taken but four mistresses. He was certain the woman at the dock was not one of them, though she may have been among the dalliances and diversions that had helped him shoulder the burden of his many campaigns. At the same time he was certain that he would not have forgotten a woman of her exotic appearance. She had black hair, fine dark eyes, a bold aquiline nose, and a hint of olive coloring beneath a discreet application of powder (Greek? Spanish? Surely not American Indian; there was nothing of the mission school about her), and she had a straightforward way of looking at a man that was unusual in one of her class—if the evidence of her attire could be accepted—that he found both disturbing and intriguing. She was about thirty, but he approved of that. The mistresses of most of the prominent men he knew were young, with large milky brows and unformed features, who if one were to unpin their preposterous hats and feel about the crowns of their heads, would reveal a soft spot where the plates of the skull had not yet joined. It was an easy enough thing for a young girl to be pretty, when life and the laws of nature had not yet discovered her, rather more of a permanent achievement for a seasoned woman to be beautiful without involving some kind of pickling process. He rejected the possibility that she was a prostitute. She appeared to be unescorted, and it was unthinkable that a courtesan of her type would need to fish for clients on Belle Isle. The police there were peculiarly adept at weeding out such women on Sundays and holidays, when families flocked to the island.

No, they had not met, he was sure of that, whatever the intimacy implied by her regard. An invitation, perhaps. Such things were not unheard of at his station. He knew full well he was no Sandor the Magnificent; without Noche's assistance it had taken him ten minutes that morning to tie his laces and button his gaiters, with intervals to catch his breath from all the bending, and notwithstanding the confidence that a dignified girth inspired at the polls, it did nothing for one's romantic attraction. But authority and fame exercised a gravitational pull of their own. It was not Jim Brady's brilliantined hair that kept Lillian Russell by his side when he rode down Fifth Avenue, but the way he shone when he entered the New York Stock Exchange.

He did not see her again when the ferry docked at Belle Isle, except as a flash of seersucker in a sea of parasols and boaters flowing down the gangplank. Charlotte and the children were waiting at the dock. He kissed his wife on the cheek, relieved her of the great wicker hamper, and they strolled to the picnic grounds, where she spread the blanket and laid out the linen and silver while the children played hide-and-go-seek among the trees. The smells of sun and water there where the river prepared to enter Lake St. Clair were intoxicating; or perhaps Dolan was simply light-headed from his cigar. He knew he should wander over to the baseball diamond and shake some hands, lose a bet or two on a pop fly or a base on balls and pay up with a genial oath as to the luck of the man and his devilish unfair knowledge of the American pastime. Instead he leaned against a great oak old enough to have stood there when Cadillac came through, his head swimming while he watched the canoers paddling down the blue canal and thought of the dark woman.

chapter six

God is a Mother

Edith Hampton Crownover was a literal woman; and even though she was happiest when she was in the morning room of the large four-gabled house on Jefferson Avenue where she had raised her three sons and one daughter, she quit it each day at noon and did not return to it until the next day after breakfast.

It was a small room with an east window, dazzling after dawn. Cabbage roses bloomed on the wallpaper and there was a pink-and-white braided rug, an upholstered rocker that had been a reluctant wedding gift from her mother, a spinet desk of cinnamon-colored pearwood, and a straight chair with a cushion for her weak back. Doe-eyed mothers and corpulent pink babies stared out of scrolled frames on the walls. The desk, below the thicket of family pictures supported on wedges and miniature easels on the stepped top, was tidy. The pigeonholes were labeled in her neat Palmer hand, stocked with ample stationery, and nothing so impractical as a tulip vase or a book of poetry rested on the blotter to interrupt her movements between the glass inkstand and the sheet before her. Every day except Sunday she wrote letters and postcards to family and friends, planned the dinner menu, and read novels in the rocker until the towering hickory grandfather clock in the downstairs hallway chimed twelve, when she went down to lay the table for the afternoon meal she shared with her husband. Abner II always dined at home during the workday on the advice of his doctor, who had told him five years ago that eating at the office or with business associates in restaurants was a criminal act upon his delicate digestive system. Not to eat at all was worse. The early days of his success, when he would pass twelve to fourteen hours at his desk or on the factory floor, working without food or gobbling sandwiches from a tin pail while he read contracts and dictated telegrams, were emphatically over. Edith, who had outgrown the romantic stage at the beginning of their marriage when she had brought meals in a basket to Abner's office, had for many years been accustomed to the quiet solitude between breakfast and dusk, when her husband came home for dinner and an hour with his newspaper before retiring. No one had thought to consult her when the situation changed. She had made the adjustment without complaint, instructing the cook that the noonday meal would henceforth be prepared for two, and ate with him in the dining room, usually in silence, conversation concerning the changeless routine of their respective days having long since become redundant. Only the chiming of the grandfather clock on the half hour interrupted the clink of silver on china.

The menu consisted invariably of leftovers from the evening before. Nothing went to waste in the Crownover household; last night's roast beef or mutton was removed from the icebox and reheated, cold boiled potatoes were peeled, cut into slices, and fried lightly in butter, ham carved too close to the bone to serve again in its original incarnation was shredded, mixed with diced carrots, potatoes, and leeks, and risen again as hash. Slightly stale bread was toasted and served dry. Thus the kitchen observed the custom of the factory, where lumber ends were turned on lathes to function as pegs, stripped bolts retapped, and wood shavings swept up and saved to fuel the heating stoves in the winter. Abner drank warm milk or water with his meal, Edith iced tea with lemon in balmy weather and coffee with a dollop of cream when coal burned in the furnace. Dessert was never present during the day, and in the evening only when they entertained guests. Abner had no sweet tooth, and his wife, who considered cakes and pies and sherbets convivial things, never ate them unaccompanied. While the table was being cleared, the Coach King removed himself to the rolled leather sofa in the parlor, where he remained recumbent for thirty minutes to avoid exciting his already overactive acids before he rose and walked back to the office. Left to herself again, Edith reviewed the dinner menu with the cook, then rested to relieve the excruciating pain in her lumbar region before attending to errands, visiting friends, or helping to raise funds for the Orphans' Asylum as part of her charitable duties as an Electra with the Order of the Eastern Star. She found the work more diverting than the company; O.E.S. ladies were boring to a degree that made Rhode Island seem as lurid as the Barbary Coast.

Edith Hampton Crownover no longer felt anything toward her husband beyond the necessity to provide respite from his various burdens. She filled her days with repetition and lived only for her sons—and her daughter, with whom she alone of all the family retained contact.

Twice each week, one of the letters she wrote in the morning room was addressed to "Katherine Crownover Gorlich, in care of Ogilvie's General Merchandise, Guthrie, Oklahoma Territory." Gus Gorlich was the name of the man with whom her firstborn child had disappeared at age fourteen, not to be heard from until a letter arrived at the Jefferson Avenue address identifying Ogilvie's store as the place where she could be reached. It went on to describe the brief ceremony that had wedded them in the home of a justice of the peace in a place called Stilwell, with a witness who signed himself Pete Stands-in-Water; she and Gorlich, a man of forty and a widower, had drawn a wagon loaded with foodstuffs and farming equipment up to a starting line at the edge of a three-thousand-square-mile section of land called the District, then at the first note blown on a cavalry bugle had raced to a 160-acre lot marked off by federal surveyors and claimed it as their own. Abner's sole comment, upon reading the letter, had been a muttered observation that she had not said whether the wagon was a Crownover. He had not spoken of their daughter from that day to this, other than to forbid his wife to answer her letters or to accept them when they were delivered.

Edith's first act had been to arrange for a box in her name at the Detroit Post Office. She then wrote Katherine, congratulating her upon her marriage, warning her of the pitfalls to avoid in farming, as outlined in various novels, and instructing her to address all future letters to her mother in care of the box number. In this manner the correspondence had continued for thirteen years. Abner, who never entered the morning room, did not know that among the pictures standing atop the spinet desk were cabinet photographs of their two grandchildren. He either did not notice or ignored his wife's grief when she received notice that both had died within three weeks of each other of cholera in 1894. She did not mention it to him, nor to her sons, for fear that one of them—most likely Edward, whom she loved equally with the others but did not trust—would let something slip to their father. She alone shared in the couple's anguish over the deaths and, six years later, when drought destroyed their crops and forced the bank in Guthrie to foreclose upon their farm, the failure of their dreams of success. Both were now living in town, where Gus worked in a livery stable and Katherine cleaned the rooms in a hotel, supplementing their income with odd jobs and the small amounts of money Edith managed to send them without alerting Abner. Katherine answered her mother's letters once a month. Invariably she apologized that her workday left her little time to do anything but sleep, and too exhausted to write.

Edith fretted that her daughter was working herself into an early grave. At night, when she lay in bed thinking, she resolved to sell off some of her shares in Crownover Coaches—an anniversary present from Abner when he was too poor to give her anything else—and send the money to Katherine. In the light of day she cowered from the scene that would take place when her actions and their purpose were discovered. She owned thirty-eight percent of the company stock, the largest single block aside from her husband's forty-two percent. With six percent owned by stockholders outside the family, the remaining fourteen had been distributed among their sons in descending increments according to their ages—excepting Harlan, whose meager promise had entitled him only to three percent, below his younger brother Edward's five. Abner was determined that none who did not bear the name Crownover would ever wield power sufficient to direct the company's fortunes. Edith had no doubt that he would divorce her if she parted with a single share.

When she allowed herself to dwell on the situation, she despised herself for her cowardice. Katherine's recent letters had been spiritless; exhausted chronicles of her daily routine containing few details that she had not already reported. Although she was too much like her mother to express her defeat in so many words, it was clear that her resiliency was gone and that she was tending to the minutiae of her life in a trance. Once, a carriage in which Edith had been riding had been stopped behind a police van and forced to wait while a band of ragged men in scrubby beards and handcuffs were driven by policemen armed with clubs up the steps of the county jail. It was an election year, and ninety days of incarceration and hard labor awaited them for the crime of vagrancy. Edith remembered the emptiness of the eyes in the gaunt faces, and the feeling that she could see clear through to the backs of their skulls. They were ambulatory dead men, nothing more. She saw newspapers rarely, but she had read in one of a tramp pursued by policemen who had thrown himself beneath the wheels of a freight train rumbling along the Michigan Central tracks. The reporter was incredulous, unable to understand why a man would choose death over a short sentence. And she remembered those empty eyes, and knew what the reporter did not, that freedom took more than one form. She wondered what Katherine's eyes looked like as she went about the unchanging details of her confinement.

On this Saturday, however, as she pinned in place an orchid-colored hat that matched the yoke of her linen dress, Edith looked forward to an hour during which she could put aside her concerns about her daughter. She had an appointment to take tea with her favorite son.

She was the only Crownover who continued to observe the ritual of afternoon tea. Nine years earlier, when the prospect of a commission to build an opera coach for the Prince of Wales appeared certain, Abner had decided to adopt the practice. He employed the services of an impoverished English baronet then living with distant relatives in Ann Arbor to instruct the family in the protocol. Edith in particular had taken to the translucent cups and saucers and round-bottomed spoons and buttery scones. Long after His Royal Highness had bowed to the pressure of an indignant British press and a stern home secretary and selected a London carriage maker to fill his order, 4:00 P.M. still found Mrs. Crownover seated in her parlor or her favorite outside venue, the tearoom at the Wayne Hotel, while Abner and his sons reverted to their previous afternoon routines. It was one more thing to fill her day, and although she would have been scandalized at the suggestion, she took a certain quiet satisfaction in the knowledge that her loyalty to the custom irritated Abner. But he had spent far too much money on the baronet's lessons to object out loud. She would never have admitted even to herself that upsetting her husband with impunity was one of the few pleasures that remained to her in life. In all innocence of this self-awareness, but with a pang of guilty joy that she convinced herself came from the anticipation of visiting with her son, she tugged on her gloves, hesitated over the collection of parasols in the wicker stand in the corner of her dressing room, then decided against taking one and descended the stairs to the foyer. There her driver waited to escort her outside to the two-seater she had ordered, an open buggy that struck her as less stuffily imperial than the closed brougham preferred by Abner.

Her upbringing in the genteel pastel society of Rhode Island had ingrained in her a distaste for ostentation. This was an unfortunate prejudice to carry into the Midwest, whose self-made millionaires emulated their New York models. These Gothamites had in turn borrowed their minareted and gingerbread-laden architecture from the Italian villas and castles on the Rhine they had seen on tours abroad. She thought the turrets and gimcracks of the Jefferson Avenue house vulgar. When she could not escape an invitation to the salons of her husband's colleagues, she smiled to herself at the spectacle of so many bricklayers' daughters flaunting their diamonds on the arms of escorts in immaculate shirtboards with old mortar-dust ground into their knuckles. These were observations she could share with no one, even if she could find someone who would understand them. Along with a love of coarse display, the circles in which she and Abner traveled shared an austere and obvious absence of irony.

Her antipathy extended to the greater Wayne Hotel. The cheap gloss of its marble floors, the depth of its carpets like sphagnum moss, and the Wagnerian massiveness of its fireplaces combined to create the sort of place where stove makers in derbies preferred to smoke cigars and talk about their trade. For this the hotel offered three bars, five restaurants, and a basement tonsorial parlor with ten chairs and all the major out-of-town newspapers. Every spring at the Shipmaster's Ball these tightly wound entrepreneurs climbed into tailcoats and trotted out their marriagable daughters for the admiration of young men with whose fathers they drank, dined, and barbered the rest of the year. None of these were things that could not be found in the East, of course. The difference out here, where less than a hundred years ago the city had maintained a stockade to keep out feathered savages, was the inflated, pasteboard quality of the pretense. The men's evening dress and women's ball gowns appeared to be wearing the wearers, like costumes in an amateur theatrical; patent leathers pinched toes that would be more comfortable in brogans, corsets creaked like hawsers, all in the name of borrowed propriety. The dog aped the master, and the cat the dog, on down to the goldfish swimming around its bowl wearing a miniature hat. It was all so much burlesque.

One of the reasons she looked forward to time spent with her second son was the conjecture that she could confide in him her feelings about the entire shabby exhibition. She did not share the general conviction that Harlan was backward. True, he was silent when others were vocal, and the male world was an argumentative one in which nonparticipation was interpreted as lack of an intelligent opinion. Nevertheless she had thought she detected, whenever the conversation had grown particularly complacent on the subject of this competitor's shortcomings or that politico's approachability, a *sparkle* in Harlan's eye. It was suspiciously similar to the one she saw in her own when something struck her as wickedly amusing while she was looking in a mirror. In every other aspect the eye was so much that of his father. But the thought that there was something so un-Abner-like behind it encouraged her to believe that her own sense of the absurd would not depart the family entirely when she was no more. It made her feel less alone.

She yearned to communicate to Harlan that he himself was not marooned, that here was the connection he could find nowhere else in the Crownover household. She had not as yet, nor did she think she ever would without some sign that the information would be welcome. There was a seriousness about Harlan, not to be confused with his father's sobriety or the pomposity of his younger brother, that kept her from committing what might be an embarrassing error. It made her question the evidence of her own eyes, and wonder if the glitter she thought she had seen was just an empty reflection from a window. She knew this was not so, yet she feared the consequences of being wrong. The discovery that he was no different from any other Crownover would be too devastating to withstand. Better not to know, and to nurture the unrealized hope.

Despite its posturing, the Wayne was very much a part of the new century, for which she was grateful. Her husband unequivocally was not, and the fact that the hotel's proprietor, Jim Hayes, had had the effrontery to host an automobile show there the previous year was another log on the fire of Abner's annoyance that his wife should take tea there. Edith had not, of course, attended the show. The prospect of bumping up against a roomful of freshly scrubbed machinists drinking champagne and throwing open the bonnets of their contraptions to point out this or that greasy feature had not appealed to her. Noisy, odiferous machines that frightened horses and children and belched great choking blue clouds into the open air with sharp reports like gunfire repelled her, but she refused to fulminate against them. What was the point? One could not reverse time and uninvent something that should not have been invented. To protest would make as much sense as a woman complaining about politics, just as if she had the vote.

In any case, she understood that Harlan had some interest in motorcars. If it was a subject that could bridge the gap that separated mother and son, then the Wayne seemed an amiable choice.

She thoroughly approved of the tearoom. It was her personal fancy that the room had been added as an afterthought and decorated by an outsider. Its proportions were anything but grand. Hayes, it seemed, had balked at wasting his over-wrought chandeliers and imitation medieval tapestries upon a space so unassuming. The person left in charge had papered it with tea roses on a black background, installed Tiffany fixtures, and stood flickering candles in rose-colored glass bowls on the tables. The stiff white linens and delicate stemware discouraged the bray and clatter that filled the other dining rooms. Even the waiters whispered, and moved about as silently as monks. To pass through those French doors was to leave behind the enervating racket of the Industrial Revolution and enter a place where quiet and repose were something altogether deeper than just an interval between steam whistles. It seemed to her that the very air was lighter and easier to breathe.

She was shown to a small corner table by a bald waiter with immaculate white side-whiskers like the late Mr. Gladstone, who held her chair and bowed when he took his leave. She was aware of the attention her arrival had drawn from the other diners; she did not acknowledge it. The celebrity of her union with the richest man in town left her cold. Back home, society cared little how much a woman's circumstances were reduced provided she belonged to an old family. In Detroit, she could have had a long past as a harlot, with a murderer for a father, without raising so much as a Japanese fan as long as she was the wife of Crownover Coaches.

When the bald waiter returned with her favorite Indian blend she informed him that she was meeting someone and would order her meal when he arrived. She sipped from the paper-thin cup, found the contents too hot, and replaced it in its saucer to cool while she listened to the muffled sounds of the Wayne. Silver tinkled, male and female voices murmured in hushed conversation, a rather insipid violin rendition of "Lorna Doone" drifted out of the morning-glory horn belong-ing to an unseen phonograph. Beneath it all, steel skate wheels rolled over the varnished boards of the rink in the Pavilion with a shuddering rumble like thunder. The windows were open on the side facing the river; the smell of sun on water reminded her of Newport. She felt a flash of homesickness. The sensation was recent, and still quite novel. After thirty years in Detroit she had thought it had died with her mother.

Harlan arrived ten minutes late, bowing over Edith's hand and spouting apologies and explanations; something about inspecting an empty factory building on Mack Avenue, with Henry Ford involved somehow. (This was a name one could not escape of late.) Harlan could be excitable, and at such times she could scarcely follow his rapid speech. He was wearing his best summer worsted, but it needed pressing, and his broad features, so much like the Hamptons' except for the disconcerting directness of the Crownover stare, looked a bit pinched.

She asked him, when he was seated, if he was getting enough sleep.

"I'll sleep when I'm dead, as Mr. Ford says. You look wonderful. How is your back?" He snapped the folds out of his napkin and laid it in his lap.

"It isn't bothering me today."

"I don't believe you."

She shook her head in argument, but smiled at his perception. She was, in fact, in considerable pain; but as that was almost always the case she saw no reason to mention it. She had an aunt, currently in her nineties, who had been dying of something particularly painful and equally unidentifiable for twenty years, and who never ignored an opportunity to apprise everyone she met of the details of her misery. Edith was determined not to follow her tiresome example.

"Are you eating regularly?" she asked. "You look as if you've lost weight. I'm afraid the North Atlantic salmon is the heartiest thing on the menu here. I can have our waiter bring a steak from one of the other restaurants."

He held up both palms in an attitude of self-defense. "I ate an enormous meal at Dolph's before meeting Mr. Ford. I was pretty sure he wouldn't feed me. I don't think the man's had honest food since he left the farm. If you wish to worry about someone, you should start with him. I think he lives on engine exhaust."

"I'm your mother, not his. You needn't snap."

He sank a little in his seat.

"I'm sorry, Mother. I'm on edge. Father and I quarreled last week."

"I thought that was what happened. He complained about his stomach for days. I suppose it was about automobiles."

"He has no vision."

The waiter materialized. Edith ordered chilled cucumber soup and the tiny crabmeat sandwiches she loved. Harlan asked for black coffee. His mother waited until they were alone again before she spoke.

"You would not have lived the life you have if it weren't for your father's vision. He saved the company."

"I've heard that story all my life. Sometimes I think we'd all be better off if Father had a little more of Grandfather's idealism. I happen to think it's a heroic thing to put one's own welfare on the line for what he believes. He opposed *slavery*, for God's sake." His mother winced at the blasphemy, and he was immediately contrite. "I'm sorry. The Dodge brothers were at Mack. Their rough manners are contagious."

"I've heard they're hooligans. You're too much the gentleman for this automobile crowd, Harlan. I'm afraid you'll be hurt."

He smiled. It was his mother's smile, and it drained the sting from his condescension. "I'm twenty, Mother. I'll look to my own scrapes and bruises."

"I know that. But you're still my son. It's an old lady's privilege to dither about."

He patted her hand.

"You don't look a day past thirty, and you know it. Don't play games with me. I'm not Ab."

She knew he was not merely flattering her. At forty-seven, Edith was without wrinkles or blemishes, and no gray showed among the red-gold, rather fine strands of her hair. She had the hooded and slightly protuberant eyes of a duchess in a Renaissance painting. Her face was heart-shaped, with a patrician nose and a mouth that was disproportionately small, which to her mind made it her weakest feature. Local legend said she had turned down an offer to use her likeness in a magazine advertisement for Pearl Drop soap. There was no truth in it, but Edith was sufficiently inspired by any story that sowed envy among the hens who kept it alive not to stir herself to deny it.

She sighed a little at Harlan's mention of her oldest son. "Young Abner fusses over me so. He makes no distinction between me and those pink-powder saints you see on the covers of song sheets."

"Or in the pictures in your morning room. You can hardly blame him for drawing the conclusion."

His smile this time, dry and tight-lipped, did not come from either side of the family. It was entirely his own, and it was vaguely troubling. She feared that he was becoming a cynic. Her only experience of that type of person was a scruffy young man in a shabby suit who had appeared in the lobby of the opera house during the intermission in *A Lady of Quality*, talking loudly about Marx and Engels and spattering the gowns and dinner jackets of his listeners with champagne from his glass when he gestured. Asked by the manager to leave, he had departed with a vile oath. Edith asked her son tentatively if he was a Socialist.

He laughed, loudly and boyishly. Heads turned at the other tables. He blushed and lowered his voice. "Not unless attending one lecture by Jack London counts. It amused me to hear the great individualist of our time talking about the will of the masses."

She was relieved, although scarcely mollified. It was a most cynical-sounding denial. "You should make an effort to get along with your father. All this rebellion can only make you bitter."

He touched her hand again, this time without patronizing her. "I'll try. I'm sorry the men in your life are so difficult."

"They're men."

"Upon my word, Mother, you're becoming quite the wit. If I didn't know better I'd swear you'd been sneaking out to the Temple Theater and watching Fields and Webber."

"I'm not my pictures, Harlan."

She had surprised him twice in the space of a few seconds. The realization filled her with guilty pleasure. She was grateful that their order arrived at just that moment. The mood dissipated as the waiter leaned forward to transfer the cups and dishes from his tray to the table.

She forced a crabmeat sandwich on Harlan, who was no match for a mother's determination. "I don't believe that story about eating at Dolph's Saloon. I don't know when you eat at all. When you're not working at your father's, you're spending your dinner break meeting with automobile men and touring manufactories. What you need is a wife who will take care of you."

"I agree. I can't think why women aren't throwing themselves at me all the time. I look so dashing in my work overalls."

"If women cared about such things, none of the men who work for you on the loading dock would be married. I happen to know most of them are. Who do you think makes up gift baskets for them and their families at Christmas? If I had grandchildren to fuss over, I wouldn't have to fuss over you." A splinter of grief stabbed her at the memory of Katherine's children, dead these eight years.

"That's bribery, Mother." But he wolfed down the sandwich and poured coffee after it.

She watched him. "I miss you, Harlan. The house has been too quiet since you moved out. Sometimes I think I can hear you moving around in your old room, pacing back and forth the way you used to. Then I go up and everything is covered with sheets."

"I couldn't very well stay after Edward got married. Without him to stand between Father and me, I'd never be able to maintain the peace. I'm not placid like Ab or agreeable like Edward. Father and I would have been at each other's throat in five minutes."

"You're too much alike."

"We might have been, thirty years ago. When I read *The Coach King*, I thought it was about someone else. If Father were in charge then, running the company the way he does now, and a young man came to him with a new suspension system he'd designed, Father would have told him he was quite happy with the old one and sent him back to his bench."

Edith drank some soup. They had put in too much onion. "Now that you've gotten that off your chest, you should have no trouble being civil to your Father."

"How do you stand it, Mother?"

The question, and the desperate expression on Harlan's usually guarded face, surprised her deeply. Close as they were, neither had ever attempted to trespass upon the other quite so directly before.

She slid her spoon back into her bowl, took a long draft of tea, and replaced the cup in its saucer without making a sound. Her eyes never left Harlan's.

"I stand it," she said.

chapter seven

The Procession

On the first day of June, Giuseppe Caesar Niccolo e Benedetti de Sorrato drew his last breath, a monster gulp of the kind that in times past he had used to finish off a plate of linguini in marinara sauce and a glass of wine poured from an earthenware jug from his own cellar. As he let it out, his sphincter released, as if he had passed gas at the end of a satisfying meal. The odor drew his wife, Dona Pronuncia, from the next room. Her subsequent wails attracted the attention of neighbors, and within thirty minutes all of Little Italy knew that Uncle Joe was dead at last. Twenty-two months and eleven days had elapsed since his last stroke, the one that had made a vegetable of Detroit's most notorious greengrocer.

The next day, a photographic portrait that had been made at the time of his election to the presidency of the Sons of Garibaldi Lodge appeared on the front page of the local Italian-language newspaper, flanked by angels with trumpets, with the dates of his birth and death printed on a scroll beneath his airbrushed chins. The obituary that accompanied the picture celebrated his successful greengrocery business, his services to the Church, and his stature as a beloved mentor and benefactor to the Italian community of Detroit. No mention was made of his conviction of arson in a fire in the shop of a tailor named deBartolo in 1874, but it was noted that he had volunteered his services as a consultant to the Detroit police in a series of disasters that had befallen the owners of small businesses in the area between Gratiot Avenue and the river in recent years. A campaign was announced to finance a scholarship at Detroit College in Uncle Joe's name, to be awarded annually to a deserving Italian-American reared in the city. The door-to-door drive to raise money for the scholarship would be chaired by Vincenzo Sorrato, Giuseppe's oldest surviving son, who with his brothers Gaetano and Giuseppe Jr., was coming up from Toledo for the funeral. Vincenzo had vowed that every local Sicilian would receive the opportunity to contribute to the fund.

The mortal remains were consigned to the care of the Palandrino Brothers Mortuary on Orleans Street. Augusto, the firstborn Palandrino and senior partner in the enterprise, personally accepted the challenge of making the corpse presentable for the visitation. Nearly a decade of illness had reduced Uncle Joe from a robust three hundred pounds to an emaciated 140; yards of loose skin hung from his frame like the canvas of a deflated balloon. First, Augusto stuffed the sunken cheeks with wads of newspaper and cotton. To prevent the padding from escaping, he dislocated the jaw, joined the upper and lower mandibles with platinum wire, and used gutta-percha to stop up the tiny holes he had drilled for this purpose. The torso itself he wound with butcher paper and unbleached muslin, around and around, augmented with a mohair cushion he had prudently saved from the last time the slumber room was refurnished; the master mortician was noted for never throwing out items which might later be put to use, thus sparing his bereaved customers the added expense of costly prosthetics. (It was whispered about the neighborhood that one client, a Mr. Tosca, who had fallen beneath the wheels of an outgoing freight on the Michigan Central tracks, was but 20 percent Mr. Tosca and 80 percent upholstery when it came time for friends and family to pay their respects.) In this way Augusto managed to fill out the trademark Sorrato white linen suit. Working from photographs, he filled in the deep wrinkles in the forehead with damp flour, inserted black rubber stoppers in the nostrils to eliminate pinching, and used a mixture of petroleum jelly and bootblack to smooth back Uncle Joe's fine hair and cover the cobwebby gray of neglect. Once he had applied powder and rouge, restored the backs of the hands to their former plumpness with an injection of Miracle-Flex Florentine Embalming Solution, and stood back to inspect his work, Augusto Palandrino reflected for the five hundredth time upon the sad fact that such artistry must eventually be concealed forever beneath six feet of earth and sod. With resignation he directed his brothers Domingo and Giovanni to transfer the corpse from the worktable to the casket and remove it to the slumber room, where he wound a rosary around Uncle Joe's hands and arranged the candles at the head and foot. The casket, made of gray-green olivewood with a gray Italian silk lining and solid gold handles, had been imported from Firenze and retailed for four thousand dollars, establishing a new record for the city of Detroit. He had obtained it for fifteen hundred dollars and placed it in storage for just such an illustrious passing. It was a source of private satisfaction that he should be able to realize so large a profit from the heirs of Giuseppe Sorrato, to whom he had been paying a premium of five hundred dollars per month for eleven years as insurance against fire and theft. In addition he charged full price for prosthetics and cosmetics he had not actually employed.

The funeral mass took place in SS. Peter and Paul Roman Catholic Church on East Jefferson, the oldest place of worship in the city, Monsignor Santino Calabria presiding. From there, the procession commenced east along the river toward Mt. Elliot Cemetery, where a six-foot granite angel waited with wings spread to receive Uncle Joe in an eight-hundred-dollar reinforced-concrete vault guaranteed to resist seepage for a century.

Leading the procession was the Palandrinos' new hearse, fashioned of black lacquered hickory on wheels with hard rubber tires, with plate-glass windows on the sides affording a clear view of the splended casket, hung all around with black tassels and crepe. The horses were matched blacks with plumes attached to their bridles, and the driver, a ten-year veteran named Caspar, wore an immaculate morning coat and a tall silk hat brushed to a liquid shine. The honorary pallbearers who loaded the casket onto the hearse were Gaetano and Giuseppe Sorrato Jr., the deceased's sons; Dr. Francis Zangara, Uncle Joe's oldest friend, a companion since Sicily and the physician who had signed his death certificate; his cousin Augustino; a brother-in-law named Olini from Cleveland—and Sal Borneo, also called Salvatore Bornea. Son Vincenzo's missing leg excused him from this duty.

Vincenzo had approached Borneo on his new pine leg at Borneo's table in the restaurant on Charlevoix to extend the invitation. With tears in his eyes he had shaken Borneo's hand and delivered a pretty speech in which he hoped by honoring years of loyal service to his late father to heal the breach between them. He had drunk a glass of wine to confirm the peace and hobbled off to seek out his brothers and finish plotting the assassination of the murderous pig who had killed their brother Carlo.

Borneo, who did not own a vehicle, had hired a Crownover brougham for his part in the procession—a choice made in the interest of solidarity with young Harlan, in whom he had invested five thousand dollars. The wood was enameled black and the upholstery was red velvet, against which the elegance of his midnight worsted was concealed from a public who could not see inside. He did not fear exposure to assassins, there being specific rules of conduct among Sicilians prohibiting murder at family occasions such as weddings, baptisms, first communions, and funerals. Since the time of his arrest, he had sought to be less visible than Uncle Joe and his kind, marching on foot as they did at the head of the Columbus Day parade and riding about the city in open phaetons, waving to admirers and bellowing traditional greetings and good wishes at acquaintances on the street. He was not and would never be as popular as the fat don, and his association with James Aloysius Dolan had demonstrated to him that fame and a conspicuous visibility were regarded as exclusive privileges of sporting figures and public servants, who were jealous men and never forgot a moment spent in someone else's shade. Borneo was determined to cultivate a reputation for humility, but not to the extent that he attracted attention to his sackcloth; a delicate performance that required concentration and a keen sense of balance. His name had not appeared in a newspaper and he had not been photographed since his apprehension in the Orosco affair.

When he helped his wife Graziella, attired in a simple black dress with modest matching hat and half-veil, into the brougham and boarded behind her, the facing seat was already occupied. The early passenger was a small man of indeterminate age, in a rumpled gray suit with crumbs in the folds and a homburg hat rather too large for him, so that only his outward-turned ears and long thick nose seemed to prevent it from slipping all the way down to rest on his narrow shoulders. With his nail-bitten hands resting on the scuffed and splitting leather briefcase in his lap, Maurice Lapel resembled a thousand other local attorneys and businessmen whose parents and grandparents had come over from Germany with the first wave of Jewish immigrants seventy years before. Upon closer inspection, his quiet courtesy, listening attitude, and in particular his black eyes that appeared to absorb light without reflecting any back, bore out his reputation—known to only a few—as one of the finest legal minds of the age. He had offered his services to Borneo at the time of the Carlo Sorrato murder investigation, and was the man who had presented Graziella and the ticket stubs bearing the date of Carlo's death to the police, who accepted Borneo's alibi and released him. Borneo's first act upon obtaining his freedom was to hire Lapel away from the two-room law firm where he was employed and place him on permanent retainer as the Unione Siciliana's chief consultant in matters of law. In the two years since his appointment, fifteen members of the Unione had been arrested for crimes ranging from malicious destruction of property to murder in the first degree. None had been bound over for trial.

"You should have worn black," was Borneo's greeting upon taking his seat beside his wife. "The Sorratos will say you lack respect."

"They won't notice me. No one does." Lapel worked very hard to eliminate a lifetime in the downtown Jewish corridor from his speech. He spoke in short sentences with almost no intonation, and thus marked himself forever as a member of a foreign culture. "We can talk?" He did not look at Graziella.

Borneo nodded. His wife's English was limited to routine exchanges with customers at Blackwell's department store, where she had worked until their marriage. They spoke Italian exclusively at home and he was reasonably assured that she had forgotten most of what she'd known.

"Vincenzo Sorrato is offering a thousand dollars for your head," Lapel said. "I heard them talking in the barbershop."

"What language were they using?"

"Italian. Sicilian dialect."

"It must be true. Sicilians think only Sicilians understand Sicilian."

"I've never found reason to put them straight. What do you intend to do?"

"To keep my head." Borneo waited.

Lapel unbuckled his briefcase and drew out a cardboard folder, from which he removed a stiff sheet of paper with holes punched in the left margin. "Handle it carefully. It needs to be back in East Park today." East Park was the site of Detroit Police Headquarters.

Borneo took the sheet and turned it toward the window. It contained photographs taken from the front and side of a man with a thick mantel of bone overhanging eyes with bloated lids and ropes of scar tissue on both cheeks. His nose was pushed flat to his face; it did not exist in profile. The man's name was George Zelos. He had been tried twice in the beating death of a quarry foreman named Constantine Butsikitis, released after his second hung jury, and had served six months in the Wayne County Jail for aggravated assault in connection with a fight at the same quarry. Note was made that the U.S. State Department was reviewing his immigration status for possible deportation. He was twenty-seven years old.

Borneo handed back the sheet. "What happened to his face?"

"He fell thirty feet into the bottom of the quarry. He was pronounced dead at the scene and woke up in the morgue wagon. His troubles with his fellow employees began when he went back to work." The attorney returned the sheet to the folder and put it away in his briefcase.

"Can a Greek be trusted?"

"I think so. I've promised to represent him at his deportation hearing if he cooperates. He's under a king's order of execution back home. Something to do with revolutionary activities against the crown."

"What do you suggest?"

Lapel said nothing, communicating much.

Borneo shook his head. "Vincenzo is smarter than Carlo was; it's often that way with second sons. Zelos will never get near him with that face."

"Vincenzo knows all the men we would use under ordinary circumstances. That's why I chose the Greek."

"You should have chosen one with a more pleasing countenance."

"It's all I had to work with. To bring someone in from out

of town would take too much time. You could be dead within a week."

Borneo turned to his wife and asked her in Italian if she were not too hot in so much black. She smiled and replied that as the color was kind to her she would suffer a good deal more before changing. Then she returned her attention to the preparations taking place outside her window.

Borneo shifted back to English. "I think we should make use of Zelos's face rather than look for a way around it. I did not see Vincenzo's daughter at the funeral. Did she come up with him from Toledo?"

"He brought his entire family. Theresa is four, too young to behave herself during a long Mass. When he lived here, Vincenzo used to place his children in the care of the sisters at St. Anne's."

"I doubt he's had time to make different arrangements. Ask Zelos to bring Theresa Sorrato to her father's hotel after the burial. Make certain he knows that she is not to be harmed."

"The sisters will not give her up to that face."

"Of course you will accompany him. I wouldn't have had you make donations to the Catholic Fund there in person these past two years if I did not want them to know you at sight."

"I'd wondered about that." Lapel's black eyes gave back nothing. "Shall I have Zelos give Vincenzo your regards?"

"No. We will not insult the man's intelligence."

The carriage began moving. From far ahead drifted the strains of the brass band, distorted by wind and distance into a swelling and fading drone. The horses' hooves clip-clopped, slow as a grandfather's clock.

"What happened on Gratiot?" Borneo asked.

"That one took some finding out. The police can be admirably obtuse when a mistake has been made. It seems an acting precinct commander named Hearndon asked for a free crack at one of the women. Ordinarily we're flexible about that kind of thing, even though the arrangements we made with Dolan don't include gratuities to the locals. However, the man was drunk and abusive. The door was shut in his face. He smashed a carriage lamp before he left and came back with a flying squad an hour later. It could have been worse. Councilman O'Dell had just left."

"Don't sprinkle sugar on it. Was the commander punished?"

"He was temporary. The department reassigned him to the Second the next day in his old position as lieutenant at the special request of Mayor Maybury."

"Not good enough."

"All the charges were dropped the next morning. The arrests themselves were erased from the blotter. It was a snag in the system. Dolan depends a great deal on the support of the police. His intervention could cost him a lot in the off-year elections."

"I'm curious to know how well that support will hold up when Vito Grapellini delivers a hundred pounds of rotten beef to the police picnic."

"You don't want to go to war with Dolan. You're not that strong. The neighborhood needs six weeks to realize Uncle Joe's dead and the Unione is their only friend. Even then you have to be discreet. Dolan's still on the way up. As powerful as he is, he isn't as powerful as he will be."

"We have that much in common."

"He won't be pleased to hear you've thrown in with Harlan Crownover. He gets nervous when his partners take on partners. Especially when the new partner is the son of the richest man in town."

Borneo, who had learned never to be surprised by anything, least of all the wealth of the lawyer's information, assumed that young Harlan had been talking. "My personal speculations are no more threatening to Dolan than they are his business to know them."

"He might not see it that way. He's been buying up land in the path of the Toledo-Detroit interurban for a year. He stands to make a fortune when he sells the right-of-way. He won't be happy when he finds out you're funding a form of transportation that will compete with the streetcar system."

The Sicilian laughed, showing his full set of even white teeth, as rare among his people as laughter itself was to him. Graziella, startled, smiled at her husband, only to divert her gaze to the window when she realized he was barely aware of her presence.

"The automobile stands as much chance of taking business away from streetcars as the hot-air balloon. I didn't lend money to Abner Crownover's son because I thought his ideas had merit."

The lawyer, too discreet ever to begin a sentence with the word *why,* said nothing. Perhaps for this reason, he was the only man to whom his client ever explained himself.

"I'm a simple immigrant. It helps my esteem to give a young man born with all the advantages a reason to feel grateful to me."

"If it's indebtedness you're after, you'd have done better to approach Edward. He's the one who will inherit the company when the old man dies."

"Harlan approached me. In any case you're forgetting my theory about second sons."

"We're discussing Dolan. He's big and fat, but he's not slow. He moves plenty fast when he suspects he's being betrayed. You've spent far too much time and money getting to where you are now to risk throwing it all away on a theory."

"I'll worry about Dolan."

"I sometimes wish you would worry about something. I'd do no more than my share if I thought you were doing yours."

A police officer in a bullet helmet was standing at the barricade at Bellevue Street, yawning into the back of a white-gloved hand. Borneo was amused by the agitated expression on the face of the driver of a beer wagon who was waiting for the procession to pass; were his customers that thirsty? Since the century's turn, impatience seemed to be the fastest-growing emotion around. It was as if everyone was waiting for something, and although no one knew what it was, the common perception was that it was taking its own sweet time. There was money to be made from such an attitude, and much power.

He faced Lapel. "Do you ever go out to Belle Isle and watch the bicycle races?"

"I never have the time."

"You should make it. There's nothing like war or a competition to bring out the best and worst in human nature. All the contestants start out at the same time, mounted on similar machines. However, many of them do not finish. At some point, one of three things will happen to narrow the field. Two or more riders will collide, or something will go wrong with a number of bicycles, or someone will give up because of exhaustion or injury or broken will. Often all three. Of the riders who finish, most are equal in strength and skill, yet they almost never tie. Why do you think only one wins?"

"That's not difficult to answer. The longer you go without something bad happening, the more the risk increases. You get nervous and make mistakes. The percentages are against more than one rider having the concentration and strength of purpose required to cross the finish line ahead of the others. It gets worse the closer you are to the end."

"Jim Dolan has pedaled a long way," Borneo said. "The race isn't over."

"Politics aren't the same as bicycles. The pressure's different."

"Then we may have to turn it up."

Lapel looked down at his ragged nails. He never chewed them except when he was alone, and then he gnawed them constantly. "Your English still needs work," he said. "I'm getting the feeling you've mixed up your tenses."

"Explain."

"You've turned it up already."

chapter eight

The Mack

Harlan Crownover had been living on the top floor of a brick colonial house on Howard for sixteen months. The move had puzzled his mother and outraged his father, both of whom believed that young men and women of good family did not leave the ancestral home except to marry. He had explained at the time that he wanted privacy, but for all the good that did he thought he might as well have told them the real reason: With Abner III and Edward married and living in their own homes, the prospect of his rattling around the Queen Anne with just his parents and the servants gave him a macabre chill.

The colonial predated the War of 1812. On clear nights when the moon was round, Harlan liked to stand at one of the tall casement windows and picture Brock's British regulars marching along Howard in their red tailcoats to lay claim to the city they had vanquished without a single shot having been fired in its defense. Without studying the matter too closely he suspected the local garrison commander had invested everything in the war machines of the previous century.

His landlords were a couple in their late sixties, the husband a former Linotypist who had retired on the generous pension provided by his guild, the wife a descendant of one of Detroit's founding French families who had lost everything in the French and Indian wars except the house where she still lived, and whose upkeep she and her husband managed by renting out the former ballroom. No partitions had been erected there since the days when gentlemen in powdered wigs and ladies in crinolines had glided across the floor to the strains of the scandalous waltz; Harlan, accustomed to the staircases and cubbyholes of the fussy building on Jefferson, could not get over the novelty of being able to drift from his bed to his parlor to his basin and stool—the last items being recent improvements discreetly hidden behind a folding screen—without climbing a flight of steps or passing through a doorway. He had celebrated his independence by laying down secondhand Oriental rugs and hanging the Impressionist prints his father had forbidden him to display even in his own room. Everything else was furnished except for the Morris chair he had found in a Michigan Avenue thrift shop, covered in scuffed brown leather and stuffed with horsehair in wads pleasing to the irregularities in his anatomy. He took his meals out when he was not invited to sit down with his landlords in the preposterously large and gloomy dining room on the first floor.

He was awakened in the gray dawn of a misty July day by a sharp report in the street below. His first thought was that one of the neighbors had set off a firecracker left over from Independence Day. Then he heard the huff and chortle of a motor and knew that Henry Ford was visiting.

He rose in his nightshirt and looked out the window just as his partner drew back on the brake lever, bringing to a stop the little six-year-old runabout he affectionately referred to as the "baby carriage." Immediately there was another report, and a puff of smoke like a ball of dirty cotton shot out the exhaust pipe in back. Measuring less than six feet from the brass acetylene lamp mounted up front to the little motor straddling the rear axle, the little wooden box perched on wire-spoked bicycle wheels put Harlan less in mind of a baby carriage than a hand-drawn delivery wagon, with Ford's angular frame propped on the open seat like a broken scarecrow. He spotted Harlan and beckoned him with a sweeping motion of an arm that was all wrist and elbow.

Harlan struggled to open the window, swollen tight by last night's heavy rain, and leaned out. "I have to leave for work in an hour," he called.

"I'll drop you off," Ford shouted back. "Come see the plant first."

"I've seen the plant."

"You saw an empty barn with pigeons in the rafters. We've started production."

His heart lurched. "A year early?"

"A month late, if you ask me. Leland's got his damn Cadillac on the street already."

"Will that thing carry two?"

"If it didn't I wouldn't have spent good money on the wide seat. Get a move on. This thing don't run on air."

Harlan put on the clothes he'd worn the day before and went out without shaving. His father, who insisted that Crownovers look like aristocracy on the job, would scold him harshly if he saw him, but he almost never came to the loading dock, and anyway, it was the *plant*. He comforted his landlords, who were standing on the second-floor landing in their robes, gummy-eyed with rats in their hair, and went down to shake Ford's bony hand and climb in beside him. The little vehicle leaned away over on its springs when he trusted his weight to it; it was just like Cheap Henry to use an inferior system of suspension and avoid paying a royalty to Abner Crownover II.

They started down the street with a snap that made Harlan grab for the edge of the seat. Intimidated at first by the noise and vibration, he held on to his grip; but as the little motorcar chugged on at a brisk fifteen miles per hour, its operator steadying its course with a hand on a knob at the end of a tillerlike device connected to the front axle, he relaxed and permitted himself to enjoy the sensation of the wind in his face. It amused him to reflect that he had invested five thousand dollars in an invention that he had not experienced firsthand until now.

Even at that early hour, people came to their doors and leaned out their windows to watch them pass. What was probably old hat in Ford's Dearborn was still a novelty in that neighborhood. He felt himself on display, and a little ridiculous; and knew his first doubts about the venture into which he had hurled himself. He had thought to emulate the knights of the Crusades, conquering superstitious hordes with unquestioning faith in the righteousness of his mission; instead he felt like a freak in a circus parade. He wondered if in his zeal to outmatch his father's youthful triumph he had chosen the wrong—well, vehicle, and managed merely to duplicate the well-intentioned folly that had ruined his grandfather. Sneaking a look at Ford's granite profile, he envied the man his fanatical belief in his course, as if it were no less simple than the brass knob in his fist. His religion was mechanics, his apostles piston rods and gaskets and butterfly valves, anointed with grease and refined oil. He had no more reservations than the heads on a totem pole.

Ford unnerved and fascinated Harlan. He was uncomfortable to be around, not warm, and clearly impatient with any company that kept him from his spark plugs and spanners. Despite his involvement in automobile races he was not a sportsman; even at the tiller of this primitive prototype he wore a three-piece suit of unseasonable winter wool instead of the jaunty cap, goggles, and duster beloved of newspaper cartoonists who liked to poke fun at the motoring community. He was not driven by the pursuit of wealth, unlike Ransom Olds and his own former partners, Henry Leland and William H. Murphy, with whom he had broken when they insisted upon rushing their new car into production over his protests in favor of testing it on the racetrack. First and last he was interested in producing a reliable machine and offering it to the public at a price that would remove it from the exclusive confines of the rich. It was, in fact, Ford's belligerent loyalty to his own vision, and not incompetence on his part or an unpopular product, that had driven him out of automobile manufacturing twice. Harlan flattered himself that he was one of the few who had seen that. What he lacked in his new partner's genius with nuts and bolts, he made up for in his ability to spot a winner.

Or so he had thought until he set foot in an automobile for the first time.

Ford's first comment after they set out, shouted above the racket of the motor, did nothing to dispel Harlan's sense of foreboding. "Well, we lost Daisy."

"The air-rifle people? What happened? I thought that was all set."

"Lawyers. Bennett's shysters told him if the car didn't sell it would hurt Daisy's stock, so he backed out. He might invest some of his own money, though."

"That's something."

"Not really. I need bodies more than I need money. I don't suppose you talked to your father about making them."

"At this point I'm lucky I haven't had to talk him out of firing me."

"Firing's nothing. I've been fired from jobs I didn't even know I had. Nobody ever got anywhere by showing up at the same place every payday."

"Well, I'm still sorry about Daisy."

"I'm not. I didn't want to name the car after a flower."

"What *are* you going to call it?"

"The Model A, to start. If we show a profit the first year we'll put out a Model B, then C. We'll decide where else to go after we run out of alphabet."

"Not very inspired."

"Inspired don't get you out of a mud hole when you're sunk in up to your axles."

"People like variety."

"In coaches and carriages, maybe. Automobiles are different from everything that's come before, except pins. The way to make automobiles is to make one automobile like another automobile, to make them all alike, just as one pin is like another pin when it comes from a pin factory."

"You make them sound dull."

"Dull is good. Dull lasts. It's the bright and shiny that fades."

Nothing more passed between them the rest of the trip. The incessant spluttering of the little car's motor and the sick-sweet smell of exhaust had started Harlan's head aching. He was depressed by his partner's mundane approach to a prospect that had excited him and felt the first gnawing uncertainty about the choice he had made. His faith remained in the future of the industry, but he wondered if, with dozens of automobile companies sprouting throughout the city, he had selected one of the inevitable failures.

The plant on Mack Avenue calmed his fears somewhat. A large rectangular frame building that had begun life as a warehouse for iron stove components, it had since Harlan's last visit acquired a sign, FORD MOTOR COMPANY, running the length of the broad side facing the street. The simple white block letters professionally painted on a black background had a permanence he would have found lacking in the bombast of a skirling circus-type legend such as was used to advertise patent medicines and phrenology. Inside, between great bay doors mounted on rollers at the opposing ends, two rows of mullioned windows on the east side allowed the first orange shafts of horizontal light to spill inside. The dust motes swarming inside the shafts appeared no less industrious than the forty or fifty laborers at work on the floor. Clad in grease-stained overalls, with cloth bill-less caps protecting their hair, teams of heavy lifters carried naked engines the size of pigs in from wagons drawn up to the dock and placed them on wooden blocks, where other workers set to work greasing and wiring them and installing spark plugs, dry cells, and coils from open crates at their feet. No sooner was one finished than a lifter carried it away, to be replaced by another engine in need of lubrication and parts.

"I'm buying old bodies and wheels from some of the other manufacturers around town so we can test the engines on the road," Ford explained, raising his voice above the clattering of hammers and clinking of wrenches and pliers. "Then we'll furnish them with new bodies and wheels and ship them out. I haven't got the bodies to spare for testing."

Harlan leaned close to Ford's ear. "Do you intend to thank my father for inventing the concept of the loading dock?"

"I'll thank him for not taking out a patent. Here are some people I want you to meet." The angular automaker strode off in the direction of a group of men assembled around a block unoccupied by a motor, looking at what appeared to be a map spread out on top and spilling over the sides. They were all dressed in business suits and hats. Two of the three men looked up as Ford approached, trailing Harlan. The third, a squat, bulldog-faced man in a slightly loud pinstripe suit, bow tie, and derby, kept his attention on the sheet of paper. He resembled a circus barker.

"Alexander Malcolmson and C. H. Wills, Harlan Crownover," Ford said.

Malcolmson, a Scot with old-fashioned muttonchop whiskers even more pronounced than Harlan's father's, had the austere features of a bishop. His firm handshake fairly crackled with electricity, as if the nervous energy that had driven him to the top of the highly competitive coal business in Detroit were too much for one man's body to contain. His gaze was mild but probing, and Harlan was very aware suddenly of his own unshaven condition and that he was wearing yesterday's clothes. The other man, Wills, was closer to Harlan's age and very tall, with the cleft chin and chiseled cheekbones of a theatrical leading man. He had an intense, searching stare and his grasp was tighter than it had to be but not deliberately so, as if he were more accustomed to handling instruments. It was impossible to stand in the crossfire of these two men's scrutiny and not feel as if one had been found out utterly.

"Wills is our engineer," Ford pointed out. "He'll be designing the Model A."

"Designed," said Wills in a clipped tone, slightly high-pitched. "Past tense." He tipped a long, elegant hand toward the sheet.

Ford pounced on it, seizing the edges and spreading it out to hold it up to the light, a way in which Harlan had never seen anyone examine a blueprint. The detailed sketch resembled a conventional coach frame, with an extension added to the front to allow for the motor. Realizing that his partner had forgotten to introduce him to the third man, Harlan smiled and held out his hand. "Harlan Crownover."

"James Couzens." The circus barker seized the hand, pumped it once, and let go. His eyes remained on the blueprint, following its motion like those of the bulldog he favored. He seemed only peripherally aware of Harlan's existence.

"We'll talk about it," Ford said suddenly, returning the sheet to the block. Both Wills and Couzens moved swiftly to catch it before it could slide to the floor.

"Couzens is my advisor," Malcolmson told Harlan. "I don't make a move without him."

Ford said, "He isn't exaggerating. Aleck won't open an umbrella in a rainstorm until Jim tells him it's okay."

Malcolmson grunted; a noise Harlan took for laughter. "I wouldn't question that, if I were you. He's the one who persuaded me to invest in this company. If it weren't for Couzens I'd still be peddling anthracite from door to door."

"Talk about what?" Wills, the engineer, appeared not to

have heard anything since Ford put down the blueprint. "The car's perfect. All it needs is a logo."

"The wheelbase is too long," said Ford. "You'd need a cornfield to turn it around in. What's a logo?"

Malcolmson said, "Henry, I want to talk to you about the Arrow. When are we going to race it?"

"I'm through with races. I'm in the business of making and selling automobiles."

"So is everyone else. How are you going to stand out from the pack if you don't schedule a public event?"

"Well, the Arrow isn't ready and the nine ninety-nine's worn out. The earliest I could race it is this winter. Oldfield won't be available then."

"Surely you can find another driver in the meantime."

"They don't grow on trees. I had to teach Oldfield how to drive. He was a bicyclist."

"Why can't you drive it yourself?"

"You won't need a cornfield with the steering wheel I designed," Wills said.

Ford said, "Just shorten the wheelbase. I can use the material you're wasting to build another car." To Malcolmson: "I'm a little too old to go haring off across the countryside in a speedster."

"I never knew you to back away from a challenge for fear of your skin," said the coal merchant.

Henry Ford's deep-set eyes retreated farther into their sockets. "I'll race the blasted thing."

"A logo is a trademark," Wills persisted. "You put it on the front of the radiator to tell the world the automobile is a Ford. I've always admired the *F* in your signature. This is it, isn't it?" Producing a yellow pencil from a row of them sticking up out of the watch pocket of his vest, the designer bent over the blueprint and wrote out the capital with a curlicue on top.

Ford stared at it for a long time. The corners of his lips

tugged out in a constipated smile. "It's a good thing I don't have any money. You could forge my signature on a check and clean me out."

Wills added the remaining three letters of Ford's name in simple script. The logo was legible and distinctive.

"I like it," Ford said. "Now all we need is an automobile to stick on the back."

Further conversation broke off as a pair of extraordinary figures strode in from the loading dock, bellowing loud enough to drown out the din of automobile construction. Outfitted identically in boaters and red-and-white-striped blazers over white flannels, the hefty newcomers put Harlan in mind of a pair of hot-air balloons broken away from the fairgrounds. He wondered if they were a vaudeville act out drumming up interest in the bill at the Lyceum Theater until he recognized the round, congested faces of the Dodge brothers, John and Horace. Both sported beer stains on their shirts. The smells of sweat and stale alcohol preceded them like a hot wind.

"What the hell is that fellow Ford doing with our dainty little engines?" John shouted to no one in particular. "We didn't sell them to him to go banging on 'em with hammers and shit."

Horace, not quite as loud—the way a clanging fire bell was not as loud as a steam whistle—agreed. "I think we ought to take 'em back and sell 'em to William Jennings Bryan. We'll tell him they're made of silver."

Both men guffawed, far beyond the boundaries of the joke. They were obviously drunk and in a bullying mood. To be in such a condition at that hour suggested that they had been at it all night. Harlan, intrigued despite himself to see how Ford's very different character would handle them, braced himself for anything. Even the burly Dodges were no match for the laborers present; but would Ford's people act fast enough to spare their lanky employer a blow from a hamlike fist? Then there was the fact that the brothers seldom ventured out unarmed.

Harlan was not so curious he wanted to see his investment go up in gunsmoke.

Ford put his hands in his pockets. "What brings you boys out so early? I heard you never rolled out of bed before noon on a Monday after a holiday."

"We ain't been to bed since before the Fourth," said John, struggling to keep his body from pitching forward when his feet stopped moving. "Anyway, we didn't want to miss the ball game. Yeager's pitching against the Orioles. We got a hundred bucks on a shutout."

"You're early. The game isn't till afternoon."

Horace said, "John figured we ought to come see what you're doing to the good name of Dodge. Also we want to buy back an engine."

"What for?"

"We're getting into boating," John said. "Pete Studer's building a racing yacht for Olds. We want one too, only we want a good engine."

"What's wrong with the ones at your plant?"

Horace said, "We want your plugs. You know all about racing, so we figure your equipment'll give us a leg up on Olds. We're looking to make forty miles an hour on Lake St. Clair."

C. H. Wills, the engineer, laughed shortly, a dry cough. "You'd be lucky to find an automobile that will go that fast, let alone a boat. It can't be done."

But Ford took a hand out of one of his pockets and rubbed his chin. "Forty, you say?"

"Damn right." Horace belched, and Harlan backed away a step. "We got the best machine shop in the country. We won't settle for anything less than the fastest boat."

"Take your pick," Ford said. "I won't accept a cent for it."

Malcolmson, Scottish to his soles, made a hoarse noise without any amusement in it. "Henry, I must say I'm glad to see you're so comfortable with my money you're willing to throw it away."

"Not a cent," Ford repeated. "Just don't be stingy about telling people where you got the plugs. Mention Ford when you win your first race."

"What if we lose?" Horace sounded sober suddenly. Harlan wondered, not for the first time, if there wasn't some method to the brothers' buffoonery.

"No Ford machine ever lost a race."

"You're out of your element, Mr. Ford," Wills said. "A lake isn't a road. The best automobile engine in the world can't compete with the second-best boat engine. The engineering's different."

"Tell John and Horace all about it. You're helping them build it."

Wills's forehead creased. "Don't I get a choice?"

"You know you want to do it. I'm just saving time." Ford looked at Malcolmson. "Are you happy, Aleck? There are two races for you."

Malcolmson looked at Couzens. The latter's bulldog face was blank for a moment. Then he nodded. The coal merchant nodded in his turn at Ford. "It's all right if you don't place first. Just don't come in last."

Ford was unsmiling. "If I don't do the one I'll do the other. That's how it's been since I left the farm."

chapter nine

The Man Who Invented the Automobile

Abner Crownover II loathed the theater. He found the seats tortuously uncomfortable both to his own unpadded frame and his wife's lumbago, despised the chattering legions of society who filed in during the overture to make sure they were seen in their shirtboards and sparklers, squirmed before the overripe emoting onstage, and hated the interminable wait in the grotesque lobby while his carriage was brought around for the trip home; which was the time when every bore he had ever met during his dealings in Detroit saw fit to approach him and discuss Washington, business, the morass in South Africa, and everything else under the sun except the play they had just seen. But he never hated it quite so much as when he made out the check each spring to reserve his season box at the Lyceum. His signature was an angry slash like a saber wound.

It was important to the continued well-being of Crownover Coaches that its owner be seen in public, particularly at such self-indulgent spectacles as concerts and the theater; in the past his absence might suggest that the company was in trouble and required his presence around the clock, but since his fiftieth birthday it could as well be construed as evidence of illness. Either situation made stockholders equally nervous and caused customers to look to competitors for large orders that might be delayed by uncertainty at Crownover. Abner III's inability to guide the company decisively was well known throughout the industry, and there was little confidence that Edward possessed the vision and fortitude necessary to succeed his father effectively. In weak moments, when he allowed himself to contemplate a rosy impossibility, Abner II wished he had a son who combined his own intelligence with Abner III's loyalty, Edward's attention to detail, and Harlan's constancy to his principles, however crackbrained. He had long since decided that he could never retire. It occurred to him more and more of late that he must never die, lest the firm to which he had sacrificed his youth and his happiness follow him into the grave. Now, sunk back into the springy plush of the Crownover Caruso opera coach, he looked up at the 150-foot towers supporting powerful arc lights that sprayed their illumination mainly into outer space. They were a civic improvement intended to celebrate the ascendancy of electric light over the gas lamps that lined the streets only two decades ago, but the fixtures were placed so high their halos extended no lower than the lofty roofs of the Majestic and Hammond buildings. He identified with the preposterous installations, things wasting their energy against a vast darkness.

No conversation passed between him and Edith during the trip from the house on Jefferson to the theater on Randolph Street. They seldom spoke these days except to exchange necessary information. Even small talk had become too much of a burden between two people who in the end had proven to have nothing in common beyond their children. The children themselves, disappointments to their father, had in fact driven the wedge so deep their parents no longer stirred themselves to peer across it. Abner blamed Edith for the way his offspring had turned out. It was not that he saw anything radically wrong with the manner in which she had reared them (although he suspected she had not disciplined them often enough or severely enough when they were small, undermining the example he had attempted to set); he had concluded that her aristocratic blood, which he had thought to be an asset, was too anemic to offset the weakness in his own, exemplified by the wronghead-edness of Abner I. And so the responsibility lay with him, the second Abner, who would have done better to wed himself to the milk-fed daughter of some obstinate rich German farmer from the wilderness north of Michigan Avenue. Whenever he came to that juncture in his reverie, his rancor receded, and he remembered something of the tenderness he had felt during his courtship, without precisely feeling it. It was the ghost of an emotion long dead, arrived too late and in a form too in-substantial to join the parallel courses their lives had taken, headed inexorably in the same direction without intersecting.

When they entered their box, he was aware of heads turn-ing their way from the orchestra, saw the glint of opera glasses trained upon Edith's pearls and the rapidly wasting face of 'America's Coach King. There was a time when he had enjoyed the attention, accepting it as approbation of his early success, like the huzzah of the people on the pavement when a native conqueror appeared on the balcony, but of late he knew they were merely measuring the evidence of his physical deteriora-tion against the standard of the young genius of local legend. Had he seen the future, he would have purchased every copy of that damned book and burned it, or sued its author, whom he had never met, when it was still in galleys. No mortal man could be expected to compete with his own shade, pressed like a blossom between yellowing pages. He held Edith's chair and sat down quickly as soon as she was seated.

The play was dreary, a faded tenth carbon of a farce that had been derivative when it premiered on Broadway, per-formed by a stock company whose male lead could not have obtained a nonspeaking role as a servant in the original pro-duction. The ingenue was too old by ten years and too hefty by twenty pounds for her part, the visiting English duchess dropped her g's like a scullery maid from Columbus, and the antagonist, an oily Spaniard with Louis-Napoleon imperials who had successfully passed himself off as an international banker in order to cheat the daughters of society out of their dowries, would have been arrested on sight as a suspicious person by the dullest of Irish policemen pounding a beat on East Lafayette. Abner excused himself during the second act, an annoying symphony of shrill voices and slamming doors, to purchase an orange juice from the concession in the lobby. Behind him the quilted double doors drifted shut against a wave of hysterical laughter from the audience. He wondered sourly if these were the same fools who bought the vehicles he built, and if it mattered whether he paneled them with the finest mahogany or that warped offal those charlatans in Nicaragua had tried to palm off on him last spring.

The orange juice had been an excuse; it was the worst thing he could pour into his tender stomach. But because he hated to lie, even to Edith, he purchased a glass, intending to stand around holding it for the satisfaction of ushers before returning to the purgatory of the auditorium. He might as well have drunk it for all the good abstaining did his ulcerated tissue. When he turned, James Aloysius Dolan was lighting a cigar in front of the door to the gentlemen's lounge.

The big Irishman wore evening dress, the tails of which alone contained enough material to make a full coat for a man of Abner's narrow build, with diamond studs in his starched shirtfront and a brilliant as large as a marble on the ring finger of his left hand. Abner, who detested diamonds on a man, particularly when that man happened to be Jim Dolan, thought of a fat crow with a glittering morsel in its beak. There was no escape. He cursed his timing. Even a dismal play was preferable to his present company.

Puffing up a thick blue fog, Dolan deposited the match in a bowl of white sand on a plaster pedestal and came his way, swaying from side to side like a frigate under full sail. He smelled of good whiskey; Abner suspected he was carrying a flask. He himself had not touched alcohol in ten years. The fumes alone were enough to pucker his insides.

"What a pleasure, Mr. Crownover. I haven't seen you since Bill Maybury cut the ribbon on the County Building."

"Dolan." Abner didn't offer his hand, and was satisfied to note that it did not seem to be expected.

"Noisy sort of a play."

"Yes."

Dolan smiled behind his whiskers. "I'm getting on. Time was when I could empty a keg and then sit through nine innings at Bennett without getting up once to drain the pickle."

Abner made no response. The big man's shanty Irish past to the contrary, he had spent enough time in society to know when he was being vulgar. For some reason he was taking pains to point up the difference in their stations.

"Charlotte's determined to win me over to the legitimate theater," Dolan went on. "The Temple's where I go to enjoy myself. I saw Eva Tanguay dance last year. One of these times she's going to bust a seam."

A fresh burst of laughter came from the other side of the wall.

"Is your wife with you?" Abner asked.

"No. One of the children is ill."

"Nothing serious, I hope."

"Too much spun sugar on Independence Day, I suspect. How are your sons?"

"They're well. Edward's wife may be expecting."

"Congratulations. I hope it's a grandson."

"I haven't given it much thought. Edith is hoping for a girl. She misses having a daughter." His stomach twisted as soon as he said it. The infernal man's obsequiousness had put him on his guard, causing him in the process to drop an older one he had taken for granted. He hadn't spoken of Katherine in years.

Fortunately, Dolan appeared to miss the reference. "I saw

Harlan a few months ago. A strapping young man."

"I heard you met."

"He's quite taken with automobiles." The Irishman drew on his cigar, watching Abner.

"He's young."

"He's about the age you were when you assumed control of Crownover, isn't he?"

Now they were coming to it. Abner fenced.

"Not quite. Anyway, times were different."

"Noisy things, automobiles." It was the same tone in which he had dismissed the noisy play. "I can't remember the last time I spent an entire Sunday without one of them bucketing down my street, stinking and scaring the horses. Did you know thirty-eight companies began producing motorcars last year?"

"I wouldn't be surprised. It wouldn't surprise me to learn that thirty of them had already closed their doors."

"That would still leave eight, more than there were two years ago all told. Strick tells me another forty-seven are expected to enter the market this year. If this keeps up, you and I will be wading arse-deep in the blasted machines come election time."

"If you mentioned those statistics to Harlan, I shouldn't wonder that he's enamored." He wasn't sure he'd succeeded in keeping the irritation from his voice.

"I did not, and would not have had I been aware of them then. I'm not in the business of encouraging young men into foolish enterprise. There are as many spiritualists in Detroit as automobile manufacturers, and more opening up in storefronts all the time, offering to put gullible old women in touch with their departed husbands as easily as ringing up Central. No one I know in the mortuary business feels threatened. That's because they recognize the difference between a genuine movement and a fancy of the season."

"I agree." Why, then, were they having this conversation?

He'd forgotten for the moment Dolan was a politico, and more than usually adept at reading minds. "Your son has invested five thousand dollars in Henry Ford's latest motorcar venture. He borrowed it from Sal Borneo. Do you know the name?"

"I do not. And I'd be interested in learning where you obtain your information."

"I'd be interested in learning where you plan to build your next plant, but I don't think that's going to happen. Sal Borneo is a Black Hander, a wop hooligan. He does favors for people, that's his business. He never says no."

"In that case, people must be asking him for favors all the time."

"You'd think so, only they don't. They have to be willing to pay the price."

"A favor you have to pay for is no favor."

"Now you understand. The man came here twenty years ago with no English and nothing in his pockets. Now he hands out wads of gelt right and left without asking for collateral. Does that tell you anything?"

"At the moment I'm more interested in hearing what it tells you."

"Borneo isn't interested in money. It's just a tool, like the pool cue he used to bash in people's heads with. He doesn't care any more about automobiles than you or I do. If he gave Harlan money, it means he wants Crownover Coaches."

Abner sipped from his glass for the first time. The acid burned his stomach, preventing him from laughing in Dolan's face. The man's oafishness made it possible to forget what a dangerous enemy he could be when sufficiently offended. "If that's his purpose, he'll have to aim higher than Harlan. My son has no control over the business."

"He owns no stock?"

"Just three percent. So you see, Mr. Borneo can say good-bye to his five thousand."

"Not if Ford succeeds."

"I thought we agreed that isn't likely."

"The streetcar companies in Toledo and Monroe aren't so sure. They're dragging their feet on the interurban project until they see which way the wind blows. All these automobiles have got them wringing their hands like old maids. They're afraid no one will ride the rails if he can make the same trip in a motorcar, and they'll lose their investment. Meanwhile I'm sitting on thirteen hundred acres of farmland in Michigan and Ohio, and I'm no farmer. The property taxes are ruinous."

"You're exaggerating."

"Those Kraut farmers drive a hard bargain. I had to liquefy every asset in order to close the deals with reasonable speed. At the time the streetcar companies were going full tilt with the interurban. If I didn't act fast, they'd have negotiated with someone else for the right-of-way."

"So you borrowed against Democratic Party Funds."

Dolan's smile put him in mind of an enormous leprechaun. "You're a great man, Mr. Crownover. Great men aren't hobbled by the laws of the land."

"We're not talking about me."

"We are. You have as much interest as I have in seeing Ford's latest attempt end in disaster. It would be a whiff of pepper in your son's nose to bring him to his senses and back into the fold."

"Perhaps. I'm curious to find out how it would benefit you. According to your own figures, Ford's failure would leave eighty-four automobile manufacturers still in business."

"Don't ask me why—he's stumbled twice before—but the man inspires confidence in unlikely places. Alexander Malcolmson's sold on him, and Malcolmson's anything but a fool. If Ford falls spectacularly enough this time, the aftershock will bring down most of his competitors. What's left couldn't frighten a kitten, much less those fellows at Detroit United Railways. He's the solution to both our problems."

Abner swirled the liquid around in his glass. "What is your plan?"

"It's a bit complicated. If you're free any day next week, I'll introduce you to the one man who can bring it all about. Do you know the Detroit Shipbuilding Company on Orleans?"

"I should think so. I went to school with the owner."

"It's a small world. The manager is a friend. He's offered me the use of his private office on the top floor for the meeting I have in mind. If you will name the day and the hour, I'll make the arrangements with the others."

"What others?"

Dolan flicked a column of ash to the floor, not without elegance. "You must allow an old politician some of his secrets. All will be revealed in the fullness of time."

"You're ten years younger than I am," Abner said. "One of the irritations of age is the number of pups who gather around me trying to convince me they belong to my generation, as if being old were some kind of exclusive club. It is not. It is a damn bore."

"I meant no disrespect."

"Respect is not your stock-in-trade. I can spare one hour Thursday at noon."

He was about to return to the auditorium without awaiting a reply when the door to the ladies' lounge opened and a striking woman glided their way on a sea of rustling taffeta. She was dressed entirely in black, with a gauzy shawl about her bare shoulders and a hat reminiscent of an old-time admiral's fore-and-aft perched becomingly on a pile of glistening black hair. She coiled an arm inside one of Dolan's and looked at Abner, lifting a pair of strong dark brows in expectation.

"Abner Crownover," the Irishman said, "may I present

Countess Maribel Louisa diViareggio. The countess is visiting from her home in Tuscany. Maribel, Mr. Crownover is our most important citizen."

"Signor Crownover's name is well known in my country. It was the fondest wish of my dear late husband to commission a coach from your great firm." She laid a cool hand in Abner's palm, extended automatically. The woman had the high cheekbones of a northern Italian and a smile Abner thought slightly mocking; but then he distrusted women who painted their faces, no matter how exotic their backgrounds. He withdrew his hand as soon as was decent.

"Are you recently widowed?" he asked.

"My poor Guglielmo was taken by fever at Christmas. I come here to visit relatives, and to forget." Her accent, like her level gaze, was somewhat masculine.

Abner noted that Dolan had shifted some of his great belly into his chest since the woman had joined them. Clearly she was his mistress. He was furious to think the fat wardheeler would parade her before him in this way, as if he were expected to approve on behalf of the society of men.

He kept his voice level. "I'm afraid you're missing the play."

"It is no great sacrifice," she said. "I did not like it when I saw it in London. Travel does not appear to have improved it."

Dolan said. "The countess knows a good deal about the theater. Her family has patronized the arts for centuries."

Abner said something about returning to his wife, declined his head in a cursory bow, and took his leave, setting his glass on the shelf of the concession window on the way to the door. He did not know if his departure was graceful and did not much care. He did know that the play taking place that evening in the Lyceum had been performed for the first time at the Lincoln Theater on Broadway in New York City in April 1901. It had never played London. The woman was an impostor.

• • •

The Detroit Shipbuilding Company, with plants in Detroit and Wyandotte, was the city's biggest employer behind Crownover Coaches and the Michigan Stove Company. Its base of operations, a great brick box of a building at the foot of Orleans Street overlooking the Detroit River, was less than ten years old but already deteriorating; the constant shuddering clang of steel beams and hammering of rivets had cracked most of the window panes on the first two floors and shaken mortar out of the spaces between the bricks into dirty white heaps at the base of the structure. Steam-operated cranes swung smokestacks and anchor winches over the heads of the workers in the shipyard, where the naked superstructures of vessels in various stages of construction resembled a fleet of Arks. In the blistering July heat, a haze of teak dust, steel and brass filings, and pulverized concrete hung over the river, a man-made fog. The fishy stench of the water, combined with rank sweat and lubricating grease, clawed at the protective lining of milk in Abner's stomach as he entered the plant through a side door and boarded the freight elevator. The operator was a squat Indian in overalls, whose brick-colored features betrayed no recognition of Detroit's wealthiest citizen; nevertheless he knew where his passenger was headed. The car started moving before Abner had time to ask for the top floor.

Cork baffles must have been inserted in the crawlspace between the ceiling of the plant proper and the offices beneath the roof. As suddenly as if a switch had been thrown, the cacophony of construction ceased the moment he stepped off the elevator. He crossed a narrow hallway with a thick Brussels carpet and opened a door with a pebbled-glass window bearing the number 300 in black numerals flecked with gold.

Beyond was an ordinary reception room, equipped with a female secretary in a starched blouse and pince-nez glasses behind a golden oak desk with a brass upright telephone on top. Five wooden file cabinets lined the wall to the left, opposite an upholstered bench upon which sat a small, balding man in an unpressed suit. The man looked up as Abner entered, but made no attempt at conversation. Abner in turn ignored him for the secretary, who left her black box of a Remington typewriter to knock at a door at the back and announce Mr. Crownover's arrival to whoever opened it from the other side. Immediately the door was flung wide and Jim Dolan beckoned Abner to enter.

Today the big man wore immaculate gray gabardine, with a platinum watch chain across his vast middle and an emerald stickpin in his tie. His left hand was wrapped around a thick glass with amber liquid in it. Abner, a rigid "sundowner" during his own drinking days, kept from scowling through an effort of will. The man seemed determined to underscore his Irishness.

"It was good of you to make time for us." Dolan stood aside.

The room was reminiscent of the library in a gentlemen's club. The desk, where presumably the plant manager conducted business, was mounted on massive cherry-wood legs carved into the likenesses of seated lions, tucked away in a corner darkened by wooden slats covering the window. Leather-bound books with titles stamped in gold on their spines gleamed on walnut shelves built into the walls. A good painting of *Walk-in-the-Water*, the first steamboat to navigate the Upper Great Lakes in 1818, leaned out in a giltwood frame from the wall above a fireplace with a gray marble surround and a bear-skin on the hearth, its fur singed in several places by wandering sparks from the grate. Morsels of white ash clung to the scorched iron, undoubtedly cold since March. A small library table supported not books but a set of four cut-crystal decanters in a portable lock rack, labeled *Scotch, Gin, Bourbon,* and *Rye*. Another decanter of polished glass with a long narrow neck and a flat base as big around as a dinner plate contained a molasses-colored liquid, as black a port as Abner had ever seen. There were in addition a tray of sparkling glasses, a leather pipe humidor, a deep carved-ash box with its lid propped open to reveal cigars stacked inside, and a brass lighter of a type popular with executives too old to have served in the war with Spain, fashioned from a machine-gun cartridge case recovered from the fighting in Cuba. The room was, even to Abner's mind, suffocatingly masculine; he thought that if a woman were to enter it unannounced, it would crack apart with a loud report, like a warm glass pitcher into which ice water was poured suddenly. He might as well have been in a barbershop or a Turkish bath.

They were not alone. In a studded leather wing chair in the corner opposite the desk, smoking a cigar, sat a beautiful man with thick snowy hair brushed back from his temples and healthy widow's peak and a vandyke beard trimmed to a perfect point. His skin was pink and unwrinkled, his eyes clear gray, and he wore a black morning coat, striped trousers without the suspicious crease that marked a garment as ready-to-wear, and gray kid spats on black patent leathers polished to a mirror, gloss. The coat was buttoned to his neck, allowing only a glimpse of white collar and burgundy satin tie to show at his throat, which had begun to sag slightly, the only flaw in his finish. Abner, who took no small care with his own appearance, felt positively slovenly against such meticulous attention to detail. It had been thirty years since anyone had managed to intimidate him; he found the sensation intriguing.

"William C. Whitney, Abner Crownover," Dolan said. "Commodore Whitney was secretary of the navy under President Cleveland."

Whitney deposited his cigar in a crystal ashtray balanced upon the arm of his chair and rose, exhibiting none of the effort associated with age, to grasp Abner's hand. The old man's grip was dry and no firmer than it had to be. Abner, who could not recall the last time he had been presented to someone else rather than the other way around (Yes, he could; it was when he met President McKinley), approved. The custom of the new century seemed to be the importance of crushing another man's metacarpi in establishing one's station; by this reasoning, circus strong man Sandor the Magnificent occupied a position higher than Oliver Wendell Holmes.

"Pierpont Morgan and I were discussing recently the relative merits of our nation's largest cities," announced Whitney, without preamble. "We agreed that Detroit boasted two strings to its bow: the birthplace of the Pullman car and the headquarters of Crownover Coaches."

Abner smiled, genuinely pleased by a statement which coming from anyone else he would have dismissed as empty flattery. "Not Michigan Stove?"

"Our wives might have insisted upon including it. It's quite possible there's one in my kitchen. Never having visited the room, I couldn't say."

"You're not a drinking man, I think," Dolan said. "I can send Aurora out for whatever you'd like."

"It's not necessary."

"Then I won't beat around the bush. I asked Commodore Whitney here because he's organizing a group in which you and I should have more than passing interest."

"I'm not a political man," Abner said.

"It's not a political group. I keep forgetting the name." Dolan turned to Whitney, who had reseated himself and reclaimed his cigar from the ashtray.

"We're calling it the Association of Licensed Automobile Manufacturers."

Abner said, "Now I know I'm not interested."

Dolan said, "The A.L.A.M. has no intention of producing an automobile. It exists mainly to prevent them from being produced, or at the very least to collect tribute from those who attempt it."

"Specifically, it's been formed to exercise one man's exclusive right to manufacture automobiles." Whitney blew a plume of smoke at the ceiling. "It may interest you to know, Mr. Crownover, that the internal combustion engine as a practical factor in transportation is not in public domain. It has been patented."

"By whom?"

Dolan, who was standing by the door to the reception room, opened it and leaned out. "We're ready now, Aurora."

A moment later, the man whom Abner had seen waiting outside walked in. He was taller than he appeared when seated, but that fact did not add to his stature. If anything, he appeared to be cowering inside himself. He had restless eyes and a habit of moving his head jerkily to take in the room and its occupants, like a particularly nervous bird. When he was introduced, his handshake confirmed Abner's impression of the man's relative unimportance in the world scheme. It was self-consciously firm, as if he practiced gripping one hand with the other in private when he should have been concentrating upon something more significant.

"William Whitney, Abner Crownover, George Selden," Dolan said. "Mr. Selden designed an automobile in 1895, and had the foresight to apply for a patent. Washington granted it. He is the only man in the United States who possesses the right to manufacture and sell automobiles. It is his intention, with our help, to prevent anyone who does not belong to the A.L.A.M. from doing so. That includes Henry Ford."

part three

The Blight

chapter ten

Fire and Ice

In the sticky July heat a haze of sawdust and iron shavings hung motionless inside the Mack Avenue plant. It stirred to admit James Couzens, then closed in behind him like shifting sand. Harlan thought the congested bulldog face a portrait of a man about to be stricken. Couzens swept past him without looking in his direction and handed Ford a copy of the *Detroit Evening News,* folded to a full-page advertisement in the first section:

NOTICE

**To Manufacturers, Dealers, Importers, Agents, and Users
of Gasoline Automobiles**

No other manufacturers or importers are authorized to make or sell automobiles, and any person making, selling, or using such machines made or sold by any unlicensed manufacturers or importers will be liable for prosecution for infringement.

Association of Licensed Automobile Manufacturers
7 East Forty-second Street, New York

Ford's deep-set eyes raced over the legend. He alone of the small knot of company executives present had kept on his suitcoat and his necktie drawn to his collar. He alone was dry of perspiration. He returned the newspaper without comment.

"Well?" Couzens' face remained red.

"Well, what?"

"What are you planning to do about this? Can these cranks really sue our *customers*?"

"Anyone can sue anyone. That's how the courts work."

"Can they win?"

"That depends on the judge and jury."

"Well, what in thunder is the Association of Licensed Automobile Manufacturers? I can't find them listed in any directory."

"That's because the directories were printed before it existed."

"You seem to know something about it."

"The automobile business is small. Not much goes on that I don't know about. A man named Selden designed an automobile in ninety-five. He didn't build it, but he did the next best thing. He took out a patent. The A.L.A.M. controls him and his patent. It intends to put out of business every manufacturer who doesn't belong."

Harlan spoke up. "Are you planning to join?"

Ford shook his head.

"Why not?"

"Because he's a mule-headed son of a bitch, that's why." Couzens accordioned the newspaper between his short thick paws.

"I am a mule-headed S.O.B.," Ford agreed. "But that's not why."

"Well, then, suppose you tell us."

A joyless smile tugged out the corners of the motorman's thin mouth. "Because I tried, when I first heard about it. They won't have me."

•   •   •

Two days after the advertisement appeared, another ran in its place:

NOTICE

**To Dealers, Importers, Agents, and Users
of our Gasoline Automobiles**

We will protect you against any prosecution for alleged
infringement of patents.

We are pioneers of the *Gasoline Automobile*. Our Mr. Ford
also built the famous "999" Automobile which was driven by
Barney Oldfield in New York this year, a mile in 55 ⅘ seconds, on a circular track, which is the world record.

Mr. Ford driving his own machine beat Mr. Winton at Grosse
Pointe track in 1901. We have always been winners.

Playing Couzens' part now, carrying the newspaper containing the advertisement rolled up in one fist, Harlan had
sought out Ford in his booth at the Pontchartrain bar, where
the automobile man was drinking a glass of mineral water opposite John and Horace Dodge. The redheaded brothers were
drinking gin.

Harlan slid in beside Ford. "Do we have the resources to
indemnify all our agents and customers?"

"Of course not. It won't come to that."

"How can you be so sure?"

"The A.L.A.M. is out to get to me. They don't care who
buys a Ford. They're just trying to scare away business."

"Then you think they're no threat?"

"I didn't say that."

"Let 'em sue!" John Dodge banged the table with his glass, slopping out some of its contents.

Ford smiled his tight smile. "I imagine they'll do just that, with or without your permission."

"When do you expect to be served?" Harlan asked.

"I'm surprised I haven't been already. I expect my advertisement is being read by their lawyers right now."

"Let 'em!" John repeated. "Horace and I have a load of money invested that says the company will do good. We ain't backed a losing horse yet."

Horace, quieter (and possibly not yet as inebriated), grinned. "I thought the whole point of this was to put all the horses out to pasture."

"They can't win, can they?" Harlan pressed.

"Maybe, maybe not. Commodore Whitney's heading them up. He knows most of the judges."

"Then we'll win on appeal?"

"We'll win in the end. Roosevelt don't hold with trusts. At the rate he's appointing judges—"

"Federal judges?" Harlan broke in. "You think it will get that far?"

"I was referring to justices of the U.S. Supreme Court."

The suit was not filed, although the threat of it hung above the plant on Mack Avenue like a guillotine blade for all to see. Infringement of patent was the charge discussed in the press. Henry Leland, Ransom E. Olds, and the makers of the Franklin, the Pierce, and the Locomobile joined the Association of Licensed Automobile Manufacturers, paying hefty fees for the privilege of making motorcars powered by gasoline. Entrepreneurs hoping to enter the field sent in money so they could show their licenses to potential backers. Ford stood alone. A lawyer representing the patent holders, granting a newspaper interview in his book-lined, cigar-smelling office overlooking New York's Fifth Avenue, put the alliance's philosophy into one succinct sentence: "When you buy a Ford, you buy a lawsuit." Sales fell off. Rows of new Model Cs stood unadmired on the grounds of dealerships, where salesmen who had been all week visiting the homes of farmers and businessmen only to come potting back in their sample vehicles without a sale sat working newspaper puzzles and making appointments for job interviews at Oldsmobile and Cadillac.

Parochial Windsor, a reflection in a delayed mirror of Detroit before the stove and shipbuilding industries came along to stretch its arms toward the sky, hunkered under a coat of flinty snow. Its docks and wooden warehouses were gaunt shadows amid white swirls whipped up from the surface of frozen Lake St. Clair. Record low temperatures even for Michigan, even for January, had constructed a thick shelf of ice as gray as iron and nearly as hard across the top of the watery international boundary. It was deceptive. The swift current of the Detroit River through the middle of the lake had hollowed it out from beneath. The mantel, two feet thick at the outer edges, thinned to six inches toward the center where the lake was deepest. There the half-buried remains of Indian dugouts, French bateaux, and American freighters rotted on the bottom, awaiting fresh arrivals. A cobwebby pattern of fine cracks intersected the surface, weaving a kind of reverse net to entrap the oblivious and foolhardy by the very nature of its weakness. Harlan Crownover, whose ears burned in the cold and whose feet had turned to sadirons in his uninsulated boots, thought of the black cold beneath the ice and knew again his childhood terror of the dark in his old tower bedroom on Jefferson.

"I don't like the look of those fissures." Bundled in a navy peacoat with a fleece-lined leather helmet strapped under his chin, goggles on his forehead, Ford spoke through his teeth, barely loud enough for Harlan to hear. He might have been talking to himself.

"Do you think it will hold?"

"I'm less concerned about that than I am about maintaining control. At a hundred miles per hour it'll be like driving over a cheese grater."

"Maybe we should postpone the race until Oldfield's available."

"Barney's chances wouldn't be any better. I'm the one who taught him to drive. Anyway, he'd refuse. He's smarter than I am." Ford's grin was a rictus.

It was a small group gathered on the snowy bank. Aside from a handful of curious spectators, stamping their feet and pounding their arms to assist circulation, it included Ford's wife, Clara, a stately chestnut-haired woman wrapped in inexpensive furs, standing still as a piling in the bitter wind; Edsel, their eleven-year-old son, jumping up and down in a combination of nervous excitement and an effort to keep from freezing; Ed Huff, a Ford Motor Company employee and Ford's copilot, whose nickname, Spider, seemed appropriate to his hunched posture and curious habit of shifting his weight rhythmically from one foot to the other in his impatience to start; and C. H. Wills, impervious to the cold as he bent over the motorcar's engine, tightening plugs, testing petcocks, and inspecting wires for signs of corrosion.

The motorcar itself, dubbed the Arrow, was a twin of the fabled 999, which Barney Oldfield had piloted to a winning five miles in five minutes and twenty-eight seconds in the Challenge Cup, and set a world's record a few weeks later when he drove a mile in 1:01. It was essentially an engine on wheels. The manifold, exposed to the elements, straddled a pair of steel rails behind a radiator shaped like a whiskey flask. The seat and T-shaped tiller appeared to have been added at the last minute. The vehicle was twice as long as Ford's little runabout and built closer to the ground; but the lake was much bigger, and the descent to the bottom was the same for everyone.

The race this time, as advertised by Alexander Malcolmson, was against not another vehicle, but the clock. Sporting reporters from the local newspapers were expected to chronicle the attempt to break Ford's own record for the mile. At length they arrived en masse on foot from the nearest streetcar stop, cheerfully profane men in long coats and hard derbies, smelling of gin and spitting tobacco at random targets in the snow. They were plainly grateful for the outing, which freed them from the overheated barns of their offices where they chucked balls of paper at distant wastebaskets and tried to fill their columns with stale speculations about off-season baseball trades during the long dormancy between football and spring training. Behind them hobbled an unkempt photographer with his box camera and tripod on one shoulder and carrying a cumbersome valise the size of a child's doll trunk. He spent some time finding a level section of bank upon which to set up his equipment, then began fiddling with his glass plates, cursing when one dropped from his stiff fingers and shattered on the frozen ground, and pausing every few minutes to improve his circulation with the help of a hammered silver flask. A reporter Harlan recognized from the *Evening News* made his way among the journalists, collecting bets on the race's outcome and recording them on a square of folded newsprint. The gentlemen of the Fourth Estate had been known to place wagers on everything from the Boxer Rebellion in China to the verdict in the trial of the assassin of King Umberto of Italy.

"When do you start?" Harlan asked Ford.

"Just as soon as my timekeeper shows up."

Ten more minutes went by, at the end of which Harlan's face had lost all feeling. Fearing frostbite, he rubbed his cheeks and nose vigorously with the palms of his jersey gloves. He could only speculate on how it would be for Ford and Huff when they sped across the lake, faces naked to the wind.

"I pray the publicity is worth it," he heard himself saying.

Ford grunted. "Prayers are a disease of the will."

A handsome carriage, with yellow wheels and decorated side panels, drew up on Jefferson, drawn by matched grays whose breath steamed as thick as meringue. When the passenger stepped down, awed conversation whirred through the crowd of spectators. James Phelan, Detroit Recorder's Court judge and Big Jim Dolan's principal rival for the chairmanship of the state Democratic Party, picked his way down the bank with his stick, his long-tailed coat spreading behind him and his Viking's mane of silver hair crawling in the wind. He made directly for the crowd, shaking hands and laughing his booming laugh from behind massive moustaches.

"I didn't know Phelan was an automobile enthusiast," Harlan said to Ford.

"He's my timekeeper."

Harlan wondered if there would come a time when the automobile maker would cease to surprise him. Phelan, quite apart from his political influence and status as a thorn in the side of the Irish Pope, was the most popular public figure in the city of Detroit. His stout figure, Byronic tresses, and round spectacle lenses as thick as jar lids were caricatured on all the local editorial pages as often as Roosevelt's teeth. With Jim Phelan keeping the time, no one in Detroit would dare to question the result.

There were cordialities to observe. Ford went over to shake the jurist's hand and answer reporters' questions about how fit he felt and whether he entertained the same confidence in the untested Arrow that he had in the now legendary 999 and if the absence of Barney Oldfield in the pilot's seat would affect his chances of meeting or breaking his own machine's record. Then it was Phelan's turn. Asked why he had agreed to accept an official role in an event so far outside his jurisdiction, he replied that nothing that took place in this great city could be so described; moreover, as it was his privilege to fish that same section of the lake in fair weather, he welcomed the opportunity to reconnoiter the area in the dead of winter, when his piscatorial opponent least expected him.

"And will Your Honor be falling out of the boat again this spring?" asked Nick Stark of the *Free Press*.

The judge riposted with nought but a frosty silence; a rare event. He had not forgiven the journalist his published observation last May that Phelan had survived "his annual narrow escape from drowning yesterday." The great man, who did not hold with the vices of tobacco, profanity, and gambling—beyond the occasional friendly wager at Bennett Park—seldom rowed away from shore without a bottle of rye packed securely among his tackle.

Finally, C. H. Wills stepped back from the Arrow, wrench in hand, and shrugged at Ford. The motorist of the hour took his leave of the press, leaned over to peck Clara on the cheek and tug down playfully on the bill of young Edsel's cap, and approached the machine with a bounce in his step. All of these acts, Harlan suspected, were showmanship. In all his meetings with Ford he had never seen the man display outward affection toward his family, or exhibit anything lighter than a preacherlike solemnity when it came to automobiles and their operation. He was, in his way, every inch the politician that Jim Phelan was, only much more insidiously subtle. The demonstrative Dodges hadn't the capacity to learn from such an example.

Ford mounted the seat and adjusted his goggles. Spider Huff climbed aboard and crouched behind him with his gloved hands gripping the backrest. The pilot looked over at Phelan, posed dramatically on the bank with a turnip watch in his palm. Ford gave the throttle lever three or four sharp jerks, mixing the fuel and advancing the spark, then flipped the ignition switch. The spark ignited the fumes with two hoarse wheezing coughs, then the engine caught with an explosive bark. Ford reduced the throttle, and the pistons settled into a chuck-chuck idle. When he was satisfied that the engine would not stall, he pushed the throttle forward. The percussive barking blended into a rumble, which when he released the brake climbed to a roar, echoing across the lake's flat surface like winter thunder as the car shot forward.

Harlan knew the instant when the vehicle struck the first of the fissures that had concerned Ford. It leaped into the air, just like a spooked horse, and struck down with a bang that Harlan thought must shatter the ice and send the car and its occupants to the bottom of the lake. But the ice held. Ford let out the throttle with a sustained, reverberating boom that surely inspired the uninitiated in Detroit and Windsor to look to the sky. The car bucked and banged, turned in the air and skidded on the ice, its tires sloughing like sled runners. At one high-flying point Huff's feet actually left the floorboards and he was holding on by his hands alone. When the vehicle landed, the copilot's knees buckled nearly to his chin. Comically, both his helmet and his attached goggles flew off and flapped behind his head from the strap around his neck. *That,* Harlan thought, was one for a cartoonist, if any were present.

But then the car was sliding again, the rear attempting to overtake the front, and Harlan forgot to laugh as he watched Ford working the tiller frantically to maintain speed without rolling over. The entire contraption tipped up on one side, then slammed down with a noise like a cannon shot, spewing white lines in every direction from the point of impact. What kept the lake from opening up and swallowing men and machine there and then, aside from Ford's own stubborn Yankee faith, was a mystery Harlan would never be able to answer.

A mile had been measured across the lake, marked at the end with a five-gallon paint can painted a bright yellow. The Arrow skidded past within inches, blowing it over with its own wind; the bucket bounded end over end three times, landed on its side, and rolled, momentarily distracting attention from the object that was spinning and sliding to a ragged stop near the Windsor side.

Now every head turned toward Judge Phelan, standing as still as Liberty with his watch resting like a compass on the flat of his palm. The old politico knew a dramatic moment when it presented itself; but in his own obvious excitement he nearly waited it out too long, at that.

"Thirty-six seconds!"

A volume of sound rose from the spectators that Harlan would not have thought possible from so small a group. An electric rush charged through his body, banishing the cold. He knew then that he had witnessed history. And any misgivings he had felt during his first disillusioning ride in a motorcar with Henry Ford at the controls were as gone as this moment was permanent.

Ford swung the Arrow around in a wide loop and headed back to shore at a cautious eight to ten miles per hour. Suddenly the ice hammocked; Harlan's stomach slipped a full notch. Ford, however, did not stop, but piloted the vehicle through small geysers of white water hemorrhaging through the network of cracks. Presently the automobile rolled to a gentle stop against the frozen berm where water met earth and Ford leaped out, followed by Huff. Wife and son embraced Ford simultaneously. Harlan, who had stepped forward to shake his hand, retreated instead as the reporters pushed in, hammering him with questions. Harlan understood then the full meaning of the word *press*.

And he realized, even if Ford himself did not, that from this time forward, the automobile man's every move and utterance would be public record. He had left the shore just another motorman in a city top-heavy with them and come back Marco Polo.

"Did you think the ice would break?"

"Let's just say I had more faith in my machine than I had in the lake."

"Does this mean you won't be employing Oldfield anymore?"

"Certainly not. At this moment I retire from racing. I'm a manufacturer, not a sportsman."

"Where do you go from here?"

"To the Hotel Chesterfield. I'm treating Wills and Huff to a dinner of muskrats."

"Are you planning to incorporate any of the Arrow's features into the Model C?"

"I'm through making the C. We've already begun production on a new model. It's easier to make and will sell for less than its predecessor."

"Is that the six-cylinder model Malcolmson and the Dodge brothers are pressing for?"

Ford scowled at Nick Stark, who had asked the question.

"A car should not have any more cylinders than a cow has teats."

Stark looked up from his notes. "Does this mean you plan to break with the Dodges and Malcolmson?"

There was a short silence, during which the wind squealed across the lake. Ford removed his leather gauntlets and flexed his long skinny fingers. "It's a mistake to make or have too strong attachments, because it weakens your will and character."

"Is that a yes?"

Harlan felt suddenly cold again. He'd never heard his partner express dissatisfaction with any of his associates in public.

The other reporters, however, took advantage of the pause to ask questions of their own, and Stark's was lost in the chorus. Nevertheless it was the quiet but persistent man from the *Free Press* who took the inquisition in a new direction.

"What defense are you planning to use against the Selden suit?"

A smudge of oil and smoke coated Ford's face, leaving only a figure eight of pale skin across his eyes where his goggles had covered. His brow darkened visibly beneath the soot.

"Who is Selden?" he demanded. "Where is the Selden motorcar? When he produces an automobile that predates the one I made in 1896, I'll retire from auto manufacture and go back to work at Edison."

More questions followed, during which Ford's native belligerence—plainly put, his love of conflict for its own sake—seemed to restore his good humor. He traded jibes with the reporters, always a friendly and boisterous crew when they had either a triumph or a crushing failure to write about, and shook hands with Wills and Huff for the photographer. It worried Harlan that Ford did not seem worried. Had he given up, without telling his partners? *It's a mistake to make or have too strong attachments . . .* Like the cold, the statement lay like metal against his spine and would not leave.

Ford broke loose from the crowd with an explosive movement and strode Harlan's way, stripping off his leather helmet. The wind caught his dark hair, usually as well maintained as his engines, and swept it into hawk's wings from the center part. There was no humor in that spare face. That had been a pose.

"I want you to talk to your father," he said.

It was the last statement Harlan would have anticipated in that time and at that place. A moment went by before he answered.

"We almost never talk as it is. He'll never connect himself with the Ford Motor Company or any other automobile maker."

"I knew that before you did. It was all there, in *The Coach King*. That's not what I want you to talk to him about. I want you to tell him to call off his dogs."

"Dogs?"

"His people. His lawyers. His money. The only use he makes of any of them anymore is to turn them loose on people. After you've got everything else out of them, that's what's left."

"I don't understand."

"There's no reason you should. But you will, if you ever get off the loading dock."

The group was migrating in their direction. Ford's bony fingers suddenly gripped Harlan's upper arm like a bundle of wires and turned him. Now both their backs were to the world.

"Selden is a wooden owl, a decoy," he said. "The A.L.A.M. paid him ten thousand for the right to exercise his patent. Any money they manage to extort from the other automobile companies is in the way of a bonus. They don't need it; they're all millionaires. They're only working together to destroy me. Why do you think they wouldn't let me join?"

"But why you?"

"Your family isn't wrong about you. You're slow. Who in this town hates me enough to close down my plant and put hundreds of people out of work?"

Harlan shook his head. "My father would never throw in with automobile men."

"They aren't automobile men. Have you ever seen Selden's car? Of course you haven't; there isn't one. His patent doesn't cover any practicable machine. None can be made from it or ever was. Or ever will. You'll hear nothing more of the A.L.A.M. once the Ford shop closes. Your father will dismantle it like a coach that's done its work."

"He's a businessman, not a buccaneer. Anyway, he's convinced automobiles won't catch on. As he sees it, you're no threat."

"Not to his business. His family is another matter. There's no telling what a man will do if he thinks his son is being stolen from him."

The others were near, reliving at the tops of their voices the details of the adventure they had all witnessed. Harlan started to say something. Ford squeezed his biceps painfully and it turned into a short cry. The automobile man leaned in uncomfortably close. Harlan felt his hot breath in his ear.

"Tell him to call off his dogs. If he won't do it, tell him to go ahead and set them loose. I'm at fighting weight and he's rusty. He can't wear me down."

Then they were enveloped. Huff piloted the Arrow up the bank to where the flatbed wagon that had brought it waited to take it away, Ford let go of Harlan's arm, and the crowd drifted toward Jefferson, Ford in the center. Harlan was left alone on the edge of the lake.

Crazy Henry, he thought.

chapter eleven

The Summit

"Cara mia, you're losing your appetite. Are you feeling ill?"

The question, delivered in Maribel's musical northern Italian accent, dripped with sincerity. There was concern in her great dark eyes, little inverted commas of worry at the corners of her wide mouth. The long fine fingers touching the back of his hand where it rested on the table held the power to love and heal. James Aloysius Dolan considered that in twenty years of politics he had never been lied to so successfully.

He smiled, feeling his face break into weary lines. "I'm right as rain, sweet child," he said. "Just a bit tired. You'll get used to seeing me this way during an election year."

She smiled then, her teeth blue-white against red lips and olive skin, patted his hand, and withdrew hers just as Fritz, the headwaiter at the Shamrock Club, came in to take away the corned-beef platter, clucking when he observed that it was still half full; the Countess, whose system would not support most Irish fare, had contented herself with a small dish of noodles and a glass of burgundy. When they were alone again she took Dolan's hand in her cool grip. They were not trying to delude anyone about their relationship; merely observing the proprieties. At the Shamrock, mistresses were regarded as a fact of life so long as the carnal nature of the arrangement was not paraded about like a shillelagh on St. Paddy's Day. Nevertheless Dolan, whose sensitivity to the opinions of others no matter how well concealed formed the crux of his success in public life, felt diminished in Fritz's esteem. True, he was just a waiter. But Dolan's standing in the community rested upon a foundation built of waiters, porters, bricklayers, coal shovelers, switchmen, domestics, and teamsters; pry loose but one and the entire structure was weakened.

What was worse, he felt shrunken in his own regard. Often when he was with Maribel, and always when he was not, he thought that the intoxication induced by the heavy spirit was not worth the feeling of misery when it wore off. In truth, she was not all she appeared on the surface, but rather inferior tobacco in a good wrapper, cheap ale poured from a decanter designed for aged claret. Her private habits were coarse. She neither shaved her armpits nor pushed the door to when she used the water closet, serenading him with the sounds of her base biology. At those times he would help himself to a slug of the good Irish whisky he bought for the sideboard in the bedroom of the flat he rented for her on Howard Street and frame his farewell speech. Then she would emerge from the bedroom wearing a floor-length sweep of diaphanous black lace, the bill for which had been sent to his office by Hudson's, drenched in the musklike imported perfume he'd paid for at Partridge & Blackwell's, and he would lose track of his golden words in the smothering moist scent of her skin, the sweet stinging agony of her nails on his back, the furnace heat of the steaming grotto between her thighs. Later, spent and self-loathing, he would slip out of the bed where she lay snoring, dress quickly, and creep downstairs and out into the light of a late afternoon sun scowling down at him, reminding him sternly what nighttime and shadows were for.

He would not, could not, go straight home to Charlotte from Maribel; thus he had formed the new habit of dropping into Diedrich Frank's saloon and washing away his sin with liquor, unaccompanied by a platter of food. He was eating less, but he was not losing weight. His full face was bloating and his complexion had gone from robust red to a liverish purple and his eyes appeared to be swimming in blood. No one he met remarked upon the change, yet he could see it reflected in their own faces, in the split second's hesitation before they responded to something he had said, as if they were preoccupied with his appearance and what it meant to his performance and their own fortunes. He wanted to shout at them, to shock them into saying what they were thinking. He did not. He was afraid they would take him up on the challenge. In the old days he had been fond of saying that he would rather have people say negative things behind his back than to his face, because that would mean they had lost their fear of him and his influence. He did not care to test his theory, because he might prove it to be correct. And so he went through the motions of his days in a clammy-cold jacket of dread.

He had been with Maribel seven months. He had first met her knowing gaze, the bottomless black shafts of the eyes into which he thought all his secrets had been poured, on board the ferry to Belle Isle on Memorial Day. Two more weeks had passed before he felt the dry cool touch of her hand, when Vito Grapellini introduced her to him at a twenty-five-dollar-a-plate fund-raising dinner at the Cadillac Hotel. The butcher, his fat face gleaming above the high white collar of his dress shirt, wearing a tailored evening jacket paid for by the prime rib he had sold to the Democratic Party for the affair, explained that the Countess diViareggio was in the midst of a tour of the United States to reduce the pain of the recent loss of her husband, and that she had asked to meet this man Dolan of whom so much was said in every quarter of the city. He had responded with equal parts self-deprecation and Old Country blarney. Charlotte was at home, looking after their daughter Margaret, who had a case of the sniffles. When later in the evening Grapellini came over to Dolan's table, pleading a problem with the refrigeration system that required his attention at the shop, Dolan agreed to escort the countess to her hotel. (The story she had told Abner Crownover at the theater, about visiting relatives, was a fabrication suggested by Dolan. He did not want it bandied about that he was keeping company with an adventuress.) He bade her good night at the door of her room and went home, but to all intents and purposes the affair had begun that night.

Charlotte, he was satisfied, did not suspect. What was commonly understood among the fifteen or twenty men with whom he associated on a regular basis was barred to her by a covenant as old as Man. She did, however, note the change in him, and the steep decline in his appetite, and had asked him if he didn't think he was working too hard. Of late she had become more insistent about his seeing a doctor. He had agreed to make an appointment with Charley Hennessey for a complete physical examination, entirely to throw her off the trail which from the time of Eve had always drawn the senses of Woman to the correct conclusion unless they were distracted. He knew what was wrong with him, and he knew the cure. Taking it was the problem.

"DeWolf Hopper is performing at the Temple Saturday night," said Maribel, scooping a forkful of apple cobbler out of a dish dusted with powdered sugar. "Will you take me? I met him in New York last winter. He told such funny stories."

"I don't know if I can get away Saturday night."

"Of course you can. It's an election year. Tell her you're meeting someone important. You will not even be telling a lie." Her eyes glinted above the fork.

"Make sure you want to see this fellow. We mustn't make this a habit. A lot of my constituents go to the Temple Theater."

"You are ashamed of me, yes?" The glint turned steely.

"You know that's not true. It's all very well for my associates to know about you and me. Voters are a horse of a different color. Their wives will never stand for it."

"Their wives cannot vote."

"They don't mark the ballots, but they might as well. No married man who values peace will vote against his wife's principles."

"You think they don't know?"

"Rumors are one thing. It's quite another to shove the proof in their faces."

"Well, I want to see Wolfie."

"Wolfie, is it, now? How did you meet him?"

"We were introduced by friends. It was a big party at the Hippodrome."

"Last winter, you said? January or February?"

"No, it was earlier. December."

Dolan set down his glass. His face felt numb, as if he had exposed it to the frigid air outside. "You were in New York December before last? How soon was that after your husband the count died?"

"Oh, weeks." She took another forkful.

"You told me he died in Tuscany at Christmas. The fastest boat in the world could not have gotten you to America between Christmas and the end of December. Just when did he die? Was he ever born to begin with?"

She looked up, startled. A swift pallor crossed her face. And then, as if by an act of will, her color returned, bringing with it a hardness he had not seen before. She let her fork slide into her plate and folded her hands under her chin, studying him as from a great distance. And in the silence before she spoke, Dolan felt it was he who had been caught in a monstrous lie.

He had an appointment with Strick back at the office, to discuss the amount in the campaign chest and how best to spend that portion not already earmarked for himself and others in the party organization, but he did not keep it nor send word that it was canceled. He asked Fritz to see that the Countess got

back to her flat and headed home, hailing a four-wheeler instead of riding the streetcar or walking the short distance. The
latter two choices presented the risk of his being recognized
and addressed, and forced to wonder how many of those with
whom he spoke were aware of his shame, the extent to which
he had willingly assisted in his own destruction. For the first
time in his life he feared human contact.

In the past, when a close and important election race had
been lost or a trusted associate had shifted his loyalties to another camp, Jim Dolan had taken comfort from a carriage ride
through the streets he loved. Baked in the heat of summer that
brought out all the pastels and straw hats and parasols like so
many blossoms, drenched in the cleansing showers of spring,
or cloaked, as today, in a fresh fall of winter snow that oblit-
erated the venial sins of broken pavement and litter, the city
had always assured him that it would go on regardless of the
transgressions of the moment, waiting patiently and with bottomless love to welcome its returning flock. Today it showed
him the hard, frozen face of a spouse betrayed one time past
forgiveness. Its ears were deaf to poetic speeches; no amount
of bouquets or baskets would penetrate the horned growth that
covered its heart. Its sterile whites and bleak grays told him he
had profaned the gift he had been given ahead of all his peers,
all for the sake of a common thing, a weakness he deplored in
his friends and attacked in his enemies. He felt low and mean
and—unheard of thing, since he had outgrown his first pair of
knickerbockers—small. And he felt on his own.

The driver drew rein suddenly, jerking him forward and
tumbling his trilby off his head to the floorboards between his
feet. Retrieving it, he saw the reason for the abrupt maneuver:
A preposterous arrangement on spoked wheels with a black
canvas top and a scrolled metal front had lurched out from a
side street, startling the horses and turning into traffic with a
clatter of pistons and an angrily bleating horn, as if the road

were its personal property and all activity that did not stop and pay it tribute had violated some natural law. The motorcar drew all his rage and self-loathing like a lightning rod; here was the thing that was to blame for his purgatory, that had warped his judgment and caused him to lose sight of the great tapestry for a single snag in the thread.

No. It wasn't automobiles.

The carriage started moving again. They were nearing his door. He raised his stick, touching the driver's arm and drawing his attention, and gave him another address.

"Are you sure, sir?" The driver, an obvious Irishman mottled with freckles from the brim of his old-fashioned topper to the heavy woolen scarf wrapped around his throat, had recognized his passenger. As was the way in such situations, he appeared to have assumed the responsibility of Dolan's entire future. "It's clear—"

"I know where it is," snapped the other. A lie; he had been doing business with the establishment at that address for years and had never laid eyes on it.

He had, it was true, visited the neighborhood, although not stopping any longer than it took to bellow the same phrases he'd been using for a decade above bumping brass, two-finger whistles, and the occasional raspberry from an opposition plant. He scarcely recognized the place in January. The vegetable carts and sidewalk stands were missing, and so were the teeming crowds that in gentle weather blanketed the streets and impeded the progress of brewers' drays and engine-company pump-wagons. The stoops and fire escapes, normally used for stadium seating, looked empty and naked, as in photographs in books of European ghettos evacuated by pogroms. Such pedestrians as presented themselves hastened across the carriage's path with hats pulled down, collars turned up, and fists thrust deep into their coat pockets, barely glancing right and left as they dashed toward shelter across razor winds blowing bits of snow like iron filings between the buildings. Dolan, who had not noticed when the names stenciled on the shop signs changed from German to Italian, was surprised when they drew up in front of a vacant-looking brickfront with a fogged display window and thought the driver had made a mistake. When he challenged him, the fellow merely pointed with his whip at the black-enameled numerals fixed above the front door. Only the first four letters of the legend GRAPELLINI'S MEATS could be read on the frosted glass.

The shopfront was shallow, ending ten feet in at a plate-glass display counter that ran the width of the room, with chops and racks of ribs and mounds of ground beef inside, advertising their prices on little signs sticking up out of the meat. The floor was paved with black and white linoleum tiles in a checkerboard pattern, kept clean with the help of a rubber runner inside the door, which collected tracked-in mud and slush from the side-walk. Homemade signs tacked to the green-painted walls above the wainscoting announced sale prices on sides of beef, whole hams, and stewing leghorns. The room was brightly lighted by a row of white porcelain bowl fixtures suspended by poles from the ceiling. Every surface shone and the smell of disinfectant was strong.

No one was standing behind the counter when Dolan stepped inside and pushed the door shut behind him, jangling a bell mounted on a spring clip atop the frame. A moment later, a door opened at the back, accompanied by a whoosh of work-ing compressors, and Vito Grapellini emerged from a thick cloud of vapor. He made an incongruous sight in a heavy cor-duroy coat, brown jersey gloves, and the summery straw boater that was part of the uniform of his profession, worn at a jaunty angle. As the thick cooler door drifted shut against the pressure of its pneumatic closer, he recognized his visitor and stripped off his gloves to reach across the counter and shake Dolan's hand. Dolan accepted his grasp out of long habit.

"Signor Dolan! What an honor and a surprise."

"Where is he?"

"He?" The butcher's fat smile remained in place, but the brightness went out of his eyes as if a veil had slid between them and his brain.

"Your partner. I want to see Borneo."

Now the smile was gone. "He is upstairs. I will tell him you are here." He squeezed his bulk through the narrow space between the end of the counter and the right wall.

"I'll go up with you."

The butcher paused, then jerked his chin in a brief nod. He went out through the front door and held it for Dolan. When they were both outside he drew the door shut.

"Aren't you going to lock it?"

Grapellini snorted rudely. "When Signor Borneo becomes my partner I throw away the key."

Dolan followed him into the narrow alley alongside the building, through a side door, and up a flight of rubber-runnered stairs between walls of mustard-colored plaster. At the top they turned down a wainscoted hallway with a hard-wood floor, lit only by the weak fixture over the staircase and a morsel of winter sunlight coming through a window at the other end, which looked out on the brick wall of the black-smith's shop next door. Ten feet short of the window they stopped before a blank door and Grapellini rapped on one of the panels. A muted voice from the other side asked who it was.

"Grapellini. Signor Jim Dolan is with me."

"Come in."

Dolan wasn't sure what he expected to find in Sal Borneo's lair. Luxury, he supposed, some Mediterranean ideal of lavish vulgarity, beaded curtains and layers of rugs and ornate carvings and castings dripping with gilt. What he found was an office of business that would have passed muster anywhere in the city.

The walls were paneled in some light wood, teak perhaps, with tasteful hunting prints hung on them in plain oak frames. An oak desk, handsome but unremarkable, stood before a leather-studded swivel, and a pair of comfortable-looking armchairs were drawn up in front of it. There was an ordinary black metal telephone on the desk and a square of pale yellow rug with a plain brown border on the floor. The only exotic touch was a marble bust of some classical figure on a barrister case in the corner by the desk, the shelves of which were stuffed with books bound in dark leather. Dolan read Gibbon's name stamped in gold on several of the volumes. A homely white-painted steam radiator shed heat beneath a window that looked out on most of Little Italy, its banners and awnings put away and the whole of the neighborhood withdrawn for the winter into a gray concrete cocoon.

"Welcome, Mr. Dolan. I believe this is the first time I have had the pleasure."

Dolan was unprepared for his first exposure to the man with whom he had been in partnership for so long. He had once seen Borneo's predecessor, Uncle Joe Sorrato, in company with Sorrato's four sons, and the memory of those elephantine men in their wrinkled white suits and broad-brimmed Panamas had fixed in his mind a matrix for the type. The man who rose from behind the desk as he entered, forty and slight in a well-cut but nondescript suit of charcoal wool with a black knitted tie on a white shirt, might have been doing business from an office on Woodward Avenue instead of a butcher shop in Wop-town. His strong features might have belonged to a Sioux In-dian but for a silken moustache whose points drooped over the corners of his mouth. Only his complexion, sallow and riddled with the shallow scars of what must have been a long and nearly fatal battle with pox, attested to a life harder than the one he was living. When he set down the book he had been reading and reached across the desk, a heavy gold ring glinted on the small finger of his right hand. It was the only extravagant thing about him. Dolan had never shaken a smoother hand.

"That's all for now, George," Borneo said without taking his eyes off his guest.

The man to whom this was addressed was the ugliest human being the Irishman had ever seen. His face was absolutely flat, like a piece of shale, and his eyes were hooded beneath thick lids and a heavy shelf of bone. Old scars braided his cheeks, paralyzing the muscles of expression so that he showed no more emotion than a big cat. His cheap suit strained at its buttons and fell inches short of his wrists. He'd have looked less grotesque in filthy overalls or the horizontal stripes of a convict. He stirred from his place beside the bookcase and headed toward the door, crouching a little with his arms bent, like a wrestler stalking his opponent. Dolan suspected he was a Greek.

"Thank you, Vito," said Borneo.

This was as much a dismissal as were his words to the disturbing George, and Grapellini took it as such without question, accompanying the other out into the hall. When the door was closed, Borneo smiled, uncovering a set of uncommonly fine teeth for an immigrant. Dolan's own were tobacco-stained and filled with gold, and he found himself resenting the man even more when he smiled.

Borneo mistook the object of his distaste. "George is a horror, but he's loyal. He did me a favor once. Nothing guarantees gratitude more than asking someone to do something for you that is within his power."

"Isn't that the other way around?" This fellow's repose was annoying. The Sicilians Dolan had dealt with in the past were either comically boastful or toadying to the point of nausea.

"It should be, but it is not. When you do a thing for someone, the response is almost always resentment. It's very difficult to secure a kindness in return for a kindness done. Integrity may already be a thing of the last century." Was that an edge to his tone, at last?

"He's an animal," Dolan said flatly.

"This animal was recommended by my attorney."

"You have an attorney?"

"You might know him. Maurice Lapel."

"Lapel's a kike!"

"When I require a barber I go to an Italian." Borneo tilted a palm in the direction of one of the armchairs before the desk.

Dolan remained standing. "You act as if you're not surprised to see me."

"Nothing has managed to surprise me since I came to this country and found that no one was waiting on the dock to hand me gold. Won't you sit down, Mr. Dolan? I have a weak back, which I will not indulge while others stand."

"I thought all you dagoes were as strong as niggers." But he sat down. The full-grain leather was as soft as a broken-in baseball glove.

"Actually it's my kidneys." Borneo lowered himself into his chair, pulling a slight face as he did so; the first sign of discomfort he had shown in Dolan's presence. "A reminder of an old visit with the police. It was one of your people, as a matter of fact."

"I doubt it. If it was one of mine he'd have finished the job."

Borneo took the challenge without changing expression. The little silence that set in when he lifted the book he'd been reading and set it down on the edge of the desk, as if to remove an obstacle that lay between them, said that it had been understood.

"I cannot vote," he said, in the bland tone he'd been using right along. "I am not a citizen. However, I follow politics closely. It's the only sport that interests me. Your candidates appear strong this year. Congratulations."

"My people are loyal, like your George. I wish I could say the same for everyone I have to deal with."

"Integrity again."

"An outmoded concept, as you say."

"It is a matter of faith, and science has replaced that. Secular times require solid measures. You must reinforce the mortar with steel. An arrangement of trust is not enough. It must be backed up with force."

"I agree. We may have to push in a few brothels and horse parlors, just to make sure the support we have continues into November."

There it was, on the table. Dolan sat back and folded his hands across his great middle. He was glad of the long carriage ride from Corktown. It had given him time to harness his rage. The game was patience.

Borneo—maddening man—withdrew. "Such a stoic art, and so suited to the Celtic temperament. This is why so few Italians succeed at it. Our love for our families distorts our judgment and weakens our resolve. Your own family must be very understanding."

"My family is not your affair."

"I apologize. We have been associated for so long, you and I, that I forget we are not old friends."

"We will never be friends."

"My great regret. You must know, Mr. Dolan, that I admire you very much. These monkeys who perform in public and make the proper faces in order to win wide regard are contemptible. Power is not a collective thing; it has never rested with the people, who have no idea what they want until someone with true power tells them."

"Thank you. I don't admire you."

"There is no reason you should. I'm only a merchant. The least of my customers is more powerful than I. If I cannot supply what they want, I cannot remain in business."

"And I tell them what they want." Dolan began to think he was gaining ground at last.

"So long as you do not misjudge. Even such authority as yours has limits. Human limits. We are all of us poor clay."

The game had reached its crisis. Big Jim Dolan leaned forward and smacked the desktop with the palm of one hand. The sting went clear to his elbow and jarred a horsehair pen out of its black onyx stand. "I sent your whore walking today." He did not shout. He kept his voice at conversation level, impressing even himself. "She made a mistake and forgot her lines."

"I can't say I'm surprised. Her career onstage was brief."

Nothing in the Sicilian's appearance or demeanor had changed. He looked and sounded as if he were still discussing the vagaries of politics and power.

"You admit she's your creature."

"It would be a mistake to call her that. She is quite independent. One might say she is more in the nature of a contract worker."

"Fancy term for a harlot."

"I hope you didn't call her that to her face. She considers herself an actress, with some justification. She had just left a touring company when she was recommended to me; a rather melancholy little farce with the unpromising title *Madame Lombardo's Confession*. I understood she had an artistic difference with the director that required twenty-two stitches to correct. Before that she was the companion of the original stage manager, who left the troupe in Cleveland. That fellow put up a bond to keep her out of the Women's Workhouse on Blackwell's Island in New York."

"That's a jail."

"Not her first visit, nor her first jail. I can provide specifics, if you're interested. The detective agency was quite thorough."

"Start with her name."

"Thelma Brown."

"That ain't Italian."

"Certainly not, although she'd be happy to learn her preposterous accent passed muster. She is a mulatto. Her father
was a janitor employed by the New York Port Authority."

"A nigger." Dolan felt the blood draining from his face.

Borneo watched and said nothing.

"Why?"

"In a way it was a compliment to you." The Sicilian picked
up the fallen pen and bent it between his fingers. "You had no
weaknesses to exploit, so it became necessary to provide one.
Oh, there was the record of your shameless corruption, but your
constituency is too loyal. It was conceivable that I could present
them with a photograph of you picking a cardinal's pocket and
they would argue that you were in fact making a secret donation
to the Church. In any case, voters expect their public servants
to steal from time to time, in order to level the field. They
aren't the fools their own candidates often take them for; they
just don't care. Adultery is quite another thing. The system is
not so far gone the electorate will tolerate a basic and flagrant
disregard for the sacred vows. Even a philandering bricklayer
will scream for the head of an incumbent who's as much a slave
to his lust as he is. The miscegenation feature was a gift. I would
not have thought of it if it hadn't plopped into my lap. Since
you had no weakness, I had to go to your strength. You are
your popularity."

"Why?" he said again.

"You know why. You're not an imbecile."

"My candidates were elected on a decency platform. Our
arrangement was founded on the understanding that you'd have
to stand for a raid on your establishments from time to time.
If we ignored you, it would only call attention to our arrangement. We'd all be out come November and you'd be back push-
ing a cart."

"This isn't about horse parlors and brothels. And you know that."

"I *don't* know." He genuinely didn't. He spread his big hands, fully conscious that it made him look like a supplicant. Which he was. He had come there as Boss Dolan, demanding answers, and the answers he got had broken him.

Borneo watched him, again in silence. After nearly a minute he opened the belly drawer of his desk, drew out a copy of the *Detroit Evening News* folded to the advertising section, and slapped it on top of the desk. Dolan read the top three lines of the full-page notice without picking it up.

NOTICE

To Manufacturers, Dealers, Importers, Agents,

and Users of Gasoline Automobiles

"The Association of Licensed Automobile Manufacturers, indeed," Borneo said. "I am not an imbecile either, Big Jim. Did you think I would not recognize your hand?"

"That's Secretary Whitney's red wagon. Your beef is with him."

"He's your cat's paw. Don't make this worse by insulting me. Where did you ever obtain the idea you could get away with prohibiting consumers from buying automobiles not built under the Selden patent? Lapel informs me no judge in this country would rule in favor of that."

"That was just to frighten away customers. We never intended to press action against them."

"If you'd wanted to attract the attention of Roosevelt's trustbusters, you couldn't have stumbled upon a better plan. Ford knows that. It's why he felt safe placing an advertisement indemnifying his customers. He knew he'd never have to make good on it. All you've succeeded in doing is make him a hero."

"This isn't just about Ford."

"I know what it's about. It's about thirteen hundred acres of Ohio farmland and half a dozen streetcar company executives with a bad case of cold feet."

Dolan remembered he was a politician in time to conceal his surprise. Where did the man get his information?

"Clumsy, Big Jim. Childish. I wish you'd come to me instead of this baboon Whitney."

This time Dolan could not help himself. His jaw worked up and down twice before he got words out. "You can't want Ford to fail. You've got money tied up in his company."

"I have money tied up in Harlan Crownover. The difference is great." Another long silence went by, at the end of which Borneo snatched up the newspaper, dropped it back into the drawer, and slammed the drawer shut with a bang that made his visitor flinch. He sat back, looking at Dolan and twisting the gold ring around his little finger. "Now. Let us discuss how we are going to retrieve your good name, accomplish our common objective, and get back to the business of making a great deal of money."

chapter twelve

Fathers and Sons

Abner Crownover III, eldest son of Abner II and Edith, was what was called, in his time and in the city in which he lived, "a creature of habit." The term "obsessive compulsive," while familiar to that specialized area of the scientific community that concerned itself with abnormalities of the brain, was not known to the general public. The principal manifestation of this condition in young Abner was in his complete inability to alter or eliminate any social habit of long standing. He could not, for example, wear his gray suit on any Wednesday, that being the day that he had stood for the final fitting of his first good black suit, and had worn it directly from his tailor's to a board meeting, two years earlier. He could not bring himself to ask his carriage driver to detour one block off his daily route to the office even to visit his regular smoke shop when he had run out of cigars, to which he was strongly addicted and endured savage headaches whenever he went without one longer than two hours; the route had been recommended to him by his father-in-law the week he moved into his marital home as the most efficient, and any deviation from it must compromise its integrity.

These and other idiosyncracies were known to most of his friends and business associates, who dismissed them as eccentric privileges afforded the sons of wealthy and powerful men. Only a very few of those with whom he worked—and these had been sworn to secrecy through a combination of salary enhancements and threats originating from the office of the founder of Crownover Coaches—suspected that Abner III's quirks were symptomatic of something far more serious: a paralyzing fear of the unfamiliar and unpredictable that threw him into a panic whenever a decision had to be made that had no recent precedent. If the boy he sent to bring back his dinner reported that Hester's had run out of the pot roast of beef—young Abner's habitual order—he flew into a hysterical rage and could accomplish nothing the rest of the day. When in 1900 a fire broke out in the warehouse in Toledo and arrangements had to be made to ship in a fresh supply of door hinges from some other source, he locked himself in his office, emerging only after an employee shouted through the door that the situation was in hand. Finally, a request for compassionate leave by his secretary to attend his father's funeral in California reduced the president of Crownover to a blubbering wreck, whereupon Abner II was forced to step in and assume his son's responsibilities in addition to his own until Edward, his youngest, was indoctrinated to take over permanently. Announcement was made to the press that Abner III had been transferred to the newly created position of executive director, whose duties were still being decided upon. In his new office on the floor below his father's, he read newspapers, circling those items connected with carriage making for Abner II's review, posed for a full-length portrait to be painted by Howard Pyle, and countersigned contracts and requisition forms previously authorized by Edward.

This latest Abner in the distinguished line was the best-looking Crownover. He exhibited neither his two brothers' inclination toward stoutness nor the simian likeness of their father, the latter's long upper lip being in his case compensated for by the thin patrician nose of the Hamptons. He had a high, intelligent brow topped by a boyish thatch of dark hair highlighted by red-gold strands, the alert Crownover eyes, and square shoulders, from which his body tapered down to a trim waist in the best Charles Dana Gibson tradition. These features, as much as his brilliant future as his father's heir apparent, had made him the matrimonial catch of the 1898 season, when Lucy Kent snagged him with the not inconsiderable assistance of her father Lionel and Abner Crownover II. Lionel Kent had left Cornwall in 1869 to work the Cliff Mine in Eagle River, Michigan, as a foreman for the Pittsburgh and Boston Company, leaving when the copper played out to stake a claim on one of the richest deposits of iron ore in the Upper Peninsula. By the time of his daughter's wedding, the Kent Mining Company owned a fleet of steamships carrying millions of tons of iron pellets down Lake Huron to the Detroit docks, to be smelted and turned into stoves by the city's biggest industry. A merger between the great ironmonger and the nation's leading provider of private transportation to the wealthy was international news, and photographs of the honeymooning couple riding down the boulevards of Paris and boarding a gondola in Venice appeared in the rotogravure sections of newspapers from Berlin to Billings.

After six weeks abroad, the newlyweds returned to take up residence in a twenty thousand-dollar Tudor mansion facing Lake St. Clair, a joint wedding present from their parents, where from their windows they could watch the hog-nosed Kent ore carriers laboring their way south beneath their awesome burdens. An interview with Lucy Kent Crownover and photographic spread showing off the custom-built Singer treadle-operated machine in the sewing room and fifteenth-century refectory table in the dining salon ran in the *Ladies' Home Journal* in February 1899. By the time it was published, the couple had been cohabiting for six months, more than long enough for Lucy to become convinced that her husband was mentally ill.

He was not violent, nor even hostile. His manner toward his wife was gentle and caring, and his respect for her opinions regarding the operation of their household bordered upon serious dependency; the man simply could not make a decision, no matter how trivial. Being of a somewhat forceful disposition herself—her father used the term *headstrong* and considered himself fortunate to have matched her with someone who was not put off by such a disagreeable trait in a helpmeet—she was pleased to accept full responsibility for the choice of wallpaper in the parlor and the dishes that appeared on the massive dining table from day to day, with the assurance that her instructions would not be contradicted, so long as they did not contradict themselves. (Mashed potatoes, she had been informed quite clearly, must not be served on Sunday, once rice had made its debut their first meal at home after church.) Nor did it alarm her when Abner sharply upbraided his valet for laying out Thursday's collar on Monday, or nearly allowing Wednesday's black suit to go to the cleaners Tuesday night. Variety, after all, was a woman's pleasure, and served only to upset the smooth gray sameness of the masculine world, in which the mere appearance of a facetious straw boater on the head of the American president instead of a good solid black derby sent the stock market plummeting. No such explanation could be brought to bear on Abner's habit of twisting and untwisting the latch to the front door twenty-three times each night before retiring, or the even more complicated business involving the wall switch in their bedroom, which had to be pressed in multiples of seven times, finishing with the light off. These maneuvers were emblematic of his day, a tissue of repetitive mathematical therapeutic exercises that were at first annoying and perplexing, then alarming, and finally unbearable. By the time they observed their first anniversary, the Young Court (as one historically minded and slightly cynical senior executive had christened the new Mr. and Mrs. Crownover) was sleeping in separate bedrooms and meeting only for meals, public appearances, and conjugal relations; however damp her ardor had become toward her mate, Lucy understood the expectations of both sides of the family, and the importance of producing an Abner IV. None, however, was forthcoming. At the end of four years, Lucy had concluded that her husband, in addition to being mad, was sterile. This was evidence, perhaps, that there was order in the universe, and a God who possessed the common sense not to repeat a mistake.

She felt no rancor toward Abner, a gentle man when not faced with the anxiety of a choice to be made or a change in the routine. She felt, in fact, a certain tenderness toward him, made poignant by the knowledge that so prominent a firstborn was barred from seeking the same help as an equally disturbed commoner. Word that Abner Crownover's son was damaged in some fundamental way must inevitably threaten the company's fortunes; and so, in the daily family intercourse, the damage did not exist. He was ill through no fault of his own, and through no fault of his own he had no hope of a cure. Lucy's experience in charity work for the poor had not prepared her for the realization that the wealthy could be as badly treated as they, without the balm of an organized sisterhood to turn to in their despair. Where was the Ladies' Christian Society for the Relief of the Privileged? She pitied her husband as intensely as she despised the symptoms of his affliction.

To distract herself she filled her days with good works. In addition to planning fund-raising events for the Orphans' Asylum with her mother-in-law (a withdrawn, eerily calm woman in whose presence she found it impossible to feel at ease), she attended meetings of the Order of the Eastern Star, her membership having been assured when Abner III was inducted into the Freemasons under his father's sponsorship, helped choose decorations and arrange an orchestra for the annual Shipmaster's Ball, where as a debutante she had first made the acquaintance of her future husband, and chaired the Junior League committee that collected old clothes for mending and shipment to the families of patriots slain in or impoverished by the fighting in Cuba and the Philippines. This last duty kept her away from home Friday nights; and Abner, after recovering from his tantrum over this betrayal, had taken to dining with his parents in the Queen Anne on Jefferson every Friday. Harlan, who was aware of this, and who as the middle son had been familiar with young Abner's peculiarities longer than anyone else, was no more surprised when his knock at the parental front door was answered by his brother than he would have been by evidence of the steady rotation of the earth.

They shook hands warmly. Harlan liked Ab, despite his shortcomings. Or perhaps because of them; intentional or not, they represented a kind of rebellion against what was expected of their generation of Crownovers, and he celebrated them as he never could Edward's lockstep loyalty to their father's credo. Ab, however, was shy in his brother's presence. Harlan didn't know whether it was because he envied Harlan's relative independence or—what was more likely—pitied him because he had been passed over in favor of the youngest brother when the time came to replace the eldest at the company helm. His smile of welcome was tentative and he met Harlan's gaze only intermittently.

"Is he at home?" The question, Harlan realized, was unnecessary. Except in times of business emergency or when he felt absolutely compelled to make an appearance at one of the city's centers of evening entertainment, Abner II could always be found at home after working hours. In his way he was as much a slave to his rails as was his namesake.

"He's in his office. Would you like to see Mother?"

"Before I leave."

Ab, whatever his problems, was not a fool, and could tell when his brother was upset. He said nothing more.

Abner II never referred to his private place at home as his study. It was an office, interchangeable in his mind with the room where he worked at the plant. Apart from a small Victorian fireplace with an arched iron surround and the absence of Abner I's photographic portrait, it was at first glance identical to the office farther down the avenue: The plain desk and yellow-oak captain's chair behind it might have shared the same workshop with their twins at the plant, the milk-white bowl fixture suspended by chains from the ceiling—scrupulously dusted and cleared of dead flies—shed the same frank light as the one at work, and even the blue unfigured wallpaper above the wainscoting looked as if it had been cut from the same bolt. The books in the built-in shelves were different. The volumes at the plant, where he received formal visitors, had been selected for display, and represented the preferred works by Homer, Virgil, Shakespeare, the two Johnsons, Emerson, and Horace Lorimer, whose *Letters of a Self-Made Merchant to His Son* attracted notice only when it failed to appear on a businessman's shelves. Here in the private sanctum reposed Abner's choice collection of books devoted to engineering and design, from the earliest known publication of da Vinci's notebooks to a six-volume set bound in green leather of technical books devoted to the inventions of Thomas Edison. In truth, Abner II would have sneered to hear his private library referred to as a "collection," although he had spent enough to acquire some of the items at auction to attract the attention of most of the collectors' journals, whose requests to interview him had all been refused. With one exception, the books were thumb-blurred and tattered from heavy use and were plainly not intended for either decoration or pleasure, but to serve as tools related to the manufacturing trade. The only truly pristine work was the green volume entitled *The Electric Car*, detailing Edison's experiments with alternative transportation. Clearly it had come as part of the set, and had just as clearly been ignored by its owner. Its continuing presence on the shelf had more to do with Abner's love of closure than any reverence for literature;

he could not abide owning anything incomplete.

When Harlan opened the door at his father's invitation, Abner looked up from the ledger he had been reading, a broad, flat, buckram-bound book as large as a plat map, spread out and propped between his thighs and the edge of the desk. The old man still had no need for reading glasses, and his bright pupils shifted their focus from the closely written figures in the columns to his son's silhouette in the doorway without apparent delay. The mummified-monkey features registered no change in expression.

"Harlan." He offered no further greeting and made no move to close the book and rise.

"Father."

The balding patriarchal head inclined an eighth of an inch in the direction of the door. Harlan pushed it shut behind him. In the silence that followed, he thought he could actually hear the house settling, one creaking micromillimeter closer to the setness of its builder's mind.

"Your mother's been asking about you. Have you seen her yet?"

"Before I leave," he said again. "I wanted to talk to you first."

Now the ledger's cover tipped shut, expectorating a visible puff of paper fibers scratched loose by the pen of the clerk who had entered the totals. Abner pushed the book up and let it topple to the blotter, like a board being added to the top of a tall stack. Harlan was reminded of last spring's altercation over how to dispose of the substandard mahogany from Nicaragua.

"Take a seat." In the fading light sifting through the oaken slats that covered the room's only window, a powder of dust showed clearly on the leather seat of the upright chair facing the desk. Abner received few visitors at home.

"I prefer to stand."

"Napoleon." It was barely a murmur.

"I'm sorry?"

"It was nothing. I forgot for a moment who I was talking to. You couldn't know, but the Emperor Napoleon had some emphatic ideas about how to handle disgruntled guests. He persuaded them to sit down, on the theory that no one could make a convincing case for tragedy from his backside. People with grievances who have read or heard that always choose standing."

"What makes you think I have a grievance?" Immediately he regretted asking the question. It had taken his father exactly two seconds to derail him. In this the Queen Anne itself was an accomplice. Harlan had, within the confines of that rabbit warren of narrow staircases, odd alcoves, and right-angled hallways, been considered the idiot of the family for so many years that he had only to reenter it to feel himself behaving as expected.

"You haven't come to this house since Thanksgiving. Since you and I see each other every day at work, and since you didn't stop to visit your mother, I assume it isn't because you miss us. It's interesting how far a person will walk to express his displeasure over some slight."

"I rode a streetcar." He felt rather than saw the exasperation this remark caused, and took petty satisfaction from it. Retreating into the family evaluation of his mental abilities had in the past provided Harlan with a weapon of retribution as well as a defense against stinging comments. The keenest barbs flattened against and slid harmlessly down the thick surface of his seeming incomprehension. His discovery of this advantage had given him his first taste of power, as well as the revelation that he could never take pride in his independent spirit. He was free from most of the conventions simply because no one thought he was worth the effort of forcing him to adhere to them.

His father changed directions, and uncannily—it could not

have been accidental, however much it represented an almost supernatural understanding of Harlan's mission—placed himself squarely in harm's way. "I read of your friend Ford's victory, a race of some kind. I suppose congratulations are in order."

"He established a record for the mile. Again. No horse in creation could touch it."

"No horse would be expected to. There are a good many more things to admire in this world than mere speed. The telegraph did not dismantle the United States Post Office."

Harlan shook his head. He felt an ineffable sadness, the source of which he could not precisely identify, but which he suspected had something to do with the bleak gulf that separated fathers and sons. It did nothing to dampen his determination to go through with what he had started. "Neither of us is going to change his opinion. I didn't come here to revive that old argument."

"Why did you come?"

"I'm sure you're aware of the trouble Mr. Ford is having with an organization that calls itself the Association of Licensed Automobile Manufacturers."

"I know something of it. I read the papers."

"It's a sham, of course. This man Selden, who claims he owns the patent, has never built an automobile. Mr. Ford insists that no working motorcar could be built from the plans Selden submitted to the U.S. Patent Office."

"I wouldn't know that."

"Mr. Ford also says no one would ever have heard of George Selden or his patent unless someone powerful offered to back him with the finances and influence necessary to pursue the case in the courts."

"That would be former secretary of the navy William C. Whitney."

"You remembered that name quickly for someone who has

only a casual interest in the story," Harlan said.

"I have a good memory. Name a successful man who has not."

"Mr. Ford says Selden is a wooden owl."

"And what is that?"

"A decoy to frighten away squirrels. In this case customers. Whitney is using him, and you are using Whitney. Mr. Ford asked me to give you a message."

"I see. So now it seems he has you running errands for him."

"He asked me to tell you to call off your dogs."

"I beg your pardon?"

"He said if you won't do it, then go ahead and set them loose. It didn't appear to make any difference to him which you did. He's prepared to fight you all the way."

"Aside from an unhealthy obsession with animals, I have no idea what any of that means."

"Don't insult me, Father. Henry Ford asked to join the A.L.A.M. soon after it was organized. He was turned down, the only automobile manufacturer who was not allowed to join. It's clear he's the target of this whole advertising campaign to frighten away his customers. Why should he be singled out among the hundreds of people who are making automobiles?"

"I suppose they thought someone had to be made an example of. Your man Ford is the fellow who's getting all the headlines, buzzing about in races and giving interviews to the press. If they can smack down someone who's that visible, all the other holdouts will fall into line. Any captain of industry knows that."

Harlan saw the flicker in the old man's eyes as soon as the last words had been said; the outside embodiment of the wish to turn back time and edit them out of the conversation. His son drew no warmth from the triumph. He felt his face stiffening as in the cold on frozen Lake St. Clair. "William C. Whitney is no captain of industry. You are. You're the A.L.A.M."

His father, whose hands had been resting on the big ledger, drew them back and folded them on the near edge of the desk. No damp spots showed on the green buckram, although the room was overheated and Harlan's own palms were sweating heavily. The old man was as dry as corn shocks tented in the sun. It was a wonder he didn't rustle when he moved. "You're overestimating my vision," he said. "The association was up and running before I was invited to participate."

"Then you admit you're financing it."

"I'm a contributor, just as I am to dozens of other funds and causes. The day of the robber barons is past. In this century, the wealthy and successful are expected to make certain gestures."

"If that were true in this case, your name would appear in the advertisements."

"I will not be induced to defend my actions." Dim spots of color appeared on Abner's sallow cheeks.

"Ford's celebrity has nothing to do with why he was targeted," Harlan said. "You only want to destroy him because I'm involved with his company."

"The world doesn't revolve around you. I blame your mother for giving you that impression. She has always doted on you."

"You can't stand having a son of Abner Crownover in the automobile business."

"This interview is over." Abner drew himself up against the desk and opened the ledger across it.

"It won't work, Father. Even if you succeed and Ford collapses, I'll raise the money again and invest it in another automobile company."

"What makes you think you'll be able to raise the money again?"

"This city is filled with people who would be honored to invest in the Crownover name."

"That's because I made it what it is." A long dry finger followed a row of figures down a column. "You have the Crownover name because I gave it to you. And I can take it away just as easily."

"If you're threatening to disinherit me, I wish you'd make it clear."

He shut the ledger. With a little shudder of effort—Harlan suspected the action was far more cataclysmic below the surface—he forced a flat calm into his tone. "You're my son. That isn't something to waste on the first shiny property to come along. Automobiles are loud, flashy things, tempting to a young man. When you're older, you'll realize the things that stay the course aren't always exciting to look at the first time you see them. The foreman I worked under when I drew up my suspension idea couldn't see the improvement even when I pointed it out; he told me to get back to work or he'd dock me for my time and his both. And he was a mechanical man, who should have understood what he was looking at. What makes you think the gasoline car is any better than the steamer or the electric? How do you know Ford is the man to back among all the rabble who are out there, chugging away and fouling the air with their stinking smoke? He's failed twice before."

"That's exactly how I know he's the man to back." His son remained calm, and was more than a little surprised to observe he was the calmer of the two. Always before his father had won his point when Harlan lost his temper and any chance of making a reasonable argument. "He doesn't give up. The fact that he's lost everything twice and is willing to risk losing it all over again is the best point in his favor. That's how I know your A.L.A.M. will fail. You can defeat Ford, even kill him, but you can't destroy him."

The silence that followed jangled like a brass bell. Muscles worked in Abner's face; Harlan knew his father's stomach had tied itself into burning knots. He did not speak until the spasm had subsided. "Is that what you came here to tell me?"

"Yes, sir, it is."

"In that case you will do me the good service to leave." He opened the ledger once again and bent his head to the columns.

Abner III was standing in the hallway when Harlan left the office. He shook his head in answer to the question on his brother's handsome face. "Tell Mother I'm sorry I couldn't see her. I have an appointment downtown." He didn't bother to make the lie convincing, a mistake. Ab had troubles, but he wasn't stupid.

Ab touched Harlan's arm. "She's in the morning room. She told me not to let you leave before she spoke to you."

"The morning room?" Although he knew it was past dark, Harlan glanced involuntarily toward the face of the grandfather clock at the end of the hall. Ab's agitated expression confirmed the message. A change in anyone's routine was enough to upset him.

Harlan climbed the stairs to the east room, tapped on a panel, and was invited inside. He had never been in the room in the evening—as far as he knew his mother had not either— and found it far less vapidly cheerful by the electric light of a small chandelier and tulip-shaped lamp on the spinet desk. The corn-fed mothers and their naked babies seemed to stare at him from the Cassatt prints on the walls with a speculative air, as if undecided whether this newcomer was welcome in their family circle. Edith Hampton Crownover was seated at the desk in a mauve dressing gown and matching suede slippers with her hair in a long braid over her left shoulder, the way she wore it to bed. Her son had not seen her thus since he had moved out, and felt a sharp pang of nostalgia at the sight. Her inkwell was capped and there was no stationery on the blotter. She appeared to have been doing nothing but sitting and waiting for her visitor, without so much as an open book for company. In that light, her son noticed for the first time the signs of age in her face. Shadows pooled in hollows beneath her eyes, and sharp lines bracketed her mouth nearly to the corners of her nostrils. He felt a cold flash of mortality then, as if the down-stroke of a dark wing had inserted itself between him and the warmth of the sun.

"Your father spent a good deal of time debating the merits of steam heat with the contractor when he built this house," she said in lieu of greeting. "In the end he decided in favor of ductwork, and there have been no secrets under this roof since that day." She inclined her head toward the scrolled bars of the heating vent in the baseboard opposite the desk.

Responding to her unspoken instruction, Harlan bent and thumbed up the lever that closed the louvers behind the bars. "I'm sorry you had to be upset," he said.

"People have tried not to upset me my entire life. You will never know how upsetting that is. I need to ask you something. Will you promise to answer without worrying about whether it will distress me?"

"I've never lied to you."

"Of course you have. We raised you to be a gentleman. Will you promise?"

He nodded. He felt more intimidated in her presence than he had in his father's. The novelty of the sensation was intriguing.

"Is your interest in Henry Ford's automobile company genuine? By that I mean to say, have you involved yourself in that industry because you believe in it, or merely because you know it will anger your father? I know a little something about rebellion, you see. I'm just enough of a coward to understand its attraction."

"Actually, it's a little of both." His response surprised him. Even as he gave it he realized he was speaking the truth.

"But not equal parts."

After a long moment he said, "No."

Her eyes searched his. Then she nodded, just as if he had told her in which direction the balance tipped. "I've heard a bit about Mr. Ford. He is no gentleman."

"No, ma'am, he isn't."

"Good." She appeared to think about her answer, then nodded again and slid a hand inside the pocket of her dressing gown. From it she drew a slim skeleton key attached to a ring with a tiny gold rose for a fob and inserted the key in the bottom drawer of the desk to the right of the kneehole. The drawer contained a large photograph album bound in black cloth with leather corners, and Harlan thought at first that this was the object of her search. But she transferred it from the drawer to the top of the desk without a second glance and took out from beneath it a sheaf of paper bound with a tasseled cord, which she lifted into her lap. The sheet on top, wider than it was long, with an ornate border and skirled lettering printed in green ink, was instantly familiar to Harlan. He kept a stack of his own in a safety deposit box at the Detroit Savings Bank, although his was much smaller. It was a stock certificate belonging to Crownover Coaches.

"I know nothing of the legalities," confessed his mother. "I assume there is something I have to sign."

chapter thirteen

Battle Lines

On rare occasions, when he had been working particularly long hours at the plant, inspecting assemblies and examining bills of lading, Henry Ford rewarded himself with a meal out. When James Couzens found him in a booth in the Pontchartrain bar, the automobile manufacturer was peeling the shell away from the first of two hard-boiled eggs he had ordered with a tall glass of mineral water.

Couzens had risen from his well-paid but amorphous position as Alexander Malcolmson's business advisor to become general manager of the Ford Motor Company. The shift had taken place at the expense of his relationship with the coal merchant, when Couzens joined Ford in opposition to the six-cylinder Model K. There was, however, little sign of self-exaltation in his strong-jowled face as he slid into the seat opposite. His collar was damp for the unseasonably cool late-spring day and his glasses were fogged. When his beer came he ignored it, distractedly mopping at his lenses with a white lawn handkerchief bearing his monogram.

"Well, good afternoon to you, too, Jim," said his employer, dusting his egg lightly with salt. "You look worn out. Have you gone back shoveling coal for Malcolmson?" For reasons known only to himself, he seemed to take delight in the rift between the two.

"You know damn well where I've been. What makes you so happy?"

"I talked the Dodges into delivering their engines in crates built to my specifications. That means after they're opened we can pull them apart and use the planks for floorboards without having to saw them. They won't cost us a cent."

"Good. It's good you're saving money. You'll need it to invest in another line of work."

Ford munched on his egg. "Did you place those advertisements?"

"No. That's what I came to talk to you about. Both the *Free Press* and the *Evening News* are refusing to carry them. They're afraid of a lawsuit."

"Bunk. Newspapers love lawsuits. The trust must have got to them." He took a sip of water.

"You seem awfully calm about it."

"We'll just go national. Even the A.L.A.M. can't silence them all."

"I wouldn't be too sure of that. For a business that doesn't make or sell anything they're pulling in money hand over fist. Every day there's a dozen new auto companies lining up waiting to give them the gelt."

"They're not alone. We should top three hundred thousand in sales next month. I hate to say it, but Malcolmson's race idea has really been selling those more expensive models. So you see, we don't need advertising."

"You can't go on winning races forever."

"I don't see why not, but we won't need to do that either. Not when we come out with our cheap model."

"How cheap?"

"I'm thinking seven hundred."

"No one can make a car that cheap."

"You can if you make 'em all the same, like pins. I've got an idea, a little thing I picked up in a meatpacking plant in Chicago. All the carcasses zip through on rollers; one man skins, the next quarters, the next slices up the smaller cuts, and the last wraps them up for shipping. The carcasses move, the workers stay put. Get it?"

"You want to run an automobile plant like a butcher shop?"

"Old bear, do you have any idea how much a good butcher pulls down on a normal day?"

Couzens, who at any given time was undecided whether Ford was a genius or as crazy as his nickname suggested, changed the subject. "I'm worried about this new A.L.A.M. move. Up until now the newspapers have been your biggest champion. Editors love rugged individualism."

"Editors don't run newspapers. Newspapers are run by their advertising staffs. If they're turning down Ford ads it means they're getting more from the Selden people."

"We can't afford to outbid them."

"We won't try." Ford leaned forward. His tiny sharp eyes glittered and his long right index finger tapped the top of the table. "Newspapers are bunk. They're in business to make money and nothing else. The news is just something they report so that their subscribers might stumble over an advertisement while they're reading. Without news, they wouldn't give them a second glance. Automobiles are news. All we have to do is keep making news and they'll have to write about us."

"Aren't we in business to make money?"

"We're in business to make money and use it, give employment, and send out the car where people can use it. And incidentally to make money."

"Like the newspapers."

"You're not listening. If they could sell advertising without having to employ reporters and editors and typographers, they would. Turn it around. If you set out to employ a great army of men at high wages and reduce the selling price of your car so that a lot of people can afford it, if you give all that, the money will fall into your hands. You can't get out of it."

Couzens smiled for the first time that day, however tentatively he felt it. "That's good. It's horseshit, but it's good. But can you get a paper to print it?"

"They'll have to. It's what I intend to say in court."

The smile fell off his face. "We've been served?"

"Not yet. They haven't the guts so far. We're going to have to force them to do it."

"How?"

The Ford finger beat a tattoo on the table. "By making and selling more cars than anyone else in the business. By making and selling more of anything that's ever been made and sold by anyone in any business. I've already made arrangements to lease a new plant on Piquette Avenue, twice as big as the Mack. We're expanding."

"With what?"

"With our profits so far. What have I just been telling you?"

"We don't use all the space we have now. It's more than adequate."

" 'More than adequate' is not this company's motto. I'm introducing a new model, cheaper and more durable than anything we've produced. It may take a couple of years to stretch out the kinks, but by the time we're through, you won't be able to throw a shoe anywhere in this country without hitting one. In five years there will be a Ford in every garage in America. And we're going to pay each and every employee five dollars a day to build it."

"That's crazy! Roosevelt isn't paid that much."

"Roosevelt couldn't hang a door on the Model C."

"If you start paying wages like that, you're either the greatest man in history or the craziest. Every manufacturer in the country will be screaming for your hide."

Ford sat back, smiling his tight smile. "Go and tell the newspapers not to write about that."

•   •   •

"I can safely recommend the linguini, although I haven't tried it," Sal Borneo said. "The chef makes his own pasta. The strands are as fine as cornsilk. It is said to be the reason Caruso accepted his last booking in Detroit."

Jim Dolan glowered at the stained menu and said nothing. The restaurant, with its murals of Roman ruins, Chianti bottles strung from the ceiling, and constant foreign jabber drifting over from the other tables, might have been in Palermo instead of ten minutes from Corktown by streetcar. He had wanted to hold this meeting in his own neighborhood, but had been unable to think of an excuse to give colleagues who saw him with the Sicilian. The bastard knew that, too, and had used his people's own low social status to gain the upper hand in his home ballpark. What was that the wop was always saying? "Weakness is strength."

"Big Jim?" Borneo's tone was polite. The son of a bitch was nothing if not polite.

He looked up and became aware of the little old waiter standing by the table. "Can I get a plate of meatballs without the spaghetti?"

He noted that the waiter glanced at Borneo before answering. "Si, Signor. Wine?"

"Beer."

The shriveled little man took his menu, paused to refill Borneo's glass from the water pitcher on the table, and withdrew.

"You're not eating?" Dolan asked.

The Sicilian shook his head, an almost infinitesimal movement. For one so thin he seemed to expend as little energy as possible. Dolan, who valued those who valued leisure, should have taken comfort from that. He didn't. "I eat once a day, at breakfast."

"Call yourself an Italian?"

"Rome was destroyed by its appetites. While others are

spearing calimari, I'm thinking. You might try abstaining from liquor the next time you visit with your friends at the Shamrock. What you learn may surprise you."

Dolan's beer came, frothing over the schuper's rounded lip. For answer he drank off half of it in one draft, thumped down the glass, and wiped his lip with a knuckle, glaring defiance.

Borneo's shrug was hardly a movement at all, and his companion was left thinking that he had come off the worse in the discussion. In a mahogany-colored lightweight three-piece with a flaring white handkerchief and pale yellow necktie, Borneo looked like a civilized Indian in a medicine act. The moustache only accentuated the hawklike lines of his face.

"I heard from Maribel this week," he said.

"You mean Thelma." Dolan hadn't seen her since they'd parted at the Shamrock Club.

"She prefers the name she used in Detroit. I think it suits her better. She writes a good letter, although her spelling is creative. She's appearing with Bert Williams at the Gotham Theater in New York. A nonspeaking part, which is a mercy."

"I didn't know you were pen pals."

"It was in the way of a thank-you note. I paid her fare east, with a bonus for her work here. Apparently I exceeded the Broadway scale."

"On her feet or on her back?"

"Your anger is misdirected. In any case the regard with which you're held in this community is more assured than ever. The November elections proved that. You have made all the right choices."

"I can't see it that way as long as I'm paying property taxes in Ohio with nothing to show for them. You told me Ford would be out of business by now. The streetcar companies are still dragging their feet on the interurban."

"I did not say that. Ford is a gamester. Give him a penny and he will play it up into thousands. You can take away the thousands, but there is always someone who is willing to give him another penny. In such cases it becomes necessary to destroy the man."

"I'll not do murder."

"I am not suggesting that. You can kill a man and still fail to destroy him. Where there is no apparent weakness you must look to his strengths. What in your opinion is Ford's greatest asset?"

"He's mule-headed. This is his third run at the same business."

"Perhaps. He is also popular. Reporters love him because there is no predicting what bold thing he will say or do next. Their editors like him because he sells newspapers. The public adores him because he came up from nothing and is a good family man besides. America is a moral nation. That's its great strength as well as its most appalling weakness. It disillusions easily."

Dolan's meatballs arrived, a heaping bowl slathered with thick red sauce, with a garlic loaf on the side. They fell silent while the waiter laid out the items from the tray. When the waiter left, Dolan remained motionless, watching Borneo. "Whatever you're chewing, spit it out."

"With your help, we've succeeded in pressuring the local newspaper advertising staffs not to accept Ford advertisements," Borneo said. "The editors and reporters aren't influenced so easily. They can be bribed, but they are not honorable about such arrangements. They have been known to take the money and print what they want regardless. Doing business with them is unstable."

"I'm sure you have methods to deal with those who won't come through in such matters."

"Of course. But they are worthless if the lesson they teach will not be learned. Journalists are lower organisms who cannot be made to understand fear. Their instincts are bestially simple:

anything for the sake of a story. Run over a dog, and if he survives he will chase your wagon again the next time you pass, if it means dragging his crippled legs behind him. Killing him will not prevent other dogs from doing the same thing. It is most frustrating to an intelligent man."

"Then what do you suggest?"

"Eliminate the wagon."

Dolan shook his head like an old bull. "You said killing was out."

"It was. It is. Dead men have a disconcerting habit of rising again as symbols, and there is no fighting a symbol. Killing Henry Ford would only cloak the automobile business in a heroic mantle. Truly destroying a man involves hollowing him out and leaving him standing, an empty wreck not even worth pitying."

"I'm beginning to get you." The Irishman's face felt hot.

"I was certain you would. You're a higher animal, able to learn from the past. George."

He spoke the name without raising his voice above the level of the conversation they'd been having, which was not engineered to carry to the other tables. Nevertheless, a man rose from his seat in a corner booth near the swinging door to the kitchen and offered a hand to someone who had been seated opposite him. The man was the shockingly ugly creature whom Dolan had first seen in Borneo's office above the butcher shop away back in January. George Zelos, the name was. A Greek, but decidedly not the kind of which statues were made. The woman he helped to her feet could not have helped but appear beautiful by comparison, although indeed she was not. She had a long, homely face, and her drab brown hair was skinned back into a tight bun behind her head under a cheap hat. She wore a dress that upon a more handsome woman might have appeared endearingly simple. On her it was a nondescript print in a shade of gray unbecoming to her indoor pallor. Her down-cast gaze and hesitant step as Zelos escorted her to his master's table convinced Dolan that she belonged to the serving class.

"James Aloysius Dolan, this is Agnes. She has asked that her surname not be used." Borneo kept his seat.

Dolan, not wishing to draw any more attention to himself than he already had, chose to remain seated also. Ordinarily he made it a point to greet every woman he met as if she were a lady. They did not vote, but many of them influenced their men, and in any case even a drunken bricklayer who beat his wife and abused his children preferred to support politicians who kept the proprieties. He nodded to the woman, who stood staring at the floor and twisting her hands in front of her.

"Agnes was once employed in the Ford household in Dearborn as a maid. She lost her place after six weeks. There is no reason I should know that, except that Mrs. Ford hired the Pinkerton Detective Agency to find her and bring her back for an interview. I'm indebted to a young Neapolitan for this information," Borneo added. "I helped him find a position with the Toledo office as a records clerk."

Dolan pushed aside the untouched bowl of meatballs. He did not want to be distracted.

"Tell Mr. Dolan what you told me, Agnes," Borneo said.

When the woman hesitated, Zelos tightened his grip on her arm. Pain flashed across her plain features.

"George." The Sicilian's tone was the same as when he had summoned the man. George released the woman's arm. She rubbed it.

Borneo said, "Go ahead, child."

"Marty saw Mr. Ford touching me." She had a strong Irish country brogue.

"Marty was the scullery maid?"

"Yes, sir."

"What happened after that?"

"Mr. Ford sent us both away."

"He fired you and Marty?"

"Yes, sir."

Dolan gripped his knees. "Where did he touch you?"

"On my hand." She stroked her right hand in a soft caress.

The Irishman sat back, disgusted. "Is this what you asked me here to witness?"

"Mrs. Ford heard enough to have her found and brought back," Borneo said. "She would not have done that if she hadn't reason to believe the rumors. Where there is smoke there is fire."

"The newspapers will laugh you out of town if this is all you have to bring them."

"That is more than likely. I am only a butcher. But you are the Irish Pope."

"No one calls me that to my face."

Borneo raised a conciliatory hand. "You have confederates on every newspaper staff in the city. If there are other Agneses, they will find them. Moral indignation sells papers. Prurient fascination sells even more."

"Even if there are other Agneses, the man's private habits have nothing to do with his business."

"That will be Ford's defense. As I'm sure it would have been yours in the case of our dear Maribel."

Dolan's fingers cramped, cutting off circulation to his knees. He had been in mudslinging politics all of his adult life and had never hated anyone as thoroughly as he hated the man who sat facing him.

Borneo's eyes, dark and nonreflective, gave the impression of absorbing everything they saw and returning nothing. The depth of Dolan's hatred for him was measured and recorded. "Agnes is staying at the Railroad Hotel as my guest. George is in the room next door. They'll be at your service whenever you want them. My advice is not to wait too long. Have you seen this morning's *Free Press?*"

"I didn't have time. I had to move up a morning meeting to make room for this one."

Borneo glanced up at Zelos, who took a tightly folded newspaper from the side pocket of his rough canvas coat and slapped it into his master's hand. Borneo refolded it and passed it across to Dolan. The headline at the top of the first column read:

CROWNOVER TO MAKE AUTO BODIES FOR FORD

•　　•　　•

The iron ferrules that were used to reinforce the wheels used in Crownover vehicles were made at the company foundry in Cleveland, where pellets from the Kent Mining Company were smelted and poured and then hammered out by blacksmiths in long strips, to be cut to the desired lengths upon delivery in Detroit and fitted by the finest wheelwrights that could be had for wages. The strips arrived in sixteen-foot-long bundles bound with iron clamps and had to be unloaded by two-man teams. Harlan, who was short a man the day the new shipment arrived, lent his back, boarding the wagon and lifting the end of each bundle and guiding it over the tailgate, where a man seized the opposite end and helped him walk it onto the dock. The bundles were heavy and awkward and the unfinished edges of the strips sliced through a pair of stout leather work gloves like razors. Very soon Harlan's palms were stung and bleeding.

"Harlan!"

He had not heard his name called in that tone in many years. When he turned, his father was standing on the dock before the entrance to the plant, with his younger brother Edward hulking behind. Abner II's simian face was as white as his stiff collar except for patches of congestion like dark bruises on his cheeks and forehead. The old man was shaking visibly; Harlan thought of one of John and Horace Dodge's engines being tested on the Ford block. He had a rolled-up newspaper clenched in one bony fist.

Harlan stepped off the wagon and approached his father and brother at a normal pace. To himself it seemed he was walking very slowly, as if wading through water over his knees. His face felt numb, the nerves dead. He would remember each of these details for many years, but would describe them to no one.

"Father. Ed. What a surprise." It was the same greeting he had used when Abner had confronted him on the dock over his meeting with Big Jim Dolan more than a year before. That it should be unchanged under the present circumstances was the real surprise.

"I wanted to talk to you about this before I demand a retraction." Abner unrolled the newspaper and held it in front of him, stretching it between his hands. The paper rattled as in a high wind. It shook so badly Harlan couldn't read the headline at the top of the lead column. He didn't need to.

"No retraction is necessary," Harlan said. "The story's true. I gave it to them right after I signed the contract with Ford."

"Then you'll call them yourself. Your final act as an employee of this firm."

"Your final act," Edward repeated.

Abner said, "You're a fool. That damned confidence man Ford has made you his instrument. I blame your mother for pestering me into giving you any part in Crownover Coaches. She's soft on weakness."

"You're a fool," said Edward.

"I signed a contract."

Abner balled the newspaper between his fists as if it were the contract. "Your signature means nothing. The signature of a loading-dock foreman."

Inspired, Edward added, "A *former* loading-dock foreman."

Harlan was aware that all work in the plant had ceased. The laborers inside the building had come out to join the dock workers watching. Harlan felt a sudden loyalty toward his father. This was no event for spectators. "Let us discuss this in your office."

"The discussion is over. Get out. You're trespassing on private property." Abner pointed to one of the dock workers, a young bald-headed Irishman with an intelligent face. "You. What's your name?"

"Jimmy Doyle."

"Doyle, you're temporary foreman. Do the job right for a week and I'll make it permanent."

"Father."

Abner turned his back on Harlan. "Edward, call the police. If he's not gone by the time they get here, swear out a complaint against him for trespassing."

Harlan slid a folded sheet of paper from the bib pocket of his overalls. "Father," he said again.

"Tell this man I'm not his father."

Before Edward could open his mouth to obey, his brother snapped open the sheet and held it out to him. "Show him this."

Edward didn't take it. "What is it?"

"It's a letter from Byron Jakes, the company attorney. It confirms that I control forty-seven percent of Crownover stock, the largest single block. Larger than Father's. Mother and Ab signed over their proxies to me last week. That puts me in charge of Crownover Coaches."

The ball of newspaper fell to the dock and bounced away. Abner snatched the letter out of Harlan's hands just as Edward was reaching for it. Before he could read it, he bent double. His knees buckled and both his sons closed in to catch him under his armpits. Parchment that he was, stretched over brittle bone, he was as heavy as a bundle of iron strips. He made a gurgling sound and retched suddenly. Spots of bright scarlet the size of pennies appeared on the white sheet crushed in his right fist.

part four

The Harvest

chapter fourteen

Targets

Go ahead, take a shot," said Henry Ford.

Harlan accepted the rifle hesitantly. It was a simple mechanism: The greasy little brass .22 cartridges were loaded flanged-end first down a narrow tube and introduced into the firing chamber one by one with a pumping action of the wooden slide, which cocked the hammer. Harlan, who had never before handled a firearm, lifted the walnut stock to his right shoulder, lined up the sights with his cheek resting against the stock the way Ford had instructed, and pressed the trigger. There was a sharp crack, and dust popped out of the rectangular bale of hay at the end of the room a good six inches to the left of the paper bull's-eye target.

"I guess I'm no Annie Oakley." He returned the rifle.

"It's your first time. You did better than Wills. He missed the hay bale."

The room was long and narrow, with a partition erected along the left side to segregate it from the rest of the plant building on Piquette. To Harlan's right was the brick exterior wall, the windows of which had been painted over recently; he could not tell if the turpentine smell was coming from that direction or belonged to the fresh pine of the partition. A shoulder-high bench had been added, with a scrap of green carpet tacked on top for the shooters to rest their elbows on when they were firing.

"The Dodges are the best marksmen," Ford said, taking his position and closing one bright eye. "They're used to shooting at bartenders' feet. I like to come in weekends and monkey with the sights. Last time I did that John got so worked up he shot out a window." Chuckling, he squeezed off a round. The bullet scalloped the edge of the black bull's-eye.

Harlan said, "I'm not clear yet on just what shooting off a gun has to do with making automobiles."

"Not a thing, that's the point. It ain't healthy to just think about automobiles all the time. Dulls your edge. God knew that and it's why He invented Sunday."

They went out and across the floor of the plant, where a number of modified Model Ns—now referred to, as Ford skipped his way through the alphabet, as the S—were in various stages of assembly. The workers banged and ratcheted and welded away without paying any attention to the visitors. Harlan had heard that Ford's reaction, upon being asked by one of his foremen to bar outsiders from the plant because they made the workers self-conscious and prone to accidents, was to schedule almost daily tours by dignitaries, reporters, and curious members of the public until his employees no longer took notice.

Ford stopped before a door in another partition and inserted a key attached to a large ring in a brass lock. On the other side he used the key again to lock the door. This room was less than one-quarter the size of the firing range—just big enough, Harlan noted, to contain an automobile (although none was present), with a little room to move around it—with a number of power tools slung from a wall rack and a blackboard mounted on a trestle. The board was blank.

The room would not have been part of a Ford operation without a discordant feature. Harlan smiled at the old-fashioned spindle-back rocking chair in the corner but did not ask about it. "Design room?"

Ford jerked his head in what passed for an affirmative nod. "You've met Joe Galamb, my best draftsman?"

Harlan said he had not. The circle around his partner was

always shifting, new faces taking the place of old ones; Malcolmson, for instance, almost never came around anymore, and it was whispered that he had broken with Ford over the coal merchant's preference for ever-pricier models. Couzens had stepped forward to fill the gap. The feisty general manager's enthusiastic support of Ford's continuing opposition to legal maneuvers by the A.L.A.M. to shut him down had drawn them into a tight conspiracy, the bulldog and the wirehaired terrier always in a corner somewhere with their heads together.

"Galamb's a world-beater," Ford said. "I never have to explain a thing to him twice. Look at what he ran up from my first rough sketch." He paused dramatically with his hand on the blackboard, then spun it on its pivot to expose the other side.

It bore a detailed sketch in white chalk of what appeared to be a bathtub on wheels. Up front was a radiator shaped like a tombstone with a curved and vented cowling behind it, folded up to expose a four-cylinder engine, as straight and simple as a shotgun barrel. The spindly undercarriage rode high upon four spoked wheels with sloping fenders and a bowl-shaped headlamp mounted on either side of the radiator. It was a homely throwback design, predating even the curved-dash Oldsmobile, and appeared too fragile to exist anywhere but on that blackboard.

". . . motorcar for the multitude," Ford was saying; and Harlan realized he'd been talking for several moments. "Large enough to transport a family but small enough for the average man to operate and maintain without recourse to a garage. Constructed of the best materials, built by the best men on the simplest design. But it will be so low in price that no man making a good salary will be unable to afford one. It will carpet the country."

Harlan found himself groping behind him for the arms of the rocking chair. He sank down onto the pressed-leather seat.

Thus spared the difficulty of maintaining his balance, he set himself to thinking how best to tell Ford he had made a mistake.

"The center of gravity is too high," he said. "What's to prevent it from tipping over when it turns a corner?"

"It won't. The wheelbase is longer than it looks."

"But will it stand up on the road? It looks as if it will break in half the first time it hits a bump."

"Wills is working on a new alloy he got from Sweden. Vanadium, it's called. More durable than regular steel and a lot more flexible. It bends, but it springs back. You'll get used to it. It will go into the bodies you build."

"Crownover has never worked with steel. We'd have to gut the plant and retool from the ground up."

"You'll get used to that too. I expect to outgrow this plant in a couple of years. I see a totally self-sufficient operation: lumber mill, foundry, glass plant, final assembly. Everything made right on the premises. No more dependency on the outside."

"Where will the money come from?"

"You're looking at it."

"I need a drink."

Ford's scowl pulled his spare features into a mask. He spun the blackboard again, making the disturbing image in chalk disappear. "That's why I set up the firing range, to discourage all you fellows from becoming sots. How is your father?"

Harlan, still unaccustomed to his partner's galvanic changes of subject, thought at first that he had accused Abner II of being a sot.

"Not well. He has a perforated ulcer. One doctor wants to operate, the next thinks it's too dangerous. He's at St. Mary's Hospital. They suggested sending him home, but he refuses. He won't accept any visitors except my brother Edward. He's the only member of the family Father thinks hasn't betrayed him."

"What did you expect? You stole his company."

"You're the one who's been encouraging me to take it over. It's all I've heard from you for more than a year. You wanted Crownover bodies."

"I didn't say you did anything wrong." Ford's tone was quieter. "Sons betray their fathers. It's a natural law. If a man is strong and his son is his son, there's no other outcome. You weren't intended to sell carriages to fat old rich women any more than I was intended to work the dirt my whole life. If we was to go against that—that would be the real betrayal. It don't mean I don't wish my father had lived a couple more years, just to see his boy didn't turn out a tramp."

Harlan rose from the rocking chair. He supposed there wasn't room for a fainting couch. "What are you going to call your little tin tub?"

"Search me," Ford said. "Whatever's next."

The Pinkerton man's name was Dibble. He wore Norfolk jackets with a belt in back and affected the British accent that would have been his by right if his mother, who was born in Chicago, hadn't bundled him away from his father's house in Mayfair when he was three years old and taken him to live with her sister two blocks from the Union Stockyards. At twelve he had run away from the stink and the tyranny of a household run by women, intending to stow away on a ship bound for England, but had got only as far as Toledo, where a conductor on the B&O threw him off a freight car. A week after that a man named Ryan collared him on an Erie dock eating a raw fish he'd stolen from a market. Ryan was a Pinkerton detective who earned money in his spare time beating up sneak thieves for the local merchants' association and tipping them unconscious into the water, to sink or swim as the fates dictated. He was also a pederast who fed and sheltered young Dibble in return for his sexual favors. This arrangement continued for two years, until Ryan choked to death on his own vomit in bed one night when he was too drunk to roll over; or so the coroner ruled at the inquest that followed.

For his own amusement, Ryan had related to the boy all the details of his work with the agency. Two days after the man's death, Dibble, wearing a suit he had stolen from a gentlemen's emporium, applied for an apprentice position at Pinkerton. The personnel interviewer was not taken in by the boy's assertion that he had passed his eighteenth birthday, but was sufficiently impressed by his knowledge of the detecting trade to employ him part-time as a file clerk. From time to time he was selected to carry messages to and from operatives engaged in surveillance work, and upon occasion to take one's place while he went for a walk or to relieve his bladder. At the age of sixteen he was installed in a permanent post as detective.

That was fifteen years ago.

His particular skill involved dealing with members of the serving class. "People talent" was looked upon as of equal value to the agency as an aptitude for forensics or for following people undetected; "Gentleman John" Stiles was celebrated for his ability to blend in with blue bloods and ambassadors, and no one got on better with pickpockets and second-story men than "Fishbait" Rudge, who had spent nine months undercover in the Ohio State Penitentiary worming the whereabouts of a cache of stolen securities out of his cellmate. "English Eddie" Dibble's background and accent, which leaned toward the cockney, bought him confidences from stable hands, assistant cooks, and chambermaids that no amount of official threats or kindly condescension could. When the agency succeeded in locating Agnes, the maid whom Clara Ford was anxious to interview on the subject of her relationship with Clara's husband, Henry, it was Dibble who talked the terrified woman into returning to Dearborn.

When the director of the Toledo office summoned him to report to Detroit and the home of James Aloysius Dolan, Dibble was unaware that his success with Agnes was the reason he had been selected. The little brown spick who answered the door had admitted him without speaking, and led him, rocking from side to side as if his feet hurt, to a modest-size room on the ground floor, where he was left alone for ten minutes.

It was the kind of place Dibble hated on sight. Shelves of books of a legal and papist nature mocked his impatience with literature of any kind. He felt intimidated by the presence of a massive painting, presumably of his host, and the lingering pungent evidence of cigars he could not himself afford to smoke. The Englishman in him (and his nightmarish memories of Ryan) distrusted anything Irish on the face of it. Finally, he disliked any assignment that took him out of Toledo and away from his small but comfortable flat, which he had decorated in an English manner, with tea things and a photographic portrait of King Edward.

Dolan entered at last, shaking the detective's hand and shrinking the room with his girth and personality. Dibble, who stood just below medium height, resented having to crane his neck to look up at his client. Big men were comfortable and confident everywhere they went. They behaved as if they had never been compelled, at the end of a belt with a square brass buckle, to kneel before a man and unbutton his fly. He was relieved when Dolan lowered himself into the huge winged swivel behind his desk and indicated the armchair drawn up in front. The leather was porous and supple, not like the cheap top-grain that covered the one comfortable chair in his flat. He noticed that he had not been offered refreshment, but he was used to that; the years he had spent relating to people of a certain station had left their mark. His hosts simply never thought of it.

"You know Sal Borneo?" Dolan began.

"No, sir." The polite address was endemic, and for years now had not required effort to sound sincere. He spoke the truth. He had never heard the name.

The Irishman nodded, as if that was the answer he had expected, and flipped open the black pebbled cover of a folder on the blotter before him. Dibble recognized it as the kind in which agency files were passed from office to office. They were never to be removed from the building. Dolan's eyes roamed over the typewritten sheets with a speed that suggested he had already read the material in detail. He stopped reading and abruptly shut the folder, resting his big hands on top of it. His eyes were as blue as Lake Erie. "Henry Ford."

"Ah."

"You spoke to the maid."

"I did."

"Did she tell you anything you didn't put in your report?"

"No, sir. I never hold out on the agency." Again he did not lie. Employees who withheld information for purposes of extortion were prosecuted ruthlessly. Dibble's loathing for authority was not sufficient to overcome his lifelong fear of it.

"Are you good with your hands?"

"Sir?" He stiffened.

"I mean, can you fix a shutter, prune a bush, oil hinges? Are you handy around the house?"

"I suppose I am." He had hung his own wallpaper and rewired a lamp he had bought secondhand that resembled one he remembered from his father's house.

"I want you to go to work for Ford, at his house. I want you to find out if there are any more maids like Agnes. They don't have to be maids, if I'm after making myself clear." Dolan lifted his brows like an instructor coaching a not-very-promising pupil.

"Yes, sir. Do I report to you or Mrs. Ford?"

"To me. Mrs. Ford knows nothing about this, nor do I wish her to."

"How long am I to stay?"

"Until I tell you to leave."

"Yes, sir."

They worked out a plan for the reporting sessions, after which Dibble rose, shook Dolan's hand again, and returned to his room at the Railroad Hotel. On the way he bought a bottle of cheap port to brighten his mood. It might be a long time before he found himself back in his little piece of the sceptered isle in Toledo.

Couzens found Ford in his bathroom in the house on Edison Street, stretched out on his back on the tile floor in his shirt-sleeves to relieve an ache caused by too many hours spent sitting in the rocker on Piquette discussing the new design with Joe Galamb.

"I just got off the telephone with Durant." Couzens stood in the doorway with his hands in his pockets and his derby on the back of his head. He looked more like a circus barker than ever.

"Bill Durant?"

"None other. He wants to set up a union with Buick and Reo, Olds's new company. International Motors, he calls it. He's inviting us in."

"What's he offering?"

"Three million."

"He can do better than that."

"How much better?"

Ford thought. "Eight."

"Million?"

"If it's all cash."

"Maybe he knows something," Couzens said. "He's close with that Selden crowd."

"Tell him I'll throw in my lumbago."

"If we lose in court we might not even get the three million."

"We won't lose."

chapter fifteen

The Payoff

First-time visitors to the home of Sal Borneo—and these were few, as the sanctity of his hearth was not to be violated with matters of business except under the most special circumstances—were always surprised to learn that the Detroit Italian community's leading citizen did not live in royal splendor. Fabulous stories had been told of the house of his predecessor, Uncle Joe Sorrato: stories of Persian rugs and tables laden with silver and a phonograph in every room, gifts from indebted admirers and mostly stolen from J. L. Hudson's and homes on Jefferson Avenue, but Borneo's four small rooms on the fifth floor of a building that had survived the spectacular fire of 1886, while comfortable, were no more opulent than the flat of a successful butcher. He had not even a study to himself, but read Virgil and Gibbon in inexpensive editions in an old chair in the parlor while his daughter sat on the floor memorizing verses for the sisters, and took his meals with her and his wife, who was also their cook, at a table in the dining room with a lace cloth made by Signora Borneo's grandmother. The kitchen was furnished with a woodstove and an icebox, and a fine old four-poster bed, a wedding gift from Vito Grapellini, left barely enough space in the bedroom for the drawers to be slid from the chest containing the husband's shirts and the wife's petticoats. Grapellini himself had an electric refrigerator and pump-up gasoline stove in his house on Heidelberg and played Caruso records on a wind-up Parlograph. Residents of Little Italy who heard of the Spartan arrangement at the Borneos' were inclined either to doubt the testimony of the witness or to conclude that Sal Borneo was not the man of influence they had thought.

At the time these disappointing stories began to be told, a joint passbook account in the name of Salvatore and Graziella Bornea at the Detroit Savings Bank reported a balance of $2,069.24. Two safety-deposit boxes in the vault of that same institution rented in the name of "Salvatore Bornea, Butcher," contained one hundred twelve thousand dollars in cash denominations of singles, fives, tens, twenties, and fifties. Some of the smaller bills still stank of the sweat of the men who had earned them in the stove foundries and carriage shops and spent them in Borneo's horse parlors and brothels. It was a comfortable sum to have amassed at a time when the average laborer earned less than a thousand dollars per year, but Borneo was dissatisfied. He desired money not for the comforts it bought (for to these he was as insensate as it was said the Duke of Wellington had been to the flavor of a rotten egg), but for the variety of its uses, and a hundred thousand was no more sufficient to this purpose than a carpenter's box half filled with tools of limited utility. The men who made things move, the Vanderbilts and Carnegies and John Jacob Astors, had millions at their disposal. He smiled at their marble libraries, their forty-room houses and mistresses girdled with diamonds, all the absurd outward ornamentation of their wealth upon which they spent so much time and money as if they needed to be reminded of it every time they read a book or opened their eyes or experienced an erection; but he envied them their monopolies. The sight of Jupiter Pierpont Morgan's red infected nose on Wall Street was rumored to have had a more positive effect upon a New York Stock Exchange in crisis than had the victory in Cuba, while a negative twitch of John D. Rockefeller's palsied head over a bit of ticker tape was all that was required to bring down the economy of a small Central American country. These men had never pumped their fists for the rights of the common man on a platform draped in bunting, nor leaned down from a caboose to shake a calloused hand that might one day check a box next to their name on a ballot, yet everything they did and said affected the lives of populations. Such might did not come from two locked boxes in the basement of a bank in Detroit.

And they were ruthless men; insatiable in their appetites, determined in their destiny, insensible to the misery of the men they ruined, the families they impoverished, the progressive ideals they crushed because they held no relevance to the bright steely light that awakened them in the night and beckoned them forward. In this they differed not at all from the lessons Borneo had learned in Little Italy, the philosophy of brutality and betrayal that had enabled him to survive in the New World. But the men were regarded differently because they were Dutch and English and French. More important, they were Not Italian. A quarter century earlier, two men named Fisk and Gould, stock marketeers and railroad men, had sought to buy up all the gold in the United States and set their own price for its sale, and in so doing brought about the Panic of '73 and a nationwide recession. They had stood trial for it, and were lightly punished, but were feted as great robber barons and inundated with invitations to Fifth Avenue balls and to speak before great crowds for huge considerations; although their audiences were the smaller for the absences of the suicides they had caused. Conversely, in 1891, seven years after Borneo came to America, a corrupt and bigoted Irish police superintendent was murdered in New Orleans, some said by Black Handers; after a jury acquitted eight Italians who had been charged with the crime and hung on three others, a mob dragged the defendants from the courthouse, lynched two, and shot the others to pieces. Theodore Roosevelt, then climbing the political ladder in New York, referred to the incident as "a rather good thing."

The episode had left a deep impression on Borneo, who at the time had been recovering in bed from his police interrogation in the matter of the assault upon the barber Gilberto Orosco. A man could rape a continent and win admiration, provided his name ended in a consonant or at least an acceptable vowel, but an Italian, like a Negro, could not take a billiard cue even to one of his own without jail and suffering even unto death. Better, then, to exert influence anonymously, through the popular anointed, and thereby gradually acquire the funds necessary to exert true power.

The process, however, seemed glacial. He was nearing the end of his second decade of enlightenment, and his dominion was small enough that he could survey it in its entirety by standing upon a chair on the terrace of the restaurant where he conducted most of his business. As much as it amused him to ridicule Big Jim Dolan for pandering to the unwashed and illiterate voters whose caprices determined the fate of his party, Borneo did not delude himself; the man was his superior in all the ways that counted. The Irish Pope was comfortable everywhere he went in the city, except of course the Italian neighborhoods, but even there his safety was assured by his celebrity. Borneo had only to journey west of Gratiot Avenue to feel his power shuck from his body; on Belle Isle, in Corktown, among the stately homes along Jefferson, and in any of the smart shops and varnished saloons that lined Woodward he was just another dago, forced to step into the gutter to make way for flying wedges of Detroit College students too caught up in their self-worship to watch where they were blundering. Resistance would only change their brainless banter to roars of indignation, followed by kicks and blows. Apart from his interest in the glory of old Rome, he took no particular pride in his nationality, which was a fractious thing even among those who did, the various cities and provinces of home having been at one another's throat since the fall of Constantinople. The oafs who gathered on the Campus Martius on Columbus Day, draped in green-white-and-red sashes and hooting above the bass drums and tubas about the contributions Italians had made to America since that Genoese opportunist had dropped anchor off Porto Rico in 1492, left him cold. Not by sermons and pageantry had the Spanish (and then the French and then the English and finally the Irish) gained sway over those who had preceded them to these shores, but by raw force, whether it was pressed by muskets or cavalry or a truncheon in the hands of a mick fireman "maintaining the peace" on election day. (The Dutch, of course, had used money, which as Borneo had already observed was the most fearsome weapon in the human arsenal.) In any case it was difficult enough for any man, let alone a dusky Mediterranean, to grope his way along the corridors of power without having to bring his whole tribe.

He had the vision, the beginnings of an organization, and the start-up funds to brave that corridor. All he lacked was a vehicle to speed the journey. It had amused him to apply that term literally and lend funds to young Crownover, fully expecting the impetuous Ford to fail spectacularly, as he had twice before, and leave the heir to the great carriage company in Borneo's debt. It pained him to admit that he had underestimated Ford. Although the business of the Selden patent was encouraging, his own small victory over the American justice system in the Orosco affair, which he, an insignificant street tough, had won through an embarrassingly transparent device, had left him with little faith in the ability or even the determination of the law to enforce itself. Ford was fast approaching the millions necessary to become an authentic force, one with the Morgans and Carnegies and Astors and Vanderbilts and Rockefellers, immune to conscience and statute. Borneo had not yet surrendered hope, but neither was he oblivious to the call of fresh opportunity.

All this he considered as he stood by the window in his

dining room, peering through the diaphanous lace of his wife's curtains at his neighborhood in full cry of the early-evening rush to home and supper. The flow of pushcart peddlers wheeling home their inventory, salesgirls with felt hats and handbags, and round-shouldered men carrying lunch buckets, some of them balancing these burdens with shiny aluminum-covered pails containing beer from the corner taproom, was as changeless and reliable as a punch clock, but almost always had a warp in it at the corner, which had become the post of choice for every type of unemployable to pitch his party line. Sometimes he was a scruffy-headed Marxist in wire-rimmed glasses and a filthy and tattered sweater, host to any number of lively vermin, reading the *Communist Manifesto* in the bored singsong voice of a streetcar conductor. Other times he was a minister with some unidentified church, gaunt and shrill in the wrinkled white suit and Panama hat of a tropical missionary, asking the workers as they passed if they were aware their daughters were under the scrutiny of white slavers like naked geese strung heads-down in the window of a market. On occasion, what appeared to be the same stout woman in a dirty frock with the same ageless and barefoot children wiping their noses on her skirts held that ground, snatching the odd sleeve and asking if anyone had seen her husband. There were others, more transient, with missions less apparent, who came but once or twice, but always left, like the others, when the traffic thinned to a trickle, with or without a handful of sweaty coins to show for their vigil. Some of the recidivists lived in the neighborhood; these Borneo knew by name. The rest were drawn from outside by the rapidly expanding Italian population. The minister, he was aware, slept in a boxcar in the railroad yard when he failed to collect enough to pay for a room, and he suspected the woman with the children made the rounds of all the other ethnic communities the rest of the time. By and large these individuals were looked upon as minor annoyances and ignored by the policeman who

walked that beat, except at election time when healthy arraign-
ment activity was desired by the party in office. The diehards
were released after a few days with a warning and were back
on the corner within a week. Out-of-towners who looked even
slightly shabby were beaten with stiff rubber hoses, transported
by police van to the city limits, and advised not to return on
pain of three months' hard labor on charges of vagrancy. No
distinction was made between the authentic hoboes who had
ridden in on the rods and those with ticket stubs in their pockets to show that they had entered respectably enough in a day
coach. A factory town did not warm to strangers with time in
the middle of the day to pester its hardworking citizenry.

Today's pest was a pleasant diversion from the normal run.
A modestly attractive young woman, rather too thin for Borneo's taste, stood on the corner wearing an old-fashioned sun-
bonnet and long full dress of pioneer gingham, handing out
leaflets. Most of those who accepted them did so out of native
politeness or because it was easier to take them than it was to
avoid her. The majority boiled past without acknowledging her
existence or altered their course to steer wide around her, and
this was what caused the warp in the flow of foot traffic. It was
a rare pedestrian—one in ten, Borneo judged—who paused
long enough actually to read the leaflet. One or two spoke to
her briefly, as if asking a question. The woman responded without breaking rhythm, snatching the sheets one by one from the
stack under her left arm and thrusting them at the passersby.
This had happened a number of times before Borneo realized
that all those who stopped were women, and that the ratio of
one in ten corresponded roughly to the number of homeward-
bound laborers who happened to be female. He became very
curious to know what was printed on those leaflets.

This thought had just formed when someone knocked on
the apartment door. He turned from the window and frowned
at the face of the china clock upon the finished pine sideboard,

the gift of a cabinetmaker whose daughter had recently married a young barber in a five-chair shop after Borneo had sent men to break the shins of a divorced Armenian to whom she had been engaged briefly. The time was ten minutes after six. In five minutes he would be sitting down to dinner with his wife. He could not think of anyone he knew who would violate the supper hour for any reason short of emergency.

He heard Graziella's low voice in conversation with a male whose own tones were pitched slightly higher; a young man, then, asking if Mr. Borneo was at home. She replied in the affirmative—dissembling was an art she refused to practice, whatever her feelings about the interruption of the domestic rhythms she held dear—and a moment later Harlan Crownover walked into the dining room.

The stocky young man wore a suit and necktie, and the crested condition of his hair suggested that he had surrendered a hat but was sufficiently unaccustomed to the accessory to think to make the necessary adjustment.

"I'm sorry to bother you at home," he said in lieu of greeting. "I missed you at the restaurant and they told me at the butcher shop where you live."

"I must speak to Signor Grapellini about that. I never conduct business at home."

"He didn't want to tell me, but I convinced him you'd be pleased." He reached inside his suit coat and slid out a thick envelope. When Borneo made no move to accept it, he turned up the flap and fanned out the corners of some of the bills inside. "Five thousand dollars was the amount I borrowed."

"I will be in the shop tomorrow morning, and in the restaurant all afternoon. You could have waited and given it to me then."

"I prefer to repay my debts right away."

He smelled the aromas from the kitchen. He seldom ate meat, but he could not resist his wife's veal. She got up very early Saturday to be sure and select the freshest cuts at the Farmers' Market.

"There is a matter of interest," he said.

"There is six thousand in this envelope. Is a twenty percent return satisfactory?"

He was silent for a moment.

"Yes."

When Borneo still did not take it, Crownover laid the envelope on the sideboard. "Do you give receipts?"

"It's unnecessary. No paperwork changed hands when we arranged the loan."

"This ends our association." The furrow in the young man's forehead was less certain than his tone.

"I'm happy you found it profitable." There was another awkward silence. Borneo, who seldom felt the need to offer empty conversation, decided to fill it. "I suppose you are in the automobile business now."

"I am."

"What's to become of Crownover Coaches?"

"The company will make more money than it ever has, as an adjunct to the Ford Motor Company. In five years—less, perhaps—we will have manufactured our last horse-drawn vehicle."

"I wonder what we will do with all those horses."

"Race them, I suppose. That should make you feel secure."

"I'm secure as long as humans insist upon remaining human. I hope your new venture brings you wealth and great happiness."

Harlan, Borneo saw, was not yet Abner II. Evidence that their encounter did not develop as expected appeared on his face for a bare instant before his expression smoothed over. "Thank you." He waited. "You don't want to count the bills?"

"Did you not count them yourself?"

"Twice."

Borneo smiled. "Good-bye, Mr. Crownover."

"Good-bye."

When the meal was over and Graziella cleared away the dishes, Borneo announced that he was going for a walk. Although it was his long-established habit to spend the evening reading in the parlor, his wife did not question him. Her plump, pretty face was as free of lines and pouches as the day she had agreed to spend her life with him; he credited this to her charming lack of curiosity. The only disappointment she had ever caused him was the absence of a male child. He never dwelt upon this, however. The mystery of who should carry on when he was gone could only make him falter in his determination to acquire something beyond a partnership in a butcher shop and the fear and respect of a few hundred immigrants who lived only to maintain a roof above their heads so they could live.

Darkness had come to Little Italy, broken by the corner lamps and the yellow glow from the windows of buildings and the absurd aloof illumination of the city system stretching above the rooftops like ineffectual Eiffel Towers. There was a sweet, tarry smell that was absent during the daytime, or more accurately lost in the olfactory jumble of ripe fruit, cheap pipe tobacco, cheaper cigars, frying meat, stale undershirts, fresh fish, wet laundry, and horseshit. As a good family man—for he loved his wife and daughter and was discreet about his mistress—he was not often abroad after sundown. Nevertheless he preferred this time to the confusion of the day, the urgency to accomplish as much as possible in a race against the sun. Night accepted one as it found one. Night expected nothing.

The woman in the bonnet was long gone. He had anticipated nothing else. In truth he had no desire to make contact with her. He was alone on the street with the sounds of domestic chatter falling out of open windows, the bubbling tinkle of a piano that wanted tuning, the nasal strain of some anonymous tenor drifting from a phonograph. (Rollo Fischetti's machine, he guessed; courtesy of a horse named Caesar's Rubicon. Borneo had taken a beating in that particular race and had learned his lesson, to place layoff bets whenever a horse with a locally popular name came to the post.)

As he had predicted, the sidewalk around the corner from the one where the woman had stood handing out leaflets was a plain of discarded paper, solid white, as if it had been hit with a fall of snow. He picked up one of the leaves and held it under the corner light. It was a song sheet, ruled and dotted with musical notes. The legend at the bottom read, "Distributed by the Women's Christian Temperance Union and the Anti-Saloon League of America." The melody appeared simple, but not as simple as the printed lyrics:

Stand up for pro-hib-i-tion, Ye patriots of the land;
All ye who love your coun-try, Against saloons should stand.
Be bold against this traffic, Your country's greatest foe;
Let word and deed and bal-lot Proclaim, "saloons must go."

There were two more choruses along the same lines as the first. He read them all, finding himself humming as he did so; marches were contagious, particularly among new Americans, who lined Woodward twelve-deep on Independence Day, souvenir flags in hand, to see the parade. The primitive two-beat rhythm, the homely naïveté of the words, were visceral. He could imagine a drunk singing the song as he wobbled home. No war had ever been won based upon the composition of a great master.

Sal Borneo folded the sheet three times lengthwise and slid it into his inside breast pocket.

•   •   •

Whatever the extent of the effect recent events had had upon his tightly controlled life, Big Jim Dolan remained secure in the knowledge that he loved his children. How else explain his willingness this Sunday afternoon following church and noon dinner to don his gabardine and boater and hike down to Fred Sanders' ice cream shop and entrust the generous Dolan rear end to the inquisition of an infernal chair with twisted iron legs and a twisted iron back, merely to remind himself every time he took a spoonful of vanilla in caramel sauce that one of his gold fillings needed replacement? The light in the faces of Sean in his Sunday serge and cap with black patent-leather bill and Margaret in her white sailor suit was impossible to resist. And Charlotte was delighted to parade her new seersucker dress and picture hat for the first time. True, it did not hurt his reputation to be seen, a man in the bosom of his loving family, participating in a Detroit summertime tradition; but he had finished a particularly busy week of Rotary Club speeches, testimonial dinners, and one photographic pose at Bennett Field, showing Red Donahue how to line up one's fingers with the stitching on a baseball for the throwing of a proper curve, and he complimented himself that the added exposure was hardly necessary. What he was doing today he was doing as James Aloysius Dolan, husband and father. Later he would reward himself with a beer and perhaps a game or two of billiards at the Shamrock Club.

"James, that funny little man is staring at me," reported Charlotte over her strawberry sundae.

She had been brought up not to point, and so he was forced to follow her gaze across the room, which was jammed to the counter with chattering families on this first truly hot day of summer. The ice cream melting on his tongue turned to sawdust when he identified the slight Italian standing with his hat in his hands just inside the door.

At first he didn't recognize him. His presence downtown was out of context, and he looked and stood far different when not in his customary surroundings; more like one of the supplicants who came to Dolan's door asking for money or favors than the dark prince of his community. Here he was just Salvatore Bornea, immigrant, and the cut of his suit did not disguise the hunched shoulders and outward-turned elbows of a wop on Woodward. Dolan found strength in that, and transferred his napkin from his collar to the round iron table with a decisive snap. "It's not you he's staring at, dear," he said. "I'll go and have a talk with him."

"Don't these people know you're not to be bothered on the Lord's day?"

"I'll remind him." He rose, and made a business of tugging down the points of his vest, shooting his cuffs, and shifting his bamboo cane from his left hand to his right before starting toward Borneo. It would give the man time to absorb the knowledge that he was in Dolan's park.

Borneo disarmed him somewhat by surrendering the point. "I am sorry, my friend, to interrupt your family excursion. Your houseboy told me I would find you here."

"Noche should have known better." He managed to make it sound more imperious than biting. The day belonged to God, after all.

"I managed to convince him my purpose is not frivolous. May I have five minutes with you?"

Dolan looked around. Three young ladies in smart hats and bustles were rising from a table ten feet away. He and Borneo reached it just ahead of two youths in linen suits and boaters carrying banana splits. One of them glared and opened his mouth, but his companion whispered something to him and the pair withdrew.

"Fame has its compensations," remarked Borneo as they sat down.

"A wee bit off your run, isn't it?"

"It is a beautiful day."

Which was no explanation at all; but Dolan chose not to ask the question again a different way.

"Harlan Crownover paid me a visit Friday night."

"Did you lend him more money?"

"No. In fact, he paid back what I'd lent him before. With interest."

"He didn't get it from his father. I hear the old boy's in a bad way. Not long for this world." This saddened him more than he let on. The Crownover plant, with its huge sign painted right on the brick tagged "A. Crownover, Prop.," had been the first thing he saw when he came to Detroit, a knob-knuckled mick switchman full of beer and piss and not much savvy about the way the gears turned. Although they had spent their lives laboring in enemy camps, Abner Junior and Dolan were both self-made men in a country that hailed the phenomenon on paper while discouraging it in practice. From the beginning, Big Jim had fixed his eye on Abner's example, the one sure landmark that would guide him out of the Yankee wilderness that had buried so many of his compatriots. A city in which an insignificant grease boy could climb hand over hand into the big office on the top floor could be made to deliver anything. He would sooner expect to see Ursa Major spill from the sky than Abner Crownover II on his deathbed.

"No, I gather it came from his first-quarter profits providing bodies for Ford," Borneo said. "People appear to want to buy Ford's machines despite the threats from the A.L.A.M. Or perhaps because of them. When judging Americans you must never overlook the fact that they are the grandchildren of rebels."

"Horseshit."

"Soon to be an antiquated phrase."

"So you made some money on the deal, and now you're a

believer. When can we expect to see you operating your own horseless carriage?"

"Not soon, I fear. All that cranking." He wasn't smiling. "The time has come, my friend, to admit we made a bad investment and cut our losses."

"Just because you lost your hold on young Crownover is no reason for me to jump the fence. You came out ahead. You're forgetting all that Ohio farmland I'm stuck with."

"Oh, that. Ford's case comes up in September. It's a New York court. When the ruling goes against him all the streetcar companies will be screaming for that property. You'll make more off it in a month than all the farmers who have worked it combined."

Dolan squinted, trying to see the Italian in an objective light. "If that's the case, why am I paying a Pinkerton detective to prune Ford's hedges?"

"He'll appeal the ruling, of course. He'll take it all the way to Washington if he's forced to. By that time it won't matter whether he wins or loses. He'll go on doing what he has since the start. He'll pay the fines out of petty cash just like Standard Oil. He's a hero to the people, like Thomas Paine or Patrick Henry. At this point a dirty little scandal might take some of the shine off his monument, but I doubt it will help. We started too late and moved too slow. We didn't know we were trying to smash quicksilver with an iron hammer."

"So you're out."

"I am out. I came here to tell you and spare you the trouble of coming to see me. I know Little Italy is not your favorite place."

"You came here to make sure we still have an arrangement."

"Grapellini really is the finest butcher in Detroit," Borneo said. "Sometimes the man who knows all the right people also knows his work."

There was a long silence, which Dolan came to conclude was wasted. The Sicilian would not be made anxious. "I see no reason to make any changes at this time," he said.

Their business was finished, but Borneo made no move to rise. Dolan could feel his wife's eyes on the back of his neck. The children would have emptied their dishes by now and would be growing restless. "Well?"

Borneo looked apologetic. "I feel that I have cost you time and money. I have a proposition."

"The last time I accepted one of your propositions I wound up in bed with a nigger."

"This would be an equal arrangement." Borneo reached inside his coat and laid a rectangular fold of paper on the table between them. Dolan picked it up and unfolded it. It was a song sheet.

He slid his glance over it, then tossed it back. "I've seen these before. Dried-up old prunes hire church halls to sing this horseshit. Are you temperance?"

"I enjoy a glass of Chianti on rare occasions. In any case I consider it poor policy to impress one's habits upon others. The woman who was handing these out in Little Italy Friday night was no prune. Neither were the women who took them. And every woman who passed her took one."

"What's the point? Women can't vote."

"We've spoken of this before. Married men who vote have to live with their wives."

"No man would ever vote to close saloons."

"I can refute that, but it's not the point I wish to make. I spent yesterday researching out-of-town newspapers in the library. Did you know ten counties in Michigan are expected to vote themselves dry next year? The Anti-Saloon League predicts that number will quadruple itself by 1910."

"They were probably drunk when they counted."

"I still have not made my point. You know our system, Big

Jim. In your heart of hearts, do you believe it is impossible to obtain an alcoholic beverage in ten Michigan counties?"

"Certainly not. Outlaw a bad habit and all you'll make is more outlaws."

Borneo sat back, smiling behind his moustache.

Dolan began to see then. That, he decided, was what he hated about the little dago; he made him feel like a potato-headed Irishman. "You invested in Harlan Crownover hoping he would fail. You're telling me you're investing in the prohibition movement for the same reason."

"Not at all. I have every hope it will succeed."

Big Jim Dolan felt the first chuckling tremors of what promised to be his first full-fledged belly laugh in many months. He shoved himself to his feet to keep the melted ice cream in his stomach from backing up on him. He was laughing out loud now, infectiously drawing grins and sympathetic laughter from the other tables. Very soon everyone was laughing, with the exceptions of his wife and children and Borneo, and only one of them knew why. He slid his chair under the table, hooked his cane over his wrist, and leaned down so the Sicilian could hear him through the mirth. He hissed the words between his teeth.

"The day the citizens of this country vote to outlaw liquor is the day the mayor of Detroit rides up Woodward Avenue in an automobile." He returned to his family.

chapter sixteen

Rouge

When Harlan Crownover heard that the judge in New York had ruled that no gasoline car could be sold without infringing on George Selden's patent, he called Ford's home and was told by a maid that her mistress was resting after the long train ride and that her master was at work. There a man whose voice he didn't recognize—Ford was always hiring and firing, taking on a man for a certain job and then transferring him to an entirely different position according to his aptitude or Crazy Henry's own whim—informed him that he had been in, but had left after fifteen minutes without leaving word as to where he could be reached. That suggested the Pontchartrain bar, and as the operator reported that line busy Harlan decided to go down there.

He found the place nearly full, mostly with strangers, although from the snatches of conversation he heard as he cruised through looking for Ford he gathered that they were mostly auto men. Every day, it seemed, more were entering the business; Harlan, who had once known everyone in the local field at least well enough to say hello to, had wondered briefly upon entering if in his preoccupation he had come to the wrong bar. At length he spotted a pair of familiar faces in a booth near the back and went that way.

John and Horace Dodge weren't hard to notice. Outfitted in identical navy blazers and yachting caps, they resembled a pair of fat babies dressed up for a studio portrait. Always husky, they were now both absolutely corpulent; two massive lumps of pink protoplasm sharing the same side of the booth as if they were joined at the hip. The table bristled with empty beer mugs and shot glasses.

"If it ain't the Coach Prince," Horace greeted.

John said, "We're taking the new scow out for a shakedown this afternoon. You want to come along as ballast?"

Harlan took their cue and responded politely. Although the brothers still owned a percentage in the company, they had ceased to supply engines for Ford cars, which were now manufactured almost entirely on the premises. Rumor said the Dodges were considering starting up their own automobile company. "This would be the *Hornet*?" Harlan asked.

"The *Hornet II*," corrected John. "This one's a hundred feet long, twin engines. Horace built 'em both with his own two hands."

His brother wrapped one around his current beer mug and finished it off. "Thousand horsepower, four cylinders, ten-inch stroke. Forty-one miles per hour. Fastest boat in the world." He belched.

"Runner-up's a torpedo boat." John grinned.

"I'll have to take you up on the offer another time. Have you seen Ford?"

The grin became a scowl. "He dropped by a half hour or so back, didn't even sit down. Son-of-a-bitch New York judge ought to be cornholed with a piston rod."

"Crankshaft," suggested Horace. They touched shot glasses and tossed down the contents in one synchronized jerk.

"Did he say where he was headed?"

The Dodges spoke in unison. "River Rouge."

Harlan blinked. Obviously John and Horace were drunk; but then they were generally yet always managed to make sense. "Whatever for?"

"Maybe he wants to drown himself." John turned his head and bellowed to the bartender for a refill.

•   •   •

The River Rouge was one of a disputed number of shallow streams that drained the flat, unfarmable plain southeast of the city into the Detroit River. French explorers had named it for the cherry trees that were in full fruit when they paddled their canoes upstream to trade with the Iroquois and Hurons. But the area had grown too marshy to sustain them after settlers had cleared the land to plow and build, altering the runoff patterns of centuries, and the last of the trees had vanished long ago. Now it was a great squishy wasteland, a breeding ground for mosquitoes and the odd massasauga rattlesnake. Harlan, who had chosen the tall, boxy Model T town car for his personal transportation, drove up and down East Jefferson several times before he spied the familiar angular figure standing all alone five hundred feet from the Rouge's southwestern bank, a startling incongruity in the same snug black suit and white collar he'd been photographed in on his way to court. The civilized gray homburg he affected in public completed the cartoon image. Harlan drew the brake, got out, and started that way on foot, choosing each step carefully. Within a few yards his feet were soaked.

"Did you bring stakes?" Ford hailed him when he drew near.

"Steaks?"

"To mark the spots. Never mind. I'll remember." He twisted his heel into the moist earth. "We'll build the steel mill here."

"Steel mill?" Harlan was turning into a parrot.

"We're going to have to dredge the river. The docks will go in there. We'll have our own ships."

Ford seemed to be in a state of deep shock. Harlan decided to go along with it until he could talk him into going home, where Clara could call a doctor. "Who's going to build the engines, Horace Dodge?"

"They'll *come* with engines. I'm not going into the ship-building business. They'll bring down ore and limestone from the Lakes and drop their cargoes right in our backyard. We'll shunt everything around on our own railroads. We'll have a separate power plant, our own telephone switchboard, our own glass plant, our own police force."

"It sounds like you're planning a city."

"A country. If the Jews take over the world the day after we cut the ribbon, we'll be able to operate independently."

"What do the Jews have to do with anything?"

"Jew judges, Jew lawyers, that Jew William C. Whitney. They can't stand to see a gentile raise himself up above them. Only they won't be able to do a damn thing about it once Rouge is built. I'll have the entire Ford business behind one fence where I can keep an eye on it and them out."

"There is no Ford business. They're shutting you down."

"I thought so too. I almost sold out to Durant. I threw back his offer when I found out he was going to sign up Buick with the A.L.A.M. Those people all stick together. I'm filing for an appeal and I'm posting bonds to protect our customers from lawsuits."

"Can the company afford it?"

"I want to show you something." Ford patted all his pockets, said, "Wup!", took off his hat, and drew something from inside the sweatband, which he held out to Harlan. Harlan studied his partner's face closely before taking the object. There was no sign of instability in his stark features, the steady burning of the eyes set deep beneath the bony shelf of his brow, but then there never was. He had heard Ford go on about the Jews before, but that was a common theme in the business world and he had not thought much about it. What he had just said was dangerously close to a speech.

The object was a brown leather postcard of the kind sold in railroad stations. Some people mailed them, but most kept them as mementoes of trips far from home. This one had a pen-and-ink cartoon of a farmer in overalls addressing a pair of motormen clad in dusters beside their generic touring car, sunk up to its axles in mud. The caption read:

Farmer—"Huh! Feller come along here 'bout an hour ago all right—with a *FORD!*"

Harlan handed it back with a dutiful chuckle. "It's cute."

"Cute, hell. I picked it up in New York. They're all over the country. And that ain't all. I bought a paper on the train and there was a piece in it about this man that was on his deathbed. When the priest asked him if he had a last request he asked that they bury his Ford with him, because he said he never was in a hole it couldn't get him out of."

That one made Harlan laugh out loud. "Is it true?"

"No. Newspapers are bunk. It doesn't matter, though. They're telling these stories in joke books and such all over the country. Did you hear about the man in Duluth who drove his T touring car up three flights of steps and won a hundred-dollar bet?"

"Bunk?"

"No, that was real. I saw a photograph. People everywhere love the T. You can't stop that in court." He returned the leather postcard to his hat, ran his finger carefully around the sweatband, and put the hat back on, squaring it off two inches above his eyes.

"That's not much evidence to build a factory on. Do you own this property?"

"I've made an offer. I'm going to build my new house on part of it. Too many people know the place on Edison Street. Everybody seems to spot me these days. I even tried false whiskers for a while, but they didn't work. I guess they recognize the car." His own town car was parked nearby at a lopsided angle with one wheel propped up on an old muskrat hut. It was one of the japan black paint jobs he'd gone to exclusively when tests confirmed that the color dried more quickly than all the others, allowing for a greater number of vehicles to be manufactured in less time. Overnight the red, blue, and green options disappeared. He'd even had the impudence to advertise the lack of choice: "Available in any color you like, as long as it's black." Sales continued to soar, and Ford advertisements encouraged the public to "watch the Fords go by." The episode of the paint demonstrated that Henry Ford was not a man to sit around waiting for anything; not even to stake out prospective buildings on real estate belonging to someone else.

"How many people are you planning to employ at this plant?" Harlan asked.

"A hundred thousand."

He nodded, as if the figure held no shock for him. He felt detached, a disinterested observer eavesdropping on a conversation between two strangers in a swamp. "What does Couzens say?"

"He's against it. He's against sharing stock with the employees as well. That's how I know it's a good idea. The old bear is against anything that hasn't been done before. If he'd been with me in '99 he'd have tried to talk me out of going into the automobile business."

"You want to make your employees stockholders in Ford?"

"It's an idea I'm playing around with. In a couple of years, automobiles will be going two abreast, in two directions on Woodward, and at the same time. The men who build those cars are going to be rewarded for their work, whether we decide to reward them or not. A shorter workday's coming, and so is a daily wage. It will be five dollars, maybe as much as ten."

"If you start paying five dollars a day, every laborer in this country will hop a freight to Detroit."

"Jews too, no doubt. But you can't open a window and not get flies."

Evidently having considered this statement a sufficient farewell, Ford squished over to his town car, cranked it into life, got in, and backed down off the muskrat hut, twisting the wheel expertly toward Jefferson as he did so. He was the best driver in the world, having had more practice than anyone else living. Harlan Crownover stood watching the boxy car's retreat with his hands in his pockets, brackish water soaking his feet to the ankles. Standing in this unlikely wonderland he could not make up his mind whether he were in partnership with the March Hare or the Mad Hatter.

And he wondered if it was worth what it had cost.

Edith Hampton Crownover filled out a form authorizing a wire transfer of five hundred dollars to Gus and Katherine Gorlich in Guthrie, Oklahoma Territory, and handed it to the clerk at Western Union, who drew a line through *Territory* without bothering to explain that Oklahoma was now a state; the error was a common one. He accepted a draft in the amount of the transfer and wrote her out a receipt. She then gave him money to send her telegram informing her daughter Katherine of the transaction, thanked the young man, and took the streetcar home.

She enjoyed the rebellion of using public transportation nearly as much as she did her new wealth independent of her husband's. Abner II, obsessed with maintaining distance between his family's present status and the indignity and poverty of his youth, had always insisted that a Crownover vehicle be employed for any excursion beyond a few blocks. The arrangements were tedious, and she had formed the habit of turning down promising invitations and sending the hired girl on errands she would have preferred to take care of herself. Abner's horror that the past might repeat itself amounted to a superstition, preventing her from confiding to anyone that she sometimes envied the working class its freedom to take advantage of those conveniences that were designed for everyone, and by implication denied those who were not just everyone. She found it liberating to board the first car that came along, pay her fare, and step off at any stop without having to instruct the driver when to pick her up. If she decided to stay longer, or finished her errand more quickly than anticipated and decided to go back early, she had merely to board the car whose schedule coincided with her own. For the first time in her life she felt a connection with the Common Man who was always appearing in the editorial cartoons in the newspapers. And standing was easier on her back.

The coin she gave the conductor was hers, as were the ones she had paid the telegrapher and the five hundred dollars she had wired. None of it came from Abner. When her husband's doctors had sent him home to an uncertain recovery at best, he had asked for his lawyer, and the two had shut themselves up in Abner's bedroom for two hours. The lawyer emerged with a new will and power of attorney over the personal finances of Abner Crownover II. As the two men were of one mind in most things, and in view of the fact that her husband had not spoken to her since he suffered his attack on the loading dock at Crownover Coaches, Edith had elected to make no contact with the lawyer for any purpose other than to forward Abner's medical bills to his office. She drew all her expenses from the dividends Crownover Coaches paid her for the use of her stock. The value of those shares had decreased alarmingly for a brief period after the announcement was made that Crownover had agreed to furnish the Ford Motor Company with bodies for its automobiles—most of the stockholders outside the family, a conservative lot, had sold out their interests quickly—but began to swing back up at the end of the first week of trading. Following the introduction of the Model T, the stock's climb was steady, and when the first-quarter profits were announced, Edith was told her 38 percent of Crownover Coaches was worth 4.2 million dollars. She had begun wiring money to her daughter and son-in-law that day.

Abner III, her eldest son, had by dint of a mother's gentle encouragement sufficiently overcome his dread of making decisions to sign a proxy form allowing Harlan to vote his six percent as well, which with Harlan's own three gave him control of the company's fortunes. His share made Abner III independently wealthy, but Harlan had had the good sense to arrange for a custodianship so that his older brother might never be burdened with the choice of what to do with it. She found bitter amusement in the knowledge that Edward, whose five percent was now worth ten times what it had been when Abner II was in charge, refused to exchange more than perfunctory greetings with her when he came to visit his father, but cashed his dividends without comment. She was not devastated. She loved all her sons equally, but she liked Edward least.

And so the world had changed, in the main for the better; but as she stepped down from the car, accepting the gracious and unnecessary assistance of the conductor, all her concerns were for Harlan. She had seen what the company had done to Abner II, wearing at him day by day almost imperceptibly, like nature's elements conspiring to destroy a building in the most reprehensible way, one molecule at a time, for suggesting that a man may improve upon a mountain. She hoped she would not live to see her middle son worn round at the edges and discolored so that none who had not known him in his youth were aware how different he had been from all the others. The kingdom of heaven belonged to the man who survived success; as yet it was unclaimed.

She removed her hat and gloves in the Queen Anne's foyer, from which she had banished the ponderous oak-and-brass

Black Forest halltree and dour portrait of William McKinley—a gift from the president in gratitude for the phaeton Crownover had designed for the 1901 inauguration—and replaced them with a Tiffany floor lamp and prints of English gardens, thus relieving the room of that somber bass note that made visitors feel as if they had come to pay their respects to an important corpse. Elsewhere in the house she had ordered rugs taken up, woodwork painted, heavy bronze replaced with airy crystal; had, in effect, breezed from room to room like Queen Mab, turning dark to light and lead to gold with the sparkling wand of her stock portfolio. She had felt like a bride—if the bride were married to anyone but Abner Crownover.

After confirming the dinner menu with the cook, she went upstairs to Abner's bedroom, where she knocked from old habit and entered unbidden from new. The male nurse, hurly and balding in his twenties, was rising from the rocking chair beside the bed when she came in. She waved him back into it. A glance at her husband, breathing loudly on his back with his eyes open, answered any question she might have put to the nurse, and as the young man interested himself once again in his paperbound book she went to the west window and opened the curtains to let in the afternoon light, smiled at her husband, whose face was thoroughly simian now in the absence of all expression, touched the hand that rested atop the counterpane—touched it with true affection—and went out to solve the problem of the paneling in the dining room.

After she left, Abner II lay absolutely without thinking, a luxury he had not known until the destruction of his stomach lining. At such times the constant clawing pain, its edges dulled by a solution of morphine in water prescribed by his doctors, seemed to be drawing all the electrical impulses from his brain. He was aware of his surroundings—the regimental-striped paper on the walls, the milk-glass fixture in the ceiling, the nurse, who smelled aggressively of Dr. Sloan's liniment and Lifebuoy soap—he had a fair idea of the time of day and even the day of the week, and he remembered, but he could not be said to think, or if he did the thoughts had no more significance than the movement of the gears in a clock whose face no one consulted. This too he attributed to the morphine, and wondered if anyone else was aware of this benefit. Without it, nothing would prevent the thoughts from shredding the rest of his insides.

He was not deluded. He knew the depth of his betrayal and the necessity of refusing communication with those who had played him false. Neither Edith nor Abner III nor Harlan—not Harlan, never Harlan, until hell burned out and was rekindled and burned out again—had heard a word from his lips or managed to capture his gaze since that day on the dock. This was their punishment, the only one he had still in his power to deal out: the denial by word or look that they existed in the world he now inhabited. It was small, but considering that eye contact and speech were his only links to the world he had once trod as one of the seven or eight Americans whose opinion counted, it was absolute. That it was not enough did not concern him, because he did not think.

He knew that Edith had been changing things in the house. The sounds of heavy furniture scraping the floors had not been heard there since they had moved in, and the conversation of workmen was never conducted in whispers. He assumed the same thing was going on at the Crownover plant. He knew there would be no more opera coaches, no doctors' buggies, no ladies' carriages with yellow wheels and pockets for their vanity things; he had said good-bye to it all when his doctors had told him he probably wouldn't recover even if he agreed to surgery. It was his office that occupied him. They could do what they liked with the desk and the ledgers and the solid, no-nonsense Stickley chairs and sofa, but he hoped they would leave the framed tintype of his father. The image of Abner I's stunned face, made between the debacle at Harpers Ferry and his miserable death, had behaved as Abner II's reverse barometer since the day he took over the company. On those rare occasions—rarer, certainly, than they occurred in romantic fiction—when a decision teetered between what was right in general and what was best for Crownover, he'd had only to look at the stricken expression of the man in the photograph to remind him which way to lean. He had never confided that to anyone; he was glad now that he had not. The realization that the surest tool in the company chest might remain available in plain sight, but that none should know its purpose, made him forget momentarily the purgatory in his abdomen.

Abner Crownover II lay absolutely without thinking in his quiet bedroom, hearing the random noises of the house and the nurse's calloused fingers turning pages and outside the window the harsh expectorant cough of a gasoline-powered automobile making its way up Jefferson.

AFTERWORD

Thunder City commemorates the most significant achievement of the twentieth century—America's transformation, in a few years, from an agricultural nation to the world's leading industrial power. In that brief span, a method of transportation that had existed relatively unchanged for three thousand years disappeared and was replaced by one that would shrink the globe and blur the lines between rural and town life, small town and city. Not until the computer revolution of the 1980s would another invention appear to lift civilization, Alexander-like, from one groove and place it in another.

It has become fashionable in recent years for certain individuals—among them a vice president of the United States—to decry the invention of the automobile, which they hold to account for destroying the environment and depleting the world's supply of fossil fuels. (Those most vocal in this belief invariably travel great distances to spread their gospel, apparently on foot.) Few have raised their voices to remind us of the introduction of the decent living wage and the eight-hour day, or the number of lives that have been saved by the gasoline-powered fire engine, police cruiser, and ambulance; numbers that far outweigh those slain in traffic accidents. Every worthwhile development in the history of man has proven itself a Pandora's box as well as a benevolent djhin, but not since the crossbow has another inspired so much strident rhetoric.

It is the theme of *Thunder City* that the true dark side of the national fantasy, the evolution of organized crime, took place at the same time as the birth of the automobile industry, and that the same combination of vision, determination, and ruthlessness that drove such pioneers as Henry Ford, the Dodge brothers, and Ransom Eli Olds existed in the handful of European immigrants and landed gentry who wedded politics, business, and vice to create what is now undeniably America's Fifth Estate. Harlan Crownover, James Aloysius Dolan, and Sal Borneo are creations of fancy, but they are by no means fanciful. Their counterparts were genuine and still are.

Other literary devices have been brought to bear in the telling of this story. In the interest of pace and clarity (but not drama, as the case of Henry Ford versus the Selden Trust provides enough for ten books), I have committed certain offenses against historical fact. Chief among these is the compression of time, so that the events of eight years must appear to the casual reader to have taken place within eighteen or so months. Similarly, I have backdated the construction of the Pontchartrain Hotel and its notorious bar a few years to create a consistent gathering place for the Detroit automaking community from the founding of the Ford Motor Company in 1902 to the conquest of the world by the Model T in 1908. The Pontchartrain Club, as the community referred to itself, met there to compare dreams and show off between the building's dedication in 1907 and 1915, when the members migrated to the Detroit Athletic Club. Sir Walter Scott set the precedent for this type of liberty and I don't think enough of myself to trumpet a higher standard.

On January 8, 1911, a judge of the New York State Court of Appeals reversed a lower-court ruling to declare the basic technology of the automobile a "social invention" that must be made available to all producers equally. The Association of Licensed Automobile Manufacturers was immediately disbanded and the industry opened to all comers. Henry Ford, for all the shocking faults of an unstable and bigoted personality, has never received sufficient credit for his valiant one-man stand against the worst threat to free enterprise in this country's history.

Thunder City closes the chronicle I have come to call, for want of a better name, the Detroit Series. In these seven books I have attempted to tell the story of America in the twentieth century through the microcosm of Detroit, the one city whose history mirrors precisely the history of the United States of America. These are, in order of chronology rather than date of publication: *Thunder City* (1900–10); *Whiskey River* (1928–1939); *Jitterbug* (1943); *Edsel* (1951–59); *Motown* (1966); *Stress* (1973); and *King of the Corner* (1990). The city since the retirement and death of Coleman Young, its mayor of twenty corrupt years, shows signs as the century turns that it is embarking upon its greatest adventure since the start of the automobile industry, in which case it may warrant at least one more book; but since time is the only guarantor of distance and objectivity, the existing titles in the series must for the time being stand alone.

—Loren D. Estleman
Whitmore Lake, Michigan
January 5, 1999

MYSTERY

ESTLEMA Estleman, Loren D.

Thunder City

$22.95

DUE DATE

2C /100